Real life is real weird and sometimes, it just stays screwed up. And ugly. Real ugly.

BOOKS BY
C.M. STUNICH

The Seven Wicked Series
First
Second
Third
Fourth
Fifth
Sixth
Seventh

Houses Novels
The House of Gray and Graves
The House of Hands and Hearts and Hair
The House of Sticks and Bones

The Huntswomen Trilogy
The Feed
The Hunt
The Throne

Indigo Lewis Novels
Indigo & Iris
Indigo & The Colonel
Indigo & Lynx

Never Say Never Trilogy & Never Too Late Series
Tasting Never
Finding Never
Keeping Never
Never Can Tell

Triple M Series
Losing Me, Finding You
Loving Me, Trusting You

A Duet
Paint Me Beautiful
Color Me Pretty

Hard Rock Roots
Real Ugly

Stand Alone Novels

She Lies Twisted
Hell Inc.
A Werewolf Christmas (A Short Story)
Fuck Valentine's Day (A Short Story)
Clan of the Griffin Riders: Chryer's Crest
DeadBorn
Broken Pasts
Crushing Summer

GET BENT

HARD ROCK ROOTS

Book Two

C.M. STUNICH

SARIAN ROYAL

for the readers who wanted to chase me down with pitchforks and torches after the ending of "Real Ugly". for those that waited patiently and stuck by my side.

all I can say is: thank you.

CHAPTER 1
❧ TURNER CAMPBELL ❧

I tap the vein in my right arm with two fingers and check the rubber tourniquet that's wrapped around my sweaty flesh, making sure it's pulled tight. I'm trying to set up a good injection site, so I can take the syringe I've got clutched between my teeth and shoot up. It's the only way I'll get through this. The only fucking way.

"Turner! What the hell is going on in there?" I slump against the wall and ignore Treyjan's hoarse shouting. He's been out there all damn morning, screaming his friggin' head off. I don't want to hear it anymore. He's driving me nuts.

I pull the syringe out of my mouth and slide the needle into my skin, hissing at the rush of white hot pain when it

punctures my vein. I press the plunger down and wait. A few seconds later, I feel it in the back of my throat. It tastes like fucking victory, like accomplishment, like I'm king of the fucking world. I yank the needle out unceremoniously and toss it into the trash can. It lands on top of a mountain of used condoms and tissue paper, and it's probably unsanitary as shit, but I don't care. I don't care about anything right now except Naomi.

Naomi.

"Turner, get your fucking ass out here now!"

I rip the tourniquet off next and lay it on the counter, clutching the sides of the sink as I lean over and cough. Good meth always makes you cough. And it makes you feel so fucking good that even a nightmare like this starts to look like a dream.

"Are you slamming dope in there, motherfucker?" Trey screams, and he sounds like he's about to burst a damn vein this time. I lift my eyes up and stare at myself in the mirror. It's not a pretty sight. *I look like shit. Jesus Christ. Have I been walking around like this for three days?* My eyes are bloodshot and ringed with purple, and my lips are pale and cracked. I look like a Goddamn zombie.

"Don't get your panties in a wad, bitch," I call out to him, standing up and sniffing, letting my eyes fall closed for another minute. At least now I don't have to worry

about how I'm going to get through another day. The drugs will take care of that for me.

Naomi.

I reach over and unlock the door.

Trey doesn't waste any time opening it and throwing me a death glare. I ignore him in favor of putting on some eyeliner. We have a show tonight, and I want to look good. Hell, I have to look good or I'm not getting onstage. My pain is private, not something to hang out for all to see. I'm not on display here.

"You got a hard-on for me or something?" I ask him, pretending that everything's alright, that my life has not just gone from bad to worse, that the breath has not just been suctioned out of my fucking lungs. "I can't even shit in peace anymore?" Trey looks down at the garbage, up at the tourniquet and sneers.

"You're just gonna get high everyday now?" I shrug, applying black around my eyes, making sure it's thick enough to hide the circles. Women love eyeliner on guys anyway. Or at least the women at my shows do, the ones with the piercings in their noses and the tattoos on their hips. I want to pick one of them up and fuck away the pain, but I can't do that to Naomi. For the first time in my life, I can't even imagine screwing another woman.

I look up at the ceiling as my brain seizures with false pleasure, misplaced hope, fatal courage.

"What are you now, Mother Theresa? We've gotten high everyday since we were sixteen." I pretend not to notice that Trey is wearing Travis' cap. Or whoever's cap. Still haven't figured that mystery out. There seem to be a whole shit ton of them floating around right now, and that's kind of the least of my worries.

Naomi.

"Not like this, Turner. Not fucking like this. What are you doing? You're gonna kill yourself." I don't tell my best friend that I don't care, that I'd rather die than live without Naomi Knox. I mean, how fucked up is that? Love sucks balls. Everybody always acts like it's the one thing worth living for, that spark in the fire that pulls you in, that strokes your hair back and lets you know that everything's going to be okay. Well now that I've fallen into it, nothing is okay. Nothing will ever be okay. I sipped from love's wine and now I'm drunk as shit without a place to lie down. My happy ending, my saving grace is lying dead in a morgue, cut up and fucked up, so mangled they can't even identify her damn body for sure. Oh, they say it's probably her because if not then, I mean, where the shit is she? Where? Where? *Where the fuck are you, Knox? With your pretty blonde hair and your sunglasses and your fuck you all attitude.*

I drop the eyeliner and shove Trey out of the way, barely managing to lift the toilet seat before I throw up

※※※ 4 ※※※

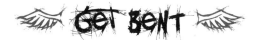

into it. He watches me with a curled lip but doesn't say anything, not until I'm done and cupping water from the faucet to splash my face with.

"Look, man, what happened to those girls is fucked up in all sorts of crazy ways, but what do you want to do about it? The cops are on it. The manager chick is in the hospital." Treyjan pauses and blows out a rush of air. His brown hair is disheveled and his eyes flick this way and that, looking for a way out of this confrontation. He knows what he wants to say to me, but he's afraid to. He should be. I stand up and turn on him quick, getting in his face, narrowing my eyes. My body is pulsing now, and I feel like I could sing from the mountaintops or some shit. But then I think of her.

Naomi.

For as long as I've been playing with fire, popping pills, shooting up, whatever, I've never had a buzzkill quite like this. I feel the urge to reach into my mouth and pull my heart up, yank it right through my throat, bleed my pain all over the damn sink.

"Say it," I tell Trey, clenching my fists, knowing I could beat the crap out of him if I wanted to. And I'm not gonna lie, I kind of want to right now.

"You don't even know her."

"Naomi. If you're going to insult her, you may as well use her name." Trey sighs and steps back, pulling a cig from his pocket and lighting up. He glances around for Milo, but our manager is off in another universe, one that has to do with hordes of reporters and TV cameras and magazine editors. There are conspiracy theorists galore, some cops, crazed fans, candlelight vigils. We're not on tour anymore, not really. Now we're part of a traveling circus, complete with freak show. Everything's gone to shit and nothing is right anymore. I feel like I'm walking crooked, like the whole world's on a tilt and I'm the only one trying to stand straight.

"Naomi was a cool chick," he begins, but I cut him off, turning away and stalking back towards the front of the bus. Ronnie, Josh, and Jesse watch me with nervous eyes.

"Is," I tell him because if I don't hold onto that last, little shred of hope, I'll crumble to pieces. I pull out a smoke of my own and light up.

"Turner, come the fuck on!" Treyjan screams, getting frustrated with me again. I think he's terrified that I'm going to turn into Ronnie, slide away into the shadow realm and become a walking, talking slice of melancholia. But he needn't worry about that crap. Knowing what I know now about this love shit, I'm surprised that Ronnie's still alive. I won't last if I find out for sure that she's gone. I'll just wither away and disappear. I take a drag and let my head fall back while

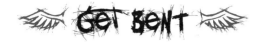
smoke curls from my nostrils in gentle spirals. "You had a week long affair with this girl. Big deal. You're not in love. Stop being an emo bitch and get over it. People die, Turner. Life fucking blows. So suck it up and get over yourself."

The bus goes silent.

I stay completely still for several long moments.

Ronnie sniffles.

I guess they think I'm going to go bat shit crazy and fuck up my friend, but I'm not. The meth is kissing me softly, teasing me with its horrible, little claws, seducing my mind from the inside out. Instead, I smile.

"The show must go fucking on," I say, dropping my chin to my chest. I flick my cigarette into the sink and snatch a pair of shades from my front pocket. When the police gave me back my personal items, these were there. I guess they might be Naomi's, but I don't want to think about that right now. I slide them up my nose and thank fuck that I didn't get booked for elbowing that cop. A few nights in jail, no drugs, no music, that would've killed me, stripped me right to the soul and bled me dry.

"What?" This is from Josh. His voice is kind of shaky, but hey, he has balls for even trying to talk to me right now.

"I'm going to sing for Amatory Riot," I tell them, and there's no collective gasp or anything; the bus stays dead

silent. They think I'm fucking nuts. "Trey, you'll play guitar."

"I don't know any of their fucking songs," he snaps back at me, taking a step forward. "Turner, they're done for. Their manager is in critical condition, their lead guitarist is dead, and their front woman is missing. Don't try to save a sinking ship. Worry about us, worry about this. Indecency needs you, man. Don't fuck us."

I roll my shoulders and reach down, wrapping my fingers around the neck of Naomi's guitar. Don't ask me how I got it or why I have it. If love makes you crazy, then the absence of it drives you insane.

"If you won't help me, I'll do it myself."

"Turner … " There's a warning in Trey's voice, but what is he going to do? Is he going to stop me? Don't fucking think so. I move over to the door and reach out, wrap my fingers around the handle and pull.

Light and sound explode like fireworks. People start to shout; cameras begin to flash. I ignore it all and step out into the fray.

✗✗✗ ✗ ✗✗✗

CHAPTER 2
& NAOMI KNOX &

Confusion. Surprise. Pain.

These are the three things that came before the blackness.

CHAPTER 3
& TURNER CAMPBELL &

"You've got to be fucking kidding me!" Dax shouts, spinning away and grabbing at his head. His bleakness mirrors my own, and I'm okay with that. He thinks he loves Naomi. Fine. But he can't. Not really. Not like I do. That's a Goddamn impossibility. "You want us to get onstage? You are nuts. Complete and utterly nuts. Do you not realize what's just happened? We are absolutely and completely screwed. Amatory Riot is over. America is practically dead. Naomi ... " Dax stops talking and leans his forehead against the wall.

Rook Geary watches on angrily, arms crossed over his broad chest. He doesn't like me on his bus, but that's where the remaining members of Amatory Riot are

staying, so this is where I've gotta be.

"How the fuck did you get her guitar?" the chick with the blonde-black hair asks me. I ignore her question because I'm not really sure. When I got back from the police station, it was just there, leaning against the cabinets. I figured one of my bandmates picked it up for me, but I never bothered to ask. I don't fucking care.

"Can't you see we've got it bad enough? We don't need you over here rubbing our noses in this crap." This comes from one of the other guys in the band. Shit if I know any of their names. I keep my attention focused on Dax.

"When she gets back, she's not going to want to see her music torn to shit." I lift the guitar up by the neck with one hand and hold my cigarette in the other. "Her fucking soul is all wrapped up in this. We can't let it just go by the wayside. That's too fucking cruel."

"She's not coming back, Turner. Naomi is dead."

"You don't know that."

"Turner, come on." When Dax turns around, he's got tears in his eyes and he's not ashamed of it. While I stand here on a false high, tuned up with meth burning in my veins, Dax stands there like the emo fag he is and just blatantly sobs in front of his band and all of Terre Haute. What an asshole. Melancholy is a private thing. It's not something you just show to everybody. It's so disrespectful, I just want to punch him in the Goddamn face and knock his teeth out. How dare he. How the fuck dare he. I squeeze my cigarette tight. "I know you and Naomi were getting close, and you're upset because of the shit that went down between you, but you've got to stop deluding yourself, man. Go onstage, pick up a girl, move on. Let us deal with this, okay?" I resist the urge to smash the guitar against Dax's face. That won't get me what I want. *It won't bring Naomi back.*

"Get onstage with me. Music heals, Dax. Even the ugliest fucking souls can take it in and heal a little. Play her songs, keep her alive." I swallow deep and lean on the drugs for support. *Naomi.* I can't even fucking think past her name. It's just there in my head on a continuous loop. Her voice plays over and over again in my head, and I swear, when the wind blows, I can feel her body against mine. I squeeze my eyes shut and look down. I'm not usually this optimistic. But I've always been this stubborn.

"Fuck the fans," Dax says, and I glance back up at him. He looks hysterical now, but I can't blame him for that, so I just stand there and let him rant. My muscles clench and anger rides over and through me, demanding respect, begging me to put him down. But I can't. I can't bring anybody else down because I'm at the lowest point there is. There's nowhere else to go. "This isn't a circus.

We're not here to satisfy their morbid curiosity. Lives were lost and destroyed, Turner. There are a thousand vultures swarming outside this bus, wanting to cut so deep into us that we bleed to death." Dax slaps his chest hard for emphasis, squeezing his fingers in their skeleton gloves so tight that his skin turns red. "And you want us to go onstage and play? Why? So every note can poison us a little more? So every strum of your fingers on her guitar can remind us that she's gone, and our life is gone, and the music," Dax laughs, but there's no joy there. Just fucking pain and agony, enough to drown an army. "The music is dead, Turner."

I look up, into Dax's gray eyes, past the wave of dark hair he uses to hide behind like a security blanket, and I give him God's honest fucking truth best as I know it.

"Music never dies, Dax. It revives and it soothes the soul. If you let this fall away, you let Naomi down, but the music will live on. The music will always live on."

The atmosphere backstage is the most cloying, depressing shit I have ever had to sit through. Even Travis' funeral

didn't feel like this. There's this sense of hopelessness that poisons the air and drags its dirty fingers through your soul. Nobody wants to be here, yet they have nowhere else to go.

The crowd is extra fucking insane today, screaming and shouting and clawing their way towards the stage, belting out questions that nobody knows the answer to. *Where is Hayden? Who killed Naomi? What will happen to Amatory Riot?* I keep the guitar slung over my shoulders and wait for Terre Haute to finish their set and get off the fucking stage. Once I get up there, this game is over. I will not allow the disrespect to continue. Those assholes will step up and shut up. They will show their support with open ears and desperate cries. They will listen and they will damn well appreciate Naomi's work, or I'll fucking destroy them onstage with her guitar. I will cut them up with this black and white axe, slice them to pieces and throw them to the wolves.

I finish my cigarette and toss it on the floor. I don't care if it burns the whole place to the ground. All that matters now is letting Naomi's voice be heard, using the music like I use the drugs, as a crutch to get through the day, a stepping stone to move across the black abyss of the horror filled week.

Nobody mentions that I'm wearing the same clothes I had on a few days ago or that I stink like shit. Not even

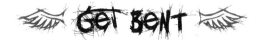

Milo. I'm not even sure I'm the only one. Dax's outfit looks pretty fucking familiar.

"You don't have to do this," Trey says to me, but I ignore him. He's really starting to piss me off. I used to think he knew me better than anyone, but this shit is starting to get old. If he can't see that I *have* to do this, then we've obviously grown further apart than I ever could've imagined.

"Trey, fuck off," I tell him, and he just sighs.

"Fine, what the fuck do I know? I only watched Ronnie fall into a lifelong depression that he's never getting out of. Screw me sideways for trying to keep you from doing the same."

"I'll be fine. Soon as I find Naomi." Even if she's dead, I have to know for sure. Until then, in my head, she's still just missing. Although missing is better than bloodless and beat up, that's for fuck's sure.

"Oh, Jesus Christ, Turner. She's fucking *dead.*" He hisses this last part out, lowering his voice so nobody else can hear. The subject of Naomi Knox is friggin' taboo back here. They're all more than willing to entertain the scenario that she's lying cold in the morgue, but too chicken shit to say it aloud. Screw them. Screw them all.

"Do you hear the crowd?" Dax asks, moving up beside me. Trey throws him a nasty look though I'm not sure why. It's not like he's at fault for all this. God help

the fucker who is. If I find him, I won't be thinking straight. There'll be his pain and his end, and I'll make it my own personal mission to see that he finds both. "This is ridiculous. We can't go out there. They're not even here to listen to the fucking music. Sorry to say this, but I think we're jumping ship."

I spin to glare at him and get up in his face, pressing the toes of my boots to his. He doesn't expect it, so he doesn't step back, just stands there and let's me get in close.

"We will demand their respect, and we'll have it. They'll either give it or they'll leave. I won't accept anything else. If you bow out now, you give in. You might be prepared to do that, but I'm not."

Rook drops the microphone from his mouth and pauses like he isn't sure what to do. The people in here have lost their Goddamn minds. Music isn't what they came here for; drama is. I don't do fucking drama.

Without waiting for a response from Dax, I storm across the stage in blood crusted boots, pausing in the center, waiting in the spotlight like I was fucking born for this. Rook gives up the mic without a fight.

"Hey." One word from me shuts the whole place up, just the way it should be. I've always been in charge, ever since I left home. My life didn't give me any other options. It was either take control or be controlled. Not

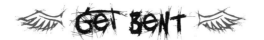

much of a fucking choice. And this is *my* tour, and it's my friggin' heart that's bleeding and my love that's lost at sea. The crowd gapes up at me with open mouths and cell phones flashing, taking pictures, recording video. Good for them. I want them to write this shit down in the history books, mark this moment as a landmark in life. If I get my way, they will remember this shit forever. Whether it's my dirty, sweaty clothes, or my sunken cheeks or my trembling hands, I don't know, but I get no backlash, just stunned silence when I speak my next words. "Shut the fuck up. We're not here to entertain you. We're here to destroy your souls and put you back together. We're here to make you remember why it's so damn good to be alive. We're here to remind you that all of the drama and the bullshit isn't worth it. So, you're gonna shut your mouths and you're going to listen, and if you don't like me saying that you can leave. And if you do stay, when you walk out that damn door later, you're going to stop gossiping and you're going to think real hard about what it is you want in life, and then you're going to take steps to fucking get it." I pause and wet my lips while equipment is shifted around me, while the members of Amatory Riot sneak out from backstage, crawl across the dirty wood floor and stand with their heads down and their hearts pounding. "I fell in love with a girl last week. I didn't expect it, didn't even know

what was happening to me until it was too late. Now that there's a chance I've lost her, I know I'd do anything to get her back." My hand falls to the guitar, and my mind scrambles to remember her rhythm, her music, the rise and fall of her voice. It's been awhile since I've played, but I will be damned if I screw this up.

From behind me, Dax starts a beat on his drums while that skinny druggy dude sneaks in from my right and blindsides the shit out of me by taking control of the lead guitar position, leaving me to play rhythm. It only takes me a second to get into the music and once it's got control, that little demon fucker screws with me hardcore and doesn't let go, sinking its teeth into my hands and sliding its tongue down my throat.

The crowd swells and breaks up into pieces before crashing together into a new whole, eliminating the us and them, becoming a single entity, one shining face shouting its joy and pain to the world, knowing that it's safe to spill secrets, that they'll get caught up in the strands of our music. Tangled webs are weaved as we unravel those motherfuckers, unleashing our fury into them and watching it get smashed back tenfold.

At first, my voice is low and weak, like I'm coming out of a Goddamn coma or something. That isn't fucking me, has never been me. If I let love make me weak, then I wouldn't be Turner fucking Campbell.

�░☓ **18** ☓░☓

"Unwitting cruelty bathed in beauty sings to me, brings me down, and lifts me back up. Takes me high, soars above, and all the while I'm falling. I am falling. Falling. Falling so far that I move right through you, and you don't, you refuse, to see me."

I get somewhere inside that maybe Naomi was singing about me. I think a lot of her songs are about me, but maybe I'm just an arrogant little bitch. There's that, too. But I like to think they're about me. All of mine are about her, whether I knew that or not. I wish I could tell her. I wish I'd done a better job of breaking my feelings to her. Jesus, I don't know what I expected, but it wasn't this. It wasn't the blood or the ambulances or the unknown. *I miss the shit out of that girl.*

"When you tried to catch me, it was all a lie. When you tried to soothe me, you only made me cry. Because I'm falling. Falling. So far into you. And I'm bleeding. Bleeding. Because you cut me through. My heart is sore."

My eyes scan the crowd and catch on smiles, tears, frowns. I pass right over all of them, trying to remember what it was like to have her onstage next to me. It might've been only days ago, but the rift between then and now is so wide that it makes it seem like years. I feel my body responding to the thoughts, the memories, and I end up with the most inappropriate, raging, fucking hard-

on. But I won't apologize for it. It's just my dick reacting to what my heart already knows.

The crowd loves the shit out of me for it.

"*And I can't go on.*"

And then as I'm scanning, as I'm pretending this call and response thing isn't happening between me and that chick with the dual colored hair, that it's Naomi that's answering me, I see the barefoot girl.

"*My life.*"

She's standing in the back, the only still person in the venue, the only one whose body isn't throbbing with the music. She hasn't lost herself in the crowd. She's still a single person, and she's looking right fucking at me. The Devil himself would cry if that girl stared at him the way she's staring at me. I almost choke on my next words. My fingers fumble a bit, but I pick it up. If anything, I'm a Goddamn perfectionist at heart. I can't fail at this. I won't.

"*It's all come undone. I can't get air.*"

I feel like the girl's trying to grab me with her gaze, trying to warn me with those crazy blue eyes that swim like the sea. I want to stop playing right then and there, call her out, have the crowd bring her to me, throw her at my feet, so I can shake the shit out of her. She knows things. What, I'm not sure, but Naomi told me about her, *warned* me actually. What if she's the one responsible?

"*And I no longer fly.*"

I keep playing, knowing that she'll be gone before I can get to her, and I try to learn everything I can from her face, from the way her hand clutches her stupid, plastic purse, the way her lips part and her face fills with fear. I see her mouthing words, and I think she's trying to tell me something. Then I realize, that's not it at all. She's singing the lyrics, the response bits, the ones Naomi would've done if she'd been onstage with that anorexic bitch, Haley or whatever the fuck her name is.

"*Because I'm falling. Falling. Falling into you.*"

When she saw the carnage on the bus, she said she was too late. That *he* got there first. Who the fuck is *he*? What the fuck is going on? The girl starts to move back, white dress dirty and torn, melding into the shadows, taking her answers with her. In my grief, I had forgotten about her and now, here she is, three hundred miles away from the last place I saw her.

I belt out the last lines of the song like a plea, like I'm praying for her to stay, to answer my questions, but if she hears me, she doesn't cut me any slack.

"*And then I know it's the end and even my descent is done.*"

The last thing I see before she goes are her lips, mouthing the words like a curse.

"*I hit the ground and I'm gone. I hit the ground and*

we're done. Forever."

CHAPTER 4
NAOMI KNOX

For some reason, I think I hear an angel singing, strumming the beat of my fluttering pulse with words that are my own, penned in a dirty, spiral notebook, born of the pain that kissed my spirit a lifetime ago. I accept that this is my end and relax into the rhythmic cadence of his beautiful breath.

CHAPTER 5

& TURNER CAMPBELL &

After the set, Trey brings a couple of girls back to the bus just to piss me off, practically forcing a little blonde onto my lap.

"Give her some of your coke, Turner," he says as he wraps himself around a brunette and smiles across the table at me. What he doesn't fucking get is that I'm not playing anymore. I don't want this girl or any other. I just want Naomi Knox back. If that can't happen, fuck if I know what I'm going to do. I just sit there for awhile and watch him make an ass out himself. I shot up again in the bathroom, but I don't feel any better, not really. The emotional charge I got from being onstage has totally fucked with my head, and I can't seem to snap out of it. I

feel like a zombie, marching along to the beat of a necromancer's drum. I'm moving, but I'm not in control. I'm functioning, but I'm not living, not anymore. "Come on, what's your fucking problem?" Trey asks as the girl runs her fingers through my hair. I let her, but only because I'm an emotional wreck right now. I'm not thinking of her or the words she's whispering into my ear or the way Trey's acting like a damn fucking fool. I'm thinking of the girl with the bare feet and the buzz cut. I looked for her. Oh, you can bet your sweet ass I looked all over the damn place. But I knew I wasn't going to find her.

I let out a sigh that the blonde mistakes for a come on. Her hand reaches down between my legs and strokes over the bulge of my crotch. I clamp my hand down on her wrist hard, maybe too hard and she lets out a yelp.

"Don't." Just that one word, stiff as steel. I push the girl off and rise to my feet. "I'm not in the fucking mood right now." I pull a cigarette out of my pocket and light up while the woman starts to screech obscenities from behind me. She even throws a tube of lipstick at the back of my neck.

"Turner, get your ass back here!" Trey shouts as I kick open the screen door and move down the steps, slamming my head against the side of the bus and sliding down to the rocky pavement. I was not expecting love, but I was

more than willing to embrace the shit out of it. This whole wallowing in the depths of despair crap? Not so much.

"You alright?" I don't have to look up to know that the voice above me belongs to Ronnie. There aren't many people on this earth who can make the gods cry with a simple question like that.

"Do I look alright, Ronnie?" I snap, pressing the back of my hand to my forehead and letting the ash from my cigarette fall onto my jeans. I think about tossing Asuka's name out there, just so he'll freak out and I won't have to be alone in my misery, but even as trashed as I am, I know better than that. There are certain lines that even I'm not willing to cross. I glance up at him as he pushes the screen door closed on Trey's rant and presses his hands flat against it.

"Don't hold this against Treyjan, Turner. He doesn't know any better. He just wants you to be happy is all."

I sigh deep and drop my wrist to the ground, letting the burn of my cherry fizzle out against the cement. My other knee comes up, and I drop my head to the rough, dirty denim of my pants, the ones that have dried, black blood splatters around the ankles.

"He's a fucking tool," I tell Ronnie, and he laughs, moving up close to me, smelling like pot and allspice. I remember the day that Asuka died, the stricken look on

Ronnie's face, the way his lips went white and the color drained from his face. My memory of those first few weeks after her death is a little shady, clouded with a lot of horrible all-nighters – girls, booze, drugs – but I'm pretty sure he didn't change his shirt for a month. He'll get it, at least. He'll offer me a joint and stand by my side, and he won't try to push some groupies on me or make me pretend that nothing's wrong.

"He is, yeah, but that's why we like hanging out with him, right? Makes us feel better about ourselves." I get that it's a joke, but I don't laugh. I feel drained. Even with the dope, I don't feel like such a big shot anymore. I feel small. Miniscule. Sitting here like this, I'm aware of how little I mean to the world, how unimportant I really am. I might have fans, a following of people who like my music, but so what? If I've made any mark on this world, it isn't a positive one. A stain, maybe. Like, look at Naomi. I left her a fucking wreck, used her and tossed her aside like I do everything and everyone else. Maybe in my quest to be respected, I forget to give it back? Maybe I've become the one thing I've never wanted to be?

"I want to believe that she's not dead, Ronnie."

"There's a chance," he tells me honestly, scooting closer, feet kicking aside loose pebbles as he adjusts himself and leans back against the bus. Inside, I can hear

Trey's false laughter, loud and raucous, full of forced cheer. I don't know what he wants from me, but this shit isn't helping. If anything, it's highlighting exactly how screwed up it is that I am.

"But nobody believes that except for me." I sink deeper into myself, wrapping my arms around my legs, halting my breathing so that it comes out slow and controlled. Inside though, inside my heart is pounding and slamming against my ribcage and my pulse is racing. My hands shake and my jaw is trembling with adrenaline.

I hear Ronnie exhaling long before he speaks. When he does, I can tell he feels bad for me, that he understands what I'm going through, that he's desperate for me to be right. He wants Naomi to be alive, so I don't have to go through the shit he went through. All of that self-loathing crap, those moments of pure terror when he'd wake up screaming her name. *Asuka.* I think the worst though was the silence that followed the screaming, the frozen slice of hell that Ronnie would sit in, eyes glazed over, sweat pouring down his face. I always knew he was remembering that she was dead, clawing his way out of nightmares and into something much, much worse. Harsh ass fucking reality.

"Does it matter then? Why not hope? Why not hope like hell until the truth comes out? If it turns out you were wrong, get depressed then. But don't get bent out of

shape yet. You can always kill yourself later, right?" Ronnie pulls a joint from his pocket and lights up with a silver lighter, casting an orange glow over his stubbled face. The crackling end of the joint makes the snake tattoos on his neck look like they're writhing, constricting around his neck and choking the life out of him. Sometimes, I think he'd like that, to die without having to make a conscious decision about it. Suicide's hard. It takes a lot of courage, and Ronnie and I both know that he's a damn pussy.

I reach my hand up for the joint, and he passes it over.

I'm about to take my first hit when Dax comes over and pauses a couple feet away, hands tucked into the pockets of his black jeans.

"Hey," he says and then looks over at Ronnie like he isn't sure he wants to talk around him. Ronnie's my fucking boy though, and there's no way in shit I'm telling him off. Either Dax says what he needs to say around him or he doesn't say anything at all. I don't want to be left alone right now. I need Ronnie here, gay as that might sound. I take my hit and hold the joint up for Dax. He ignores it. "Can I talk to you for a minute?"

"Listening," I say, leaning my head back against the bus and breathing in the sweet scent of sweat, smoke, and alcohol. Oh yeah, the party is on tonight. The crowd is whipped up into a riotous frenzy, screaming outside the front entrance, tossing shit over the gate. The press isn't helping much either, reporting on rumors and spreading them like forest fire. If I were to go searching for the little bald bitch now, I'd get torn to shreds by my own fans. They would freaking trample me to shit. I take another hit and hand the joint to Ronnie.

Before Dax gets a chance to speak, Jesse moves up between us in his red skinny jeans and baggy tank, wearing a bunch of stupid, rubber bracelets on his arm, you know the ones they give out for fundraising and whatever.

"Check this shit out," he says, flashing me his wrist and the white writing that adorns all eight of the bracelets he's squeezed onto his skinny arm. They all say the same damn thing: *Mrs. Turner Campbell.* Huh. "They're passing these out by the dozen."

"Who is?" I ask, lifting up my shades and looking closer. Jesse shrugs and withdraws his arm, casting a curious glance over at Dax.

"Dunno. Chicks in a blue van? Looks like you're even more popular now. Nice job, Turner." He picks at the bracelets again and pauses, biting at the black stud in the center of his lip. Jesse doesn't know what to do with me now. Every other thing he says to me is punctuated with an *I'm sorry* or some shit. Doesn't make me feel any better. All his awkwardness does is make me worse. It's

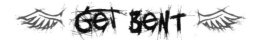

a constant reminder that things are not right, that they might not be right for me *ever.* Naomi Knox had this … this *something* inside her that made me think of puppies and kitty cats. I want to kiss her face off and make babies with her, and she is the only damn woman on this earth that I would give the title of Mrs. Turner Campbell to. Fuck the rest of them groupies.

"Well, glad you're interested in the position, but I don't do dick. Thanks." The joint makes its way back to me, and I take a hit. "And tell the rest of the crew that anybody I see wearing those damn bracelets is getting fired."

"Can I please talk to you seriously for a moment?" Dax growls, sounding pissed. I glance over at him and wish that the drugs did it for me like they used to. Guess the pain of losing the only spark I've ever had lit in me sort of diminished that. Now, they take the edge off, but that's about it. I think about getting up and snatching the bottle of vodka from the cabinet. Maybe if I mix a few choice substances, I'll pass out? Seems better than the alternative.

"I'll see you inside," Jesse says, getting the hint. I notice he doesn't take the bracelets off as he goes. A few seconds later, Josh slides by, but he doesn't say anything. Good. He's starting to learn his lesson and stay the hell out of my way. Ronnie thinks we should get along better,

but I just don't have the energy to try right now. Maybe when Naomi comes back, I'll give it a go? *If* she comes back.

"What do you want, Dax? Kinda busy right now, okay?" Dax wrinkles up the left side of his face for a moment and then grabs control of himself, sucking in a deep breath and shaking out his hands. He's wearing fingerless red gloves with black stitching today. I think they're made of leather, but who the fuck knows?

"The band and I have been talking," he pauses and looks over his shoulder like he expects Naomi or Skinny Bitch to pop out of the crowd of roadies at any moment. "And we'd like it if you took over, at least until Hayden comes back. I mean, if she comes back. If not, then until we find somebody new." He doesn't have to ask twice.

"I'm in until Naomi comes back," I say, and then before the asshole can speak up, I add the next bit. "However long that takes, you catch my drift?" Ronnie whistles under his breath. Being a front man for two bands? Maybe not such a good idea, but I'm making this pledge on a bet, on the idea that Naomi Knox *will* come back, that she's out there somewhere, alive.

I'm making this pledge out of love, stupid or not, because without that, there ain't nothing in this world worth living for.

CHAPTER 6
✧ NAOMI KNOX ✧

How cruel is it that after I've accepted my defeat, surrendered to the dark and allowed myself to slip to the other side, that I wake up? That I come to with a gasp that never escapes my lips, that gets caught up in something constrictive, that chokes me as I flail and struggle, desperate to determine the purgatorial hell I've been caught up in?

It's wicked cruel. Wicked cruel and real ugly.

I kick and fight and snarl, but it doesn't do me any good because I'm caught. In what, I don't know. It could be rope, could be chain, could be threads of demonic power, or shit, if I'm lucky maybe it's angel hair? Maybe I'm waiting at the gates of heaven, wrapped up and ready

for judgment? If so, then I know I'm screwed. So I struggle some more, and I scream, and I scream, and I scream. And in the background of my mind, I hear a response, a chant coming from all around me, echoing in response to my cries.

And the chanters are repeating one thing and one thing only, two little words that mean nothing and everything all at once.

Turner Campbell.

CHAPTER 7
& TURNER CAMPBELL &

The next morning, I wake up to rain that plasters the windows with moisture and leaves room for really inappropriate sketches from my bandmate's fingers. The windows in the back all have giant dicks drawn on them. I swipe them away with my hand and smoke a cig, hoping that Milo's still feeling sorry enough for me that he won't bitch. It's my bus anyway.

I sigh and wonder where it is we're going now, what city's next. I stopped caring after Naomi went missing, but I can't help but feeling like I'm getting farther away from her, like maybe she's still in that blood drenched bus back in Denver. I tap my ashes into a glass tray and put the cig between my lips.

If the woman in the hospital is Naomi's manager, America, and she's *not* the girl in the morgue, then who the fuck is that? That's the question that's been bothering me all night. I figure the police should have DNA or some shit, and I wonder what's taking so long. Or maybe if they know and they're just not telling me. It'd make sense. I mean, who the fuck am I really? A rock star? A drug addict? They don't fucking care. In all reality, she and I have nothing to do with each other. The police don't know I'm in love. And even if they did, love doesn't mean shit in the real world. It opens you up inside, fucks your soul crazy hardcore, but outside, it's just a weakness to be exploited.

And right now, I'm being shit all over.

I crush the cigarette into the ashtray and spin around, moving between the bunks, past Jesse's snoring ass and into the front where Trey is sitting shirtless, nursing a rank ass hangover and glaring daggers at me. He's mad, I get it. I'm not acting like myself, but you'd think he could cut me some slack considering the circumstances. I pause and look over at Milo who's typing away furiously on his laptop. I know last night created some buzz; I heard my name being chanted in the parking lot. I bet he's got his hands full. At least I know I'm paying him to do something other than bitch. On a whim, I reach over to the counter and grab one of the stupid *Mrs. Turner*

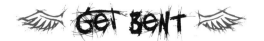

Campbell bracelets, sliding it on my wrist. I snap a photo with my phone and post every-fucking-where.

Only woman that could ever hold this title is missing. Help me find Naomi Knox and keep the music alive.

"Turner," Milo warns when he sees what I'm doing. When I glance over at him, he looks tired, and I feel guilty for maybe the first time in my life. The man's infuriating, but he's a good manager. I guess.

"It wasn't a picture of my dick this time, I swear," I tell him, and he almost smiles. The little crinkle between his brows takes over quickly enough and wipes that bit of humor away. I move over to the fridge and grab a beer.

"Turner, if you're going to be singing for Amatory Riot, there are some things we need to talk about, legal things." I take a swig from my bottle and set it down on the counter, folding my fingers around the edge of the countertop. Up front, I catch snippets of the song our driver is listening to. It's something old, something that I recognize vaguely that I've heard before. *Hiding from you in the most obvious way, giggling behind my hand I pray, that'll you'll see me. Oh baby, just see me. See me.*

"I don't want to talk about legal things, Milo," I tell him, letting my chin drop to my chest. "Work it out for me, will you?" And then I stand up and start to move towards the back. Ronnie's finally done in the bathroom, leaving it open for me.

I head straight in there with a single purpose in mind: getting high. Last night, I had a dream that Naomi was sprawled out on a bed in front of me, eyes rimmed with liner, face sweaty and lips parted. In it, I crawled on top of her, kissed her and found my way down her throat, between her breasts. I tasted her, and then I fucked her hard, and we ended up coming together and lying twisted, arms and legs tangled. When I woke up, I wanted to blow my fucking brains out. I give Ronnie a look as I move past, finally feeling for the first time that I understand what he went through all those years ago. If it's this bad with an unknown hanging around my damn throat, how would it be to actually know that the one you're so desperate to see is dead?

I can't even fucking imagine.

I don't want to.

So I'm going to get high, so what?

But then I pause with my feet on the tiled floor and my mind starts to spin. With only a few sips of beer in my system, this is probably the most sober I've been in a long time. Wheels start to turn, clues click into place. The blonde in the hospital is the manger. By my faithful pledge, Naomi Knox is *not* in the morgue. There's another woman then, dead, cut up so that she looks like Naomi, or rather doesn't look like much of anything. And nobody's reported her missing, so nobody's made the

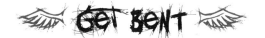

jump yet.

I slam the bathroom door and head back to the front, ignoring Treyjan's glare and Milo's frantic typing. The old song winds its way through the air and crawls into my skull, getting me thinking.

See me, baby. Oh, oh. See me, baby, so you don't miss me. If you miss me, then I'll have never been there.

The driver. The roadies. The groupies. There are a whole host of people that follow us around, who come and go so often that they're not ever really missed. If one of them were to end up toe tagged, who would know? That's right. Fucking nobody.

"Milo," I begin, setting my beer down in the sink. I might not get it then, but I don't have as big of an urge to pick it back up. Whether this is a trend that'll continue, who the shit knows? I'm not saying I want to go straight-edge or anything, but if I have to stop using to think straight, and thinking straight leads me to Naomi, I'll become a damn priest. "Can you get me a list of all the people approved for travel? Anybody that has a backstage pass that might've had access to the buses during a show?" He stops typing for a moment and looks up, obviously baffled. His blonde hair is stuck to his eyebrows with sweat and his lips are pale. Again, I get that little niggle of guilt, that whispering voice on my shoulder that says maybe I'm too hard on the guy. I try to

smile, but it won't come out, not without Naomi. Still, my face ends up neutral which is better than a straight-up frown, right? "I need the records from the day before Naomi went missing up until now. Can you do that for me?" Milo opens his mouth to respond when I interrupt him with a word I'm pretty sure he's never heard pass between my lips. "Please?"

He pauses, fingers resting on the keys of his computer, and then sighs.

"Alright, Turner," he says, and I try not to get too excited. This could mean nothing. But then, it could be fucking everything. "Let me finish what I'm working on and I'll get that together." Milo looks down at his screen and then back up at me. "Is this important?" he asks, like maybe he already knows the answer to that question.

"The most important fucking thing I've ever asked from you."

A couple hours later and I'm holding a stack of printed pages in my hand. On page ten, I find exactly what I'm looking for.

CHAPTER 8

❧ NAOMI KNOX ❧

I'm pretty sure I'm not fucking dead.

If I were, I wouldn't have to piss so bad, right? My shoulders wouldn't be aching, and my stomach wouldn't be growling. If I were dead, I wouldn't have an IV in my arm, and I wouldn't be bouncing around in this darkness.

I think I'm in a car. Or a van maybe. A truck? Wherever it is that I am, I'm on the open road, that's for sure. And I'm tied up. It's nothing magical, no unicorn hair or fairy dust, just rope and tape. I think I've been kidnapped, but who the hell knows? I try to pull up memories, try to piece together what happened to me, but all I can see when I close my eyes is Turner Campbell onstage with me, grinding against me, mixing his voice

with mine and screwing the crowd with his words. After that, everything's a big, fucking blank.

But I'm not dead.

I'm pretty damn sure about that.

CHAPTER 9
❧ TURNER CAMPBELL ❧

I don't tell anybody about my find. Not yet. I want to wait and see what happens tonight at the show, if that bald girl will show up again. I make the decision in advance that if I see her, I'm going after her, everything else be damned. I might have figured something out, or at least think I figured something out, but I won't really know anything until I talk to that girl. Knowing that the woman in the morgue is *not* Naomi doesn't tell me where Naomi is. For that, I've got to dig deeper. I feel like freaking Sherlock Holmes or some shit, like I should be walking around with a damn magnifying glass. Everywhere I look, everything I see is calling out to me, promising me that there's a puzzle here to be solved if I

just get closer to the core of it all.

Everything changes when we get to San Antonio.

We pull into the lot behind the venue and already, there are news crews everywhere, blocking the roads, clogging the sidewalks. It's raining, but fans have shown up in the hundreds and the show's already sold out. I always wanted to be popular, but shit. I didn't want to get there like this. These people aren't just here for the music or the sex or the drugs. They're here for tragedy, showing up in flocks to absorb the mystery and the heartache. Some of them wave signs that say things about Naomi, none of it helpful or useful. My post probably made things worse instead of better.

"It's like a zombie apocalypse out there," Trey says, coming up to me with his brown hair slicked up, spiked out with gel. He's got on a *Burning the Bleeding* tee, reminding me that there are other bands on this tour besides Indecency and Amatory Riot. Kind of easy to forget that sometimes.

Hands slap the windows as we slide through the crowd, inching our way into the gated area our roadies have set up in advance around the back lot behind the old building. This place is sick, and I've been looking forward to playing here for ages. Now, though, doesn't seem so damn important. My mind's all wrapped up in other things.

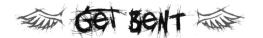

GET BENT

"Worse, maybe," I say as I get out a cig and light up. Trey follows suit and we stand there in silence, puffing out gray smoke and casting glances over our shoulders to make sure that Milo isn't about to pop in and yell at us. "Zombies just bite, right? I'd rather get eaten alive or turned then go out there with these crazy bitches. Kind of have a feeling I'd get raped."

"Probably," Trey replies. More silence. Outside the windows, my name is chanted like a curse. I've just become more than a rock star. I'm a damn superstar now. Not that it really matters, but I checked some of my shit on my phone earlier. I have ten times as many likes on Facebook, a dozen times as many Twitter followers, and my name is actually trending on Google. How about that? If I wasn't heartbroken and bloody inside, I'd probably be in the middle of a damn orgy by now. *Damn you, Naomi Knox, with your fuck all attitude and your pretty orange eyes. Who the fuck are you to disrupt everything, to tear up my soul and leave me wanting and searching without my ever knowing I wasn't whole?* I step back into the bathroom and grab some eyeliner, scribbling the words out on the mirror before I forget them. Might make for a good song if I ever get the chance to write a new one. The way things are going, I'm feeling hopeful.

Marta Yadley.

Signed up to join the tour and passed a background check, started with us in Seattle our first day and didn't show up for work the day after Naomi went missing. She wasn't the only one. No, lots of crew members bolted that day. I don't blame the fuckers. I mean, who wants to ride around on a tour if you might get your head bashed in? Drugs and easy fucks aren't worth dying for. But Miss Yadley is the only white female that disappeared that day. Nobody else fits the bill.

I drop the eyeliner in the sink and grin at myself in the mirror. I look much better today, less like a corpse and more like a man with a fucking mission.

I will find Naomi Knox. A real man never lets his lady slip by the wayside. If she's out there, I'm going to fucking get her back.

"Hey, man," Trey says as I put out my cigarette. "I want to apologize for last night. Don't know when I turned into such an asshole." Silence falls between us again, punctuated only by the crowd outside the windows. Trey and I have never been any good at this heart to heart shit.

"You've always been one," I say and he gives me a lopsided grin. "Not your fault. You can't help acting out when you're named after a fucking condom."

"Screw you, Turner," he says, but I know then that there's not bad blood between us. He'll give me some

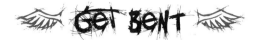

space as I long as I don't drive myself into the ground. If I try to, then he'll be there kicking my ass until I stop. That's what friends fucking do.

Once the buses are parked and the equipment is being dragged in, covered in plastic and hauled through the sudden downpour at record speed, I head out with an umbrella over my head and a pair of thick, leather boots on my feet. I'm looking for Dax and end up running into him in a vulnerable position, bent over on Terre Haute's empty bus sobbing his fucking eyes out.

When I open the doors and climb up the steps, he raises his face to look at me and wipes the back of his hand across his eyes, not apologizing for the tears or making up justifications. I don't ask him to either. I get it, whether he knows that or not.

"They found her blood," he says before I can speak. I shake some water off my umbrella and close it up, pulling it inside behind me before I slam the door.

"What the fuck are you talking about?" I ask as I stand there staring at Dax's damp hair and tired eyes. He's not wearing any makeup, and he's got on the same damn gloves from the night before. I don't even think he's bothered to change his clothes.

"But not her," he continues, sniffling hard and taking a deep breath. "They found Naomi's blood on the bus, but it doesn't match the body. The girl in the morgue, it isn't

her."

"Marta Yadley," I say and he startles, glancing up at me with a wary expression. He's got stubble all over his jaw, and the skin on his cheeks looks sallow. The Little Drummer Boy is not faring well in all this shit. Guess I'm made of tougher stuff. I try to thank my momma in the back of my mind, praise her for beating the shit out of me all those years. It was enough to prepare me for this. But then, fuck the bitch. I'm not thanking her metaphorically or otherwise.

"How do you know that?" I resist the urge to go for the joint in my pocket and glance around. There are bags everywhere, guitar cases, empty beer bottles. Looks like shacking up together hasn't been kind to either band.

"Good gumshoe work," I say which is sort of a smart ass thing to do. Looking at Dax's bloodshot eyes and trembling hands, I decide to add, "I went through all the missing roadies and found a girl that matched Naomi's description." I shrug, but inside, I'm shaking, too.

It isn't her. It isn't her. It isn't her.

The mantra plays through my head on repeat and brings the first real smile to my face that I've had in days.

"But they don't know where she is?" I figure that Dax wouldn't be bawling his eyes out if they did, but it never hurts to ask.

"The police don't know shit," he tells me which isn't

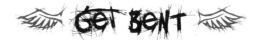

surprising. I don't expect them to help out much. Dax sighs deeply and lowers his chin to his chest. "Or if they do, they haven't told us. That's all I know. They found her blood. A lot of it they said. There's a pretty good chance she's dead based on the amount." I don't respond to that. What the fuck am I supposed to say? Dax is lost in his own world, mourning the loss of his love. I'm determined to find mine.

"That's why I came here to talk to you," I tell him, looking up at the ceiling. This bus isn't nearly as nice as ours. The appliances are black, not silver, and the floor is covered in linoleum, not hardwood. Maybe if Rook Geary spent a little more time on his music and a little less fucking groupies, he'd have a better rig. "But I guess the point's moot now."

"Don't dig into this, Turner," Dax tells me, voice so low it's almost a whisper, lost in the patter of rain on the metal roof. "Let it go. Let the experts handle it." I smile again, not a pretty one, but a bitter one. If Dax had lived the life I had, he'd know that the police don't always get it right.

"See you onstage," I say, and then I'm descending the steps and sprinting through the rain. When I hit the back door to the venue, the bouncer nearly tears my fucking head off and then apologizes profusely when he sees my face. That's when I know that something is changing inside of me, mutating, shifting, becoming something different. I would've fired that man before, beat the ever living crap out of him. Now though, I'm having a hard time justifying why. I've got a purpose now, and it feels *damn* good. Everything I do between now and the moment my lips meet Naomi's again, is focused wholly on that task. Nothing else matters.

Inside, I search around until I find the girl with the dual colored hair. I have no friggin' clue what her name is, but the thing I'm looking for, if it's here, she'll have it. She's the only chick I ever saw Naomi hang around with.

"Hey," I say, and she spins around to face me, black and white polka dot dress swirling around her hips. She's pretty in an old school sort of a way. Had somebody introduced us a few weeks back, I might've fucked her. Not anymore. "You're Naomi's friend, right?" The girl looks down at my outstretched hand and then back up at me.

"Blair Ashton," she says and then shakes it. "What can I help you with, Turner Campbell?" Her expression is neutral, resting in a place where each word I say could tip the scale, convince her that I'm one way or the other. Right now, I want her to like me. I *need* her to.

"Well, hello there, Blair," I say, trying to switch on the charm to half-mast. If I go all the way, she'll be repulsed. Pull it all back, and I might as well spit in her face. "I

wanted to ask you a question." She blinks her long eyelashes at me and waits with her red lips pushed out and her cheeks sucked in.

"Shoot," she says, scooping some hair over her shoulder and letting her eyes flicker around behind me, taking everything in. Blair is not in a good place right now. Anybody could see that. She's nervous, and she has a right to be. Nobody knows who attacked America and Marta, and even more frightening, no one knows why. She could be next; she might not be.

"Do you have access to any of Naomi's things? Anything that the police left behind?" Blair gives me a once over that says she isn't sure what to make of my questions. One thing I do notice right away: she doesn't like them.

"Why?" she asks suspiciously, fanning faux eyelashes as she keeps her gaze traveling around the room, hooking onto unknown roadies and local staff with a nervous flicker of her tongue over her lips. "I mean, what would they leave behind that would be of any use to you? They're cops, Turner." I squeeze my fists tight at my sides. I am so not used to taking shit from people. I'd sort of like to punch Blair in her tiny nose. But I'm not going to. I'm over that crap. It's not worth it. The only thing that's worth it is this. I sigh and release my frustration into the humid air. It's so fucking *hot* in air.

Should be fucking illegal. Christ. *I can't even breathe right now.*

I stare at the exposed beams overhead, the untreated wood. This building is old as sin. I don't know anything about the history of it, don't care at the moment, but it would be kind of cool to find out. I run my hands down my face and count cobwebs twenty, thirty feet up. The acoustics in this place are going to be off the hook.

"Is this like, some souvenir sort of a thing? Do you need something to remember her by?" Blair sounds bitter when she asks these questions, but I don't let it bother me. Naomi isn't dead. Marta is. Naomi is out there, somewhere, and I'm going to fucking find her. I drop my chin down and stare Blair down hard. She can't hold my gaze, good sign.

"If you can think of anything Naomi left, I'd like to see it. Sometimes the cops look at things one way and the bad guys look at it another."

"Are you a bad guy, Turner?" she asks me, tilting her head slightly, pursing red, red lips. She's got that rockabilly look going on that I'm not a fan of. She's pretty, but she'd be prettier in a pair of jeans and a tee. Whatever. I've only got eyes for Knox at this point. Seems like a one-fucking-eighty for me, but it's not. It's just a natural progression. I've been through a lot of girls, hundreds even, and I don't give a shit about any of them.

For Naomi, I'd chop off my own dick. Pretty simple.

"I don't know, Blair. I'm still figuring that bit out. When I find an answer, I'll let you know. For now, I just want to search Naomi's stuff." Blair shakes her head and pulls out a cigarette from the pocket on the front of her dress. She lights up and doesn't offer me one. I notice absently that her hands are shaking.

"There's nothing, Turner. The cops took everything. Stop worrying about it, okay?"

And then she walks away and leaves me there more curious than ever. I might be an asshole, but I'm a perceptive asshole. Something's up with Blair Ashton. I smile. Any clue is good, any new mystery is helpful because it means progress. I take another breath of the humid air and listen to the drone of the crowd out front. After this is all over and Naomi's back, we'll be crowned the freaking King and Queen of Rock. I pause. *No, I* think as I get out a cig for myself. *The fucking God and Goddess of Rock 'n' Goddamn Roll.*

I look around for awhile, letting the sea of workers and musicians swarm around me, keeping their distance, tucking in elbows and scooting past. They'll do anything, *anything,* not to run into me. I wonder how long I've been a colossal jackass without even knowing it. I go to drop my cigarette on the floor and pause. *Baby steps, Turner. Baby steps.*

I turn around and go searching for an ashtray.

For awhile there, nothing happens. I walk around and I run my fingers over the staccato walls, dig into guitar cases, open abandoned bags. I'll admit, I have no fucking clue what I'm doing. I'm not one of the Hardy boys or some shit. I ain't no Nancy Drew. But there's a driving force inside of me that won't rest, a burst of passion for someone other than myself. I've never had these urges before. At least not like this.

"Five minutes, Turner," Milo says when he finds me later, slumped in a chair, pretending to be dazed out of my Goddamn mind. In reality though, I'm more aware now than I've ever been. I haven't smoked a joint today, haven't slammed any dope. Today, it's just me and nicotine and a single beer. One fucking beer. I'm proud of myself, even if I don't have anyone to share my accomplishments with. I nod and pass him a shaky salute, my arms covered from wrist to elbow in those stupid bracelets. Every time I find one, I put it on. Don't know why. Just seems important somehow.

When he hesitates and stops to stare at me, I give him a thumbs-up and stay seated, watching, waiting for God only knows what.

But I never expect what comes later. Never would've even fucking guessed.

I pull out a cigarette but don't smoke it, instead

thrusting it behind my ear and rising from my chair, watching as the back door opens and rain splatters the cement floor. Dax comes in, moving slow, eyes hollow and empty. He's the kind of guy that gets kicked in the nuts and cries about it. Maybe it makes him deep or whatever, but all I can think is that there's no way in shit he loves Naomi. If he did, there'd be no such thing as giving up.

I slip the sunglasses on my face. They've become sort of a thing for me now, a trend. Plus, I can think all sorts of nasty things behind these glasses and nobody will know. The windows to my soul have shades now, baby.

"I hope you're ready to tear this shit up," I tell Dax, feeling good. My adrenaline is pumping and I'm *ready* for this. When I sing her words, her spirit wraps around me, caresses my shattered soul and sews me up, keeps me going another day. Dax shrugs, looking just as pathetic as the rest of the band. Amatory Riot is a broken window, and if I'm not careful, it's going to blow out. "Well, just follow my lead and you'll be alright."

At an imperceptible nod from Milo, I storm the stage, raising my arms up to get a rise out of the crowd. Doesn't take much when they're like this. Below me, no human stands, only beasts. Below me, the last vestiges of control humanity maintains to keep themselves separate from nature, is gone. It's all instinct and wild rage down

there. Music is the metaphysical representation of our shredded hearts, all of our pain and anger, our love and joy, ground up and blended together. It saves people, and it destroys them. If it's anything in between, it's not really music at all, just noise.

I grab the mic hard, wrap my fingers around it and wish it was my cock. I haven't been able to masturbate or fuck since Naomi went missing, so I've got all of this pent up energy inside of me, nibbling at my soul, feeding me dark thoughts. I French the shit out of that microphone with my tongue, getting in close, nipping it with my teeth.

"Good evening," I growl, letting the anger and the sex and the confusion out through my mouth. "How y'all doing tonight?" I let a bit of a twang hit my voice. It's as fake as half the tits in this room, but what the hell. I just go for it. "They say everything's bigger in Texas." I pause. Grin. "If that's true, then I guess I'm right at home here."

I swing the guitar around, not as epically as Naomi, but it works. Screams fill the auditorium as I slam the strings so hard it feels like my fingers are going to get sliced off at the tips, garroted by raging riffs and epic melodies.

"*Who the hell are you?*" I scream at the top of my lungs, missing that high shrieking pitch that Skinny Bitch

managed to hit. Crowd seems okay with it though, jumping up and down, pounding the floor and tasting the bass through their feet. "*Eating me, bleeding me, fucking me.*" I eat those words, change 'em up a little with a silent apology to Knox. "*He's not me, that fucking dick with the perfect kicks. I saw his reflection in a mirror, smashed it to pieces. Eating me, bleeding me, fucking me. Make a picture perfect, unbend his soul. Where were you the day I turned myself invisible?*"

With a small amount of guilty relief, I pull my hands from the strings and grab the mic, snarling into it with animalistic intent while Wren rocks a solo meant for Naomi. He's good at it, enough to get everybody excited, pump their blood up to their brains and blind them with passion and rage, but he's no Knox. Not by a long shot. If she were here, this crowd would be laid out flat, killed by it.

I spin in circles and slam the soles of my boots against the old wood, wondering what this place was originally built for. Certainly not this, this shedding of blood and sweating of souls. Oh God, I bet there are ghosts fucking *weeping* in here, spinning in their graves and crying foul.

I pause and tap my foot, waiting while Wren winds down and the Little Drummer Boy starts up, slamming his cymbals, pounding away. The other guy, What's-His-Name, smashes the bass to his crotch and screws the crap

out of it. I'm impressed.

"*I'm calling you out. Calling out to the guy within, the person buried deep that's eating me, bleeding me, fucking me. I'm picking up the pieces and the edges don't look good. Sharp points of pain are tasting me, slicing me, dicing me, and I can't ... I won't ... I will NOT let you go, let you get lost deep down inside of me.*"

The crowd is pumping their fists, swaying like barley in a Goddamn summer breeze. Some eyes are closed, diving deep, others are open, spreading out. It's like a damn orgy in here – bodies mixing, sweaty hands sliding over hips, up backs, across tight asses and throbbing cocks. I would not be surprised if this whole thing just spiraled to shit.

I get ready for the harmony that's coming up, for Blair to jump in and soften the edges of my voice.

Instead, I get something else altogether.

"*Eating me,*" whispers out of the speakers, soft and feminine, familiar but not familiar enough. "*Bleeding me.*" I pause and the crowd goes silent, just like that, like a candle snuffed out. The absence of noise is almost painful to my throbbing ears, like a punch to the gut, sudden and unexpected. "*Fucking me.*"

It's like a murder mystery play here now, but the joke's not just on the audience, it's on the players, too. I stand frozen in place, guitar hanging loosely around my neck

while a woman enters from stage left, crying out the words to this painful song like she's sung 'em before.

And she has.

Fucking Christ.

Wet and dirty, covered in cuts and dried blood, there she is. Hayden Lee.

Amatory Riot's missing leading lady is back.

CHAPTER 10
NAOMI KNOX

I hear my music again, booming loud, like some sort of
fucked up call from Heaven. It pours down around me
and infuses my soul with rage. That's when I really start
to fight, when I scream against my bindings and strain
my muscles to breaking, push until blood seeps from my
wounds and sweat sluices between my lips.

An angel is singing my music from a devil's lips, and I
know who it is, even in this state. It's Turner Campbell,
the man I loved, that didn't love me back when I needed
him most, who says he loves me now. Why is he stealing
my lyrics, crying my pain? Does he know I'm here?
Does anybody?

I think back, *hard.* I imagine my hand clamping

around the door handle to the bus, pausing at the sound of voices within.

"Next time I ask you to do something, I expect it to get done. Smoking pot behind the bus doesn't equate to work in my book. When you're on the clock, you belong to me. Afterwards, I could give a shit less what you do."

America. Being a bitch. Nothing unusual about that.

In my memory, I keep climbing, yanking open the door and ascending the steps to find my manager, hands on her hips, looming over a young girl that looks like she's about my age. I've never seen her before, but that's not unusual. There are lots of staff members I've never met.

They both look up when I come in, but they're not looking at me. They're looking at someone behind me. America opens her mouth to speak and pain slashes through my skull, dropping me to my knees. I fall forward as a crushing weight grinds into my back. My mouth makes no sounds; only my mind is capable of screaming. And it does. It shouts and fights, lashing out at my attacker, but failing to move my limbs. My eyes go dark, and I pass out.

And then I wake up here.

I can taste blood and smell it, too. It's dark, but it's not a trunk. There's too much space above and around, and below, it's too soft. A bed? Am I on a bed?

A sound jerks my head around, draws my shuttered eyes towards a flash of light. I must be blindfolded because I can't see anything but the change in shadow. A prick in my arm stings painfully, and I scream again, crying out to that angel to come to my rescue. I don't know why. I have no clue how, in my most terrible moment, I could rely on that wolf in sheep's clothing.

But I do.

With every slowing beat of my tired heart, I do.

CHAPTER 11
TURNER CAMPBELL

Seeing Skinny Bitch alive and well is like watching a zombie rise from the grave. When this chick went missing, I just sort of assumed she was dead. Unlike Naomi, Hayden has a hole inside of her. Basically, she's weak. Seeing her walk onstage is a shocker to be sure. To their credit, the band keeps playing and finishes the song with a beautiful high note from Miss Lee. Me, I just stand there like an asshole and stare.

"That happy to see me?" she chokes, coughing and gagging as Dax gets up from his kit and races over with a water bottle for her. The band gathers around.

"Naomi?" I ask, hoping beyond hope that wherever Hayden was, that maybe Naomi is with her, that maybe

we've got a solid lead. She ignores me for the moment and downs the bottle while the crowd's silence fades to murmurs and then rises to deafening screams.

"What about her?" Hayden asks, looking around at the band with a bit of blood dripping from her scalp towards her eye. She doesn't seem to notice it. Her hair is tangled and she's wearing clothes that look like they've seen better days. What the fuck is going on? Ain't nobody going to shit with me and tell me that her disappearance had nothing to do with Naomi's. Nuh uh. I might be stupid, but I'm not fucking retarded. I resist just barely the urge to reach out and shake her hard.

"Oh my God," Blair whispers, getting tears in her eyes. "You haven't heard."

"Heard what?" Hayden sniffs, wiping her hand across her face. She's shaking and her cheeks look gaunt, but in her eyes, I don't see any pain or fear, just confusion. "What's going on? Where's Naomi? Why is Turner here?"

"Where the fuck have you been?" bursts out of Dax's mouth. He, too, looks like he wants to shake the bitch. Hayden tucks some brunette hair behind her ear and sniffles, shaking her head wildly. The buzz in the crowd has gotten so bad that it's almost impossible to hear what she says next.

"In Hell." And that's it. Hayden stops talking, and

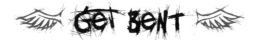

tears fill her eyes. Blair wraps her arms around her bandmate.

"It's okay, baby. It's okay."

"I just want to sing," Hayden whispers and then starts to full on sob. I stand there watching unsympathetically as the rest of the band looks around like they're not sure what to do. They have no manager now and their leading lady is obviously suffering some sort of trauma. Naomi, their real leader, is nowhere to be found. I turn around and move off the stage quick as I can.

"Milo," I say, and I'm not ashamed of the words that fall next from my lips. I might never live 'em down, but hey, what's a man to do? "I need you." Milo nods and moves forward, stepping into that role he's so damn good at, taking the stage and wrapping his arm around Hayden's shaking shoulders. He escorts her off and tosses a look over at me, worry lines crinkling his face.

"I think it's time for Indecency to put on a show," he says, and I nod, sucking in a huge breath and really missing the rush of drugs in my system. *I can do this.* Milo starts barking orders at the crew and they rush around me, splitting in half as they hurry to haul off the equipment. One of them even grabs a rag and scrubs away some of the blood that Hayden's dripped across the floor.

"What the shit?" I hear Trey ask from behind me. But

I don't have any answers for him. Whatever shit Hayden's been through will have to wait. The show must go on, right? I scrape my teeth against my tongue ring so hard that it bleeds, filling my mouth with a tangy copper taste. When I glance over my shoulder, I see cops. Don't know where they came from, probably the mess outside, but they're already hovering around Lee and whispering soft spoken questions.

My mind struggles with this new bit of information, trying to digest it as I move to the right and try to grab a glimpse of the heaving crowd. The bouncers all look nervous which is a bad fucking sign. The metal gates up front are rattling and shifting forward as people attempt to climb up and over them, desperate for a taste of this drama. If they only knew what it was like to drink the stuff, they would't be so eager. My eyes scan the colorful mess of misfits and miscreants quickly and then go over them again, just in case. I don't really expect to see her.

But I do.

The bald girl.

Turner Campbell's never really been that smart. I admit it. Yeah, I'm fucking stupid sometimes, but when I set my mind to something, I go for it. And this, this I've set my fucking heart and soul on. I move across the stage in a sprint and hit the edge with a bunching of muscle and tendons, launching myself forward and into the frothing

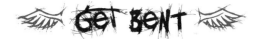

mass.

The audience fucking *loves* this, and their hands come up, like the demons of hell, reaching and grasping for a taste of me. I hit this hot wave of flesh and sweat and land like I'm floating on fucking clouds. The crowd lets me surf for a price, running their hands over me, molesting me with greedy fingers and touching me all over, rushing me back and forth, up and down, pulsing me with the beat of their hearts. The whole time, I struggle to keep my eyes on the girl who tries to turn and flee. But the crowd is thick, dense and immovable. My movements might be frenetic, uncontrollable, but at least I'm moving. The girl gets stuck between the exit and the bathrooms, choosing the easier route and sliding her body past a bouncer and into the heavy swinging door.

And then things get bad.

These people are riled up crazy, salivating for blood, desperate to eat a piece of me and become *something*. I said worship me; they said yes sir. And now I'm paying for it. My own arrogance is fucking the ever living shit out of me.

The crowd surges and engulfs me, dropping me to the floor where I hit the wood hard with my knees. People press down on me like an avalanche, knocking my palms to the ground, scraping my skin along the splintered wood. I hear my name echoing around me, and for the first time ever, I see my fame as a curse instead of a blessing. Hiding behind the walls of my bus, behind the fog of the drugs, the whisper of sweet, anonymous lips, I haven't seen this side of it. And let me tell you, it's real ugly. Real fucking ugly.

There's this pain and this sadness, this tragedy, and they don't care about any of it. They see me how they want to see me, refuse to acknowledge my pain. *This is hell. Destroyed by your own dream. Brilliant, Turner. Look at you now, you fucking fool.*

In the heaving mass of faces and greedy, grasping hands, something stands out at me.

A pair of bare feet, frozen and still in the kicking and the scrambling, the stampeding.

I fight through to it, crawling beneath the sea of followers I've always wanted, who believe everything I've ever told them. They all want me but now they can't find me; I'm hidden in plain sight beneath their feet while bouncers fight to get through from the sides. *What a fucking mistake this was.* The last time I was out in public, before this tour started, I'd get recognized sure, but it was nothing like this. Oh God, not at all like this.

I crawl slowly, aware that hands are touching me, feet kicking me, some on accident, some on purpose. Looks like a damn riot's stirring up in here. I keep moving, focusing my eyes on pale, white toes and a shiny, silver

anklet that I swear I can hear tinkling, even with all the noise.

When I get to that island of stillness, I reach up and out and a hand brushes mine, wrapping gentle fingers around my wrist, pulling me forward with a surprising amount of strength. I surge to my feet just in time, just as the crowd starts to explode in screams and angry shouts. I don't look where I'm going, just follow the whisper of flying feet as the girl – Naomi's foster sister I presume – drags me forward, making a lot more headway than she had before. My guess is that she wasn't trying then. She sure as fuck is now.

We hit the women's bathroom and slide inside.

Almost immediately, I'm bombarded with memories of Naomi, and my heart constricts painfully, leaving me bent over and leaning against the wall panting for breath. Bald Girl doesn't give me any time, just snatches me by the wrist again and drags me to the stall at the end, pushing me inside and slamming the door behind us. She slides the dead bolt into place and spins to face me, chin up and eyes stormy as the fucking sky outside. Where Naomi's eyes are dry, this girl's are wet. Soaked. She's drenched in pain and melancholy, a walking, talking slice of abuse and mistreatment.

"You could've been killed," she says and her eyes flicker over to the door as the roaring sound of the crowd booms and then fades. Female voices chatter wildly, and Bald Girl snaps her gaze back to mine. "Stand on the toilet," she whispers and I give her a *what the fuck?* look. But this girl doesn't take shit. Looks like maybe she's had enough of that in her life. *"Get on the toilet,"* she hisses under her breath, like a vulture or something. "If they see you, you'll get tied down and raped. Up, up, up." I frown, but I oblige. Just barely.

"Who the hell are you?" I whisper as Baldy gives us a courtesy flush. "What's your name?" The girl walks in a circle and wraps her arms around herself, sucking in a harsh, gasping breath. She's obviously a few cigs short of a pack, but what can I say? She knows things. I know she does. When she doesn't answer, I hazard a few guesses. "Kathleen? Karen? Kim?"

"Well, it's not Rumpelstiltskin," is her response. Huh.

"Kerrie?" The girl hunches over and closes her eyes so tight I can see the skin on the back of her skull crinkling. "Katie?" She whirls on me then, dirty dress flapping, eyes blazing like fucking firecrackers.

"Yes!" she breathes, the word quiet but powerful, pitched just so that I can hear it over the din outside the tiled shit hole we're standing in. *Naomi's hot body wrapped around mine, her fingers on my skin, her sweet breasts.* I shiver and try to ignore the hard-on that's scraping the inside of my pants. Kind of think I might

need to start wearing underwear one of these fucking days. "And you're Dakota, am I right?" I shrug and get out a cig.

"Turner Dakota Campbell, in the flesh," I say and pause. The voices outside the stall have paused to listen. I flush the toilet again. I don't ask how she knows that. My name is plastered across a thousand websites, blogs, Twitter feeds, Facebook timelines. It's fucking everywhere, and that's not just my arrogance speaking; it's a fact. "And now that we've played the damn name game, I want to know. Where's Naomi?" The girl's eyes fill with tears and she starts to shake. That damn purse is hanging over her shoulder, swinging like a pendulum. The dress she's got on is the same one I saw her in a week ago.

"I don't know," she whispers, shaking her head. "I don't know. I tried to get here in time, I did. But it was too late. It's too late."

"Shut up," I snap at her, maybe a little too harshly. She cringes and right away, I feel bad. I adjust my boots on the toilet seat and hope the piece of crap doesn't crack and break my damn ankle. "It's not too late. It's never too late. Where is she? You said *he* got to her first. Who the fuck is he?"

"The Devil," Katie says and then drops to her knees. Something rolls from her purse and disappears under the door.

"You alright in there, sweetie?" asks a nasally voice. "You dropped your pills."

"Keep them," Katie says, looking up at me from her position on the floor. I'm gettin' uncomfortable crouching here on the damn shitter, but I don't move. I stay, and I wait, eyes scanning the girl's tired face for clues.

"This is some good shit, you sure?" asks the stupid bitch outside the door. I have the urge to tell her to fuck off, but then I might end up with a mob on my hands. I stay quiet. It takes a hell of a lot of effort, but I manage.

"I said KEEP IT!" Katie screeches, grabbing at her head with crooked fingers, clawing at the fine buzz of hair there. She starts to keen and ends up rocking back and forth like a crazy person, moaning under her breath, whimpering pitifully.

"Fuck, okay, your loss," says Nasal Bitch, and then her heels clomp away across the tile. "I hear Turner Campbell's in the audience somewhere," she says and I hear a few sets of giggles. I block the girls out.

"The Devil doesn't exist, Katie. Who did this to Naomi and America, to Marta? You've gotta know something."

"All I know is that you better find her before he gets his claws in her."

"Who, Katie? Who the fuck are you talking about?"

I'm getting frantic now, feeling adrenaline pump through my veins. *He, he, he.* The thought of some guy touching Naomi just makes me bat shit crazy. I see red; I want to fucking *destroy.* Nothing bad can happen to her or Turner Campbell will cease to exist and Vengeance will take his place.

"I've seen what he can do, and it isn't something you survive. It's something you run from the rest of your life. I'm still sprinting, Dakota."

"Goddamn it," I shout, stepping down from the toilet and slamming my boots against the dirty floor. There are syringes everywhere in here. Looks like a damn biohazard room. "I can't do shit with vague little hints. Spell it out for me!"

Katie looks up at me and stares through waterfalls of pain that run down her cheeks and stain her dirty dress. She's a pretty girl, this Katie chick. She has a heart shaped face and round eyes, lips like a rosebud. There's a fiery spirit in there, too, one that makes me sick when I see the haze covering it, like the fog over the sun. Somebody really screwed this chick. *Not somebody, her parents, the ones Naomi killed.* If I'd been bothered at all by the thought of Naomi killing someone, I needn't have been. Seeing this girl, I know why she did it, why she took justice into her own hands, channeled it into a pair of scissors and ended things. For what they did to this

girl, Katie's parents got off light.

"I don't know anything for certain. But if he finds me, he'll destroy me. I only have a few pieces left. If he gets me again, there'll be nothing to put back together. I *need* Naomi to be okay. Please, help her." I clench my fists at my sides and try to hold back a rush of anger and rage and helplessness. Standing here in this stall chatting it up isn't going to save the woman I love, that I never got to actually show that to. I have to take action but how can I when I have nothing to go on?

"What's the devil's name?" I ask, hoping she'll give me something concrete. Katie wipes her hand across her face and clutches her plastic purse against her chest.

"He goes by many names. Beelzebub, Antichrist, Satan … " The girl is obviously off her rocker. I'm not getting *anything* out of her. I spin around and punch the wall in anger, letting out a growl of frustration. The tile cracks and blood oozes down my knuckles. Too late, I spin back to Katie to apologize, but she's already gone and I hear Heaven crying for her pain, drenching the earth in tears as she explodes into the auditorium and disappears into the crowd before I can take a single step forward. When I do, my boot crunches down on something. I pause and take a step back.

Beneath the rubber sole is a car key.

CHAPTER 12
NAOMI KNOX

Voices wake me from my foggy stupor. They're familiar, but I can't place them. All I know is that I haven't heard them here before. I can't make out any words; the drugs won't let me. What I can tell is that the music has stopped. All around me is quiet, a few sputtering generators but not much else. *Where the fuck am I?* I wonder as I shift to my side and feel a painful tug in my arm. The IVs are still attached, pumping God knows what into me. Food? I know I haven't eaten in days. Moisture certainly because I haven't had anything to drink either.

Footsteps come toward me, growing so loud it feels like my eardrums are going to burst. The swishing noise

of curtains sounds again and light flashes bright against my blindfold. *Curtains. An enclosed bed. Generators.*

I'm on a bus. Or an RV, I guess. But probably a bus. A tour bus maybe?

This time, instead of the usual arm prick, a hand tangles in my hair and brushes it back gently in a soothing gesture. Only it doesn't soothe me. It pisses me off. I want to get up. I want to know where I am. I want to know who the fuck has the audacity to tie me up like this? I start to scream and the hand becomes rough, jerking me around and smashing my cheek against the rough fabric of jeans. Behind the fabric, I can feel a hard bulge that can only really be one thing. *No. No. No.* I start to struggle and the hand reaches down for my gag, digging fingers beneath the fabric, getting ready to tear it away.

Whoever this is wants to rape me.

My body explodes with panic, adrenaline taking over and making me kick and flail like a wild animal. The hand slaps me hard, but I barely notice, shrieking and bucking, arching my back and hitting the wall with my feet.

More footsteps sound toward me and the hand retreats. A tense moment of silence reigns overhead and then the prick comes, digging into my arm painfully. As I fade into a forced slumber, I cry out to the world around

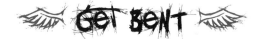

me, praying that someone or something has enough mercy to care about a girl who thought she was broken, who only just now realized she's merely bent.

Who, who, who will come for this girl who doesn't know how to love anymore?

Who?

CHAPTER 13
TURNER CAMPBELL

I bail on our set.

It's fucked, I know, but I can't sing when my heart's in my throat. If I were to open my mouth now, the only thing that would come out would be a strangled cry of rage. That's it, all I got right now. I sneak around the front, using the advantage of the bathroom to escape into the drizzling rain outside. Above my head, thunderclouds crack and snarl, warning me out of the mess. But I ignore it all, key clutched tight in my hand. The weather may not realize it, but I'm the one with the advantage right now. The crowd's been cut down to the barest minimum and even the few people left are huddled under umbrellas and inside tents. I make an easy beeline to the customer

parking lot and stand stone still, eyes scanning the dripping vehicles.

The key's nondescript. The only reason I know it goes to a vehicle is because it has that black rubber bit on the end. Otherwise, I'd have never even known. I hold it so tight that the metal cuts into my palms and bleeds my red blood into the puddle below my feet. The task in front of me seems downright fucking impossible, but I can't talk myself out of it. So in the dark, in the rain, I move forward and I start testing vehicles. I try doors and trunks, moving from one end of the row to the other, then onto the next. I figure if anybody catches me, I'm Turner Goddamn Campbell. They'll back off. If not, there's always money. Last I checked I had a whole shit ton of it.

Each failure pisses me off, making me grit my teeth and bite at my tongue ring, tasting blood on my mouth, feeling like I want to beat the shit out of someone. No. Not someone. *Him.* Whoever the fuck is that took Naomi. God, when I find him, he better run because if I get my hands around his throat, it is lights fucking out.

"Turner!" A sharp voice cuts through the rain and draws my gaze up and over to a figure jogging through the drizzle towards me. As he gets closer, I can see that it's Ronnie. His face is pale and his hands are shaky, but he looks lucid enough. I stick the key in the next lock

and turn. Nothing. "What the hell are you doing out here?" he asks, watching as I move to the trunk of a silver Miata. I pause for a moment, trying to figure out how the hell to answer that question.

"Looking for my woman," I say simply because well, that's all there is to it. Ronnie should understand better than anybody. I move onto the next vehicle, and he follows, hair sticking to his pale forehead and sunken cheeks. Ronnie used to be a good looking guy. Not so much anymore. He better chill on the damn drugs or he's going to rot from the inside out. Even I fucking get that.

"Trey is not happy with you," he says, but he doesn't mention Milo, so I figure everything's alright. With Hayden's sudden reappearance, the crowd will get over it. They got to see me sing, a ghost rose from the grave, and I crowd surfed the shit out of their asses. They'll remember this concert for a long time coming.

"I figured as much," I say as I keep at it, inserting the metal, twisting it, feeling that surge of disappointment. From behind me, I can hear the sounds of the crowd filtering out of the building. I'm not going to be able to keep this up for much longer. "But that doesn't mean shit compared to this." Ronnie doesn't question me, just holds his hand out for key and examines it carefully. Being the God of Gossip has honed his skills and refined his knowledge of useless shit, so when Ronnie looks at

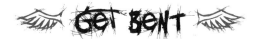

the key and squints hard, I know he's come up with something for me.

"This isn't a car key, Turner," he tells me as he nods once and hands it back. His shirt is sticking to his body, showing me how skinny he's gotten. It makes me feel like a shitty fucking friend. How did I miss this downward spiral? Where the shit have I been?

"Then what is it?" I ask as the masses disperse and start moving towards their respective vehicles. Probably a good time for us to leave. But I won't. Not until I get an answer from Ronnie. He licks his lips and glances around like he expects somebody to be listening in on our conversation. When he looks back at me, I can see the curiosity and the fear in his eyes. He doesn't know exactly what's going on, but he can guess, and he doesn't like it. I don't blame him.

"If my instincts are right, and they usually are, I'd have to say that this key … goes to one of the tour buses."

Ronnie and I leave the parking lot running, pausing only

when the big burly bouncer out front looks like he's about to blow our friggin' brains out. I don't flash him any ID, just swipe the hair from my forehead and look him in the eye. He lets us right in.

Pausing there in front of the chain link fence, I look around the mostly empty parking lot. Nobody really wants to be out in this dark, miserable weather, so it gives me time to think, to scan. There were five buses before; there are four now. This key could go to my bus or even to Naomi's. In that case, it isn't really a clue at all. But then there's the chance that it goes to one of the other buses. There's Terre Haute's over on the left, closest to that side of the fence. In the center, I see the bus for Burning the Bleeding. To the right of that, Ice and Glass.

I twirl the key around my finger, using the empty ring it's attached to and just watch, watch and wait. Lightning crackles in the distance, snaking through the blackness of the horizon like a warning. *Stay out of this,* it tells me. *If you don't want to get hurt.* I smile. Not even God herself could stop me from taking on this task.

"I'll walk you back to the bus," I tell Ronnie, but he's already shaking his head. When I look over at him, I see something in his face. In that gaze, the one that's been empty for too long, there's hope. There is seriously fucking *hope* in Ronnie's gaze.

"Man, if I let you do this alone, I'd be putting a gun in

my own mouth. I have to have something, and this it.
You've got to be happy, Turner. If I can't make things
right for you, then what chance do I have?" He rubs at
his nose, a habit from snorting all the crack. His eyes are
wet but maybe that's from the rain or whatever. "After
Asuka, I … " Ronnie shakes his head. He's not ready to
talk yet, but he will be. Eventually. If this all works out.
If Naomi's dead, then I'm giving up and I'll probably be
taking Ronnie along for the ride. *Can't think about that
right now, Turner. Cannot even consider that.* "Anyway,
I don't want to go back to the bus and hear Trey bitch.
Let's just pound this out, so we can sleep tonight. I am
tired as fuck."

Ronnie starts off towards our bus, dragging me along
in his wake. We don't talk when we get close in case
Trey or Milo are inside, and test the lock. Not our key.
One down, three to go. Next bus belongs to Terre Haute.
I highly fucking doubt that this is theirs. We have to test
it though or I won't rest easy. I won't even go to the grave
easy if I don't know in my fucking heart that I did
everything I could to find Knox.

As we approach the silver and green walls of the bus,
we can hear voices buzzing inside, hovering around
Hayden like she's the most precious Goddamn thing the
earth has ever seen. Personally, I don't think the world
would've suffered much to lose her, but what do I know?

"You hear any gossip about this?" I ask, tilting my head towards the foggy window on the side. Ronnie nods but puts a finger to his lips. We manage to successfully test the key without anybody noticing us. They're too busy cooing at Hayden to pay much attention to anything else. Their Barbie doll is back, and that's all that matters. I doubt any of them are even thinking about Naomi right now. Except for Dax. Maybe emo boy is sobbing away in his bed, I don't know.

"She's telling everybody she spent the last week tied up. Says she doesn't know where or why, but that she just woke up lying on the ground near the dumpsters, heard the music and wandered in." I raise both brows.

"Bullshit."

"That's what she's saying. She doesn't have many details, just keeps repeating the same things over and over again. She said she was on her way from the bus to the venue in Denver when somebody hit her over the head and took her." I crinkle my brow. That shit doesn't make sense to me, not with what Naomi said before the show. She said she was filling in for Hayden, like she knew something else. I look at Ronnie, but he's just shrugging.

"Hey, I'm not a lie detector. All I'm telling you is what I heard, and it's second and thirdhand information anyway. Could be dead wrong." Ronnie's never wrong,

and he knows it. I rub at my chin, but I can't figure out why Hayden would lie. Maybe she's just getting her shit mixed up considering the circumstances. If she's telling the truth as far as she knows it, it would make sense. If not, it's too much of a coincidence. There is no way in hell she was off doing her own thing and just *happened* to be kidnapped the same night that all the rest of the shit went down. Nuh uh. I call bullshit.

"And the police?" I ask. Ronnie shakes his head, dark hair plastered to his skull like a cap.

"Don't know crap about the police," he tells me and we both stop talking. The other two buses are easy enough to get access to, a lot less activity goes on over here. We try two locks, get two misses. I'm about to toss the key to the ground and smash it when Ronnie makes another suggestion, one I've obviously overlooked because I'm a fucking tool.

"What about the staff RVs?" he asks as he glances around with squinty eyes. "I don't see them here, but the key could belong to one of them. They're off refueling right now." He turns and looks at me as we make our way back to the bus. "Or it could be nothing. I don't know where you got the key, but maybe it belongs to some old lady in Oklahoma or some shit. You never know."

"No," I say automatically, spinning the bit of silver

around in my hand. "I do know. This key is a piece of the puzzle, a bit of the map that's going to lead me to Naomi, and I'm not going to stop until I find out where it came from." Ronnie nods and sighs deeply, reaching out for the door handle and pausing as his fingers wrap around the cold metal.

"If you're right, Turner, then what?" he asks, but I think he already knows the answer to that question.

"Then?" I say as I look up and watch the gray clouds moving across the dreary darkness of the sky. "Then I kick some serious ass."

CHAPTER 14
❧ NAOMI KNOX ❧

Everything stays stagnant for awhile. How long, I'm not sure. With my eyes covered, in this stifling darkness of blankets and rope, I have no way to judge the passing of time. Some people might be able to weather longs period like this by accessing happy memories, days at the beach or nights out with the girls. They might be able to escape the physical hell they're in by retreating into the glowing depths of joy that they've stored away, the past that glows bright and beautiful, that guides their way into the darkness of their futures.

But for me, my past is not so happy, my memories not so beautiful. I lay there in that blackness, drugged up and

terrified. I don't want to get raped. I don't want to be used. It goes against the very nature of my character. Lying here, helpless and trapped, I feel like a different person. Naomi Knox always finds a way out, always triumphs despite adversity. She might do it with a dirty mouth or a fist to the face, but she always manages. Maybe not this time. There's going to be no epic escape for me. The ropes are tied tight and the drugs are solid. My captors are no movie villains, leaving me alone in an unlocked room with a single guard. There are no chances here for daring escapades or hair raising triumphs.

I have to wait to be saved. Not because I want to, not because I'm lacking somehow, but because I can't move. I can't see. My shoulders have transitioned from painful to numb, not a good sign. I'm being kept alive artificially. How fucked up is that? And the most fucked up part of all this is that I don't know why. Have no fucking clue. Am I hostage? Don't think so. A sex toy? Is this human trafficking? But then why do I keep hearing music? The last logical part of me, the bit that's beyond the reach of drugs, gets that I'm still probably following the tour. My music is playing, and Turner is signing it. I want to slap his face and kiss it at the same time. He's keeping my soul alive while my body lies here and rots. I don't know why he's doing it. Is it because of that … that dirty *L* word, that thing that makes hearts beats but also stops

✗✗✗ 🞨🞨 ✗✗✗

them? I suppose that if … no, no, no … *when* I get out of here, I'll have to ask him.

So I lie there in forced silence, desperate to keep my mind away from all the horrible what-ifs it wants to play in my head, images of me broken and bleeding, close to death but denied the peace. I shiver and sniffle, trying to think of a moment in my life where I was actually happy. They are few and far between for sure, but there is one that keeps coming to mind over and over and over again.

The night I met Turner Campbell for the first time.

It should be my darkest nightmare, but it's not. Somehow, when I think of that night, I smile.

God, I must really be desperate.

CHAPTER 15
& TURNER CAMPBELL &

I finger that key while I sit at the table and listen to Milo go on and on about publicity and the police and blah blah blah. I don't really give a shit. All I care about is the rumble of engines. Ronnie and I keep exchanging glances, and he keeps shaking his head. Feels like those fuckers have been gone forever.

"When do they get back?" I ask, interrupting Milo and drawing everyone's eyes to mine. My manager runs a hand through his blonde hair and adjusts his red tie. He always wears one, even in this humid hell hole. It's like he's impervious to weather, a walking, talking symbol of civil obedience and corporate upstanding. Gotta love Milo Terrabotti, right?

"Who, Turner?" he asks me, sounding frustrated. He often sounds like that when he talks to me. I spin my new phone around on the table and stare at the image on the background. Naomi. I'm not a fucking creeper or nothing. I got the damn thing off Amatory Riot's website. It's a group photo, but she's the only face I see. I touch a finger to her lips.

"The RVs, the ones the staff use." Milo checks his watch with a perplexed frown. He doesn't understand my request, but at least he'll answer the question, if only to prove that he knows. "I thought they were just refueling. What the fuck is taking so long?"

"They're not just refueling, Turner. If that were the case, they could do it on the road. They have to shop for things, you know. Food, pleasantries, items that *you* requested." Milo gives me a look. "They'll be back before sunrise. That's when we're leaving." My manager looks up from his watch and stares straight at and through me. "Why?"

"Need to know basis," I tell him, squeezing the key tight. He sighs and shakes his head, rubbing at the crinkle of skin between his eyebrows.

"Okay, Turner. Fine." Milo takes a breath and tucks his small hands into the pockets on the front of his slacks. He doesn't like anybody to know, but he has to take them up because he's so damn short. I keep my gaze on the

bottom of his pants and try to pick out the hand stitching while my mind wanders.

Why would any of the staff want to kidnap Naomi? It this a crazed fan thing? Did Marta and America get in their way? And if so, how did we all miss them taking her back there?

I squeeze the key even harder, grinding it into my palm while I try to imagine how big this is and how far it goes. There's the video of Naomi, Travis' hat. I mean, how deep is this thing? How many people are involved?

"We have some renewed interest in the album. It seems this whole tragedy, as horrible as it is, has gotten the attention of some very important people." Milo clears his through and gets ready to launch into his *Professionalism, Practice, Progress* speech. We can always tell when he's about to get into it because he snorts like a damn pig and shuffles his feet.

Fortunately, he gets interrupted by a knock at the door.

Glances are exchanged and then Milo goes to open it, revealing Hayden Lee standing in front of our bodyguard, hair dripping around her freshly washed face. She smiles at us all and then focuses her gaze on me.

"Oh God, please come in," Milo says, ushering her through the door. In the distance, I can see some of her band members hovering under umbrellas and watching carefully. Milo closes the door on them and helps Skinny

Bitch get a towel to dry off with. She's not as wet as you'd imagine, making me think she probably walked here with one of her friends.

"What do you want?" I ask her, not trying to sugarcoat shit. I don't trust her. I'm going to be honest. Bitch disappears the same day Naomi goes missing and comes back remembering nothing? Hah. Fat load of crap. If she's involved, I'll destroy her. A good throat punch could end her career.

Hayden licks her lips and touches the bandage on her forehead with tentative fingers.

"I was hoping we could talk," she says and then glances around the room at my friends. It's obvious she wants to have a little one-on-one. Fine with me. I have a lot of questions for her. Without responding, I reach out and grab her wrist with one hand, snatching an umbrella with the other. The key remains in my hand, clenched tight against the wooden handle. I kick the door open and we move out before Milo can finish his protest, splashing through the rain and moving away from the bus.

"Better start talking," I tell her as she struggles to keep up with me.

"You have a problem with me or something?" she snaps as she wraps her hands around my arm and slows me to her pace. I let her touch me. But only just so she can keep up. "I do something to personally fucking

offend you, your majesty?" I look around and lick some stray drops of moisture from my lips.

"Yeah, actually. Now that you ask, I am a little suspicious, princess." Hayden slams her palm on my chest and jerks away from me. I whirl around and feel my muscles burning with adrenaline. I want to hit her fucking *hard,* but I'm not going to. I am done with that shit. *Breathe, Turner, breathe.* I let my eyes flicker closed and then open them again.

Hayden watches me struggle to get control of myself and smirks. She doesn't look or act like a girl who's been tied up for a week. I resist the urge to spit in her face as she looks up at the rain and lets it drizzle down her gaunt cheeks and thin lips. The rain surges and starts to pour, sticking her white ribcage tee to her chest and revealing little hints of the real thing underneath. If the bitch was skinny before, she's halfway to the grave now.

"Do you remember fucking me?" she asks which knocks me off my guard a bit. I sniffle and run my hand across my face. My tattoos look neon out here in this gray light. You'd think they'd be muted, but they're not, they're staring me straight in the face, blazing with color, a stark contrast to the monotone all around us. I examine the stars across my fingers, the paw prints. I curl them tight and slip the key into my pocket, just in case this gets ugly.

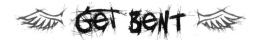

"I don't remember shit. Why do you ask?" Hayden shrugs and scratches at the gauze around her wrist. Her smirk falters a little, but she tries not to let me see it.

"I heard about Naomi," she says as she moves forward, drawing me along behind her, swaying her hips like she's trying to bait me. Not a chance that's going to happen. I get out a cigarette and fight the wind as I try to light up. The absence of chemicals in my system is really screwing with me. I feel shaky and dizzy and weak at the same time that I feel free, clearheaded. It's fucking odd. "And America. And whoever that dead chick is."

"Marta Yadley," I say and Hayden glances over her shoulder with a wet frown, moisture running down her pointed chin and hitting her erect nipples like they're bull's-eyes.

"I thought the cops weren't releasing her name to the public?" I get the cherry to light and snap my lighter closed, tucking it in next to the key and assuring myself that it's still there, still safe.

"They're not," I say, but I don't explain how I know who it is. I just take a drag on my cig and keep walking. I have no clue where we're going, but I follow along, trying to see what information I can glean before Hayden decides to clamp up about it. It doesn't escape my attention that we're moving in a circle, heading back around towards the dumpsters behind the venue, the place

where Hayden says she woke up. There were cops out there earlier, but they've gone now. I can see some of them milling around the fence, trying to figure out how to deal with this shit. Since we're on tour, they're having a hard time fitting us into their fucking jurisdiction and politics bullshit. We crossed state lines, but the murder happened in one place, so it isn't FBI territory. The county where it happened is still in charge of the investigation, but although they held onto Knox's bus, they couldn't keep the rest of us there after questioning. Some of them came along with us, but I haven't seen them do shit while being here. They mostly stand around and drink coffee, glare at us all. It's really put a damper on the fucking fun factor. I hear the roadies grumbling about it backstage.

"Where did you get it?" Hayden asks me as we get close to the building and pause. Her face lifts up and her blue eyes lock on the boarded up bell tower. Whoever did the construction tried to make it look like it'd always been that way, but it's still obvious that something isn't right, that something's missing.

"Get what?" I ask her as she wraps her arms around herself and shivers. I hand her the umbrella and she takes it, but I don't join her beneath it. Instead, I take a step back and start to move away. In the distance, I can hear the rumble of engines. This is a private road and the

show's over. There's only one thing that could mean. *The RVs are back.*

Hayden looks over at me and curls her lip.

"I liked you, Turner," she says, and I shrug. That isn't something I haven't heard before. "You were what I always wanted to be. Now, I don't know anymore." I drop my cigarette to the ground and it fizzles in a puddle. "You're the God of Rock 'n' Roll, a sexual beast to be reckoned with." Hayden smiles again, but it falls flat. "But you're also full of shit. Where the fuck is Naomi, you psychopath?" My head snaps up and I glare daggers at her.

"Are you fucking accusing me?" I ask, thoroughly disgusted. Hayden sucks in a breath and licks her lips. The next thing she says blows me the fuck away.

"That guitar you have, the one you claim is Naomi's. That's bullshit, Turner. Dax told me they all saw her smash it up onstage, so what is it you're trying to get at? What are you trying to pull?"

My body goes cold and my blood freezes in my veins, leaving me a statue in the roiling blackness of the rain and the sharp flashes of lightning. Hayden's right. In all the commotion and the shit, I wasn't thinking clearly. The guitar. Fuck. The guitar. It *can't* be Naomi's.

That is a fucking impossibility.

I hit the stairs to the bus in a blinding rage. I'm not exactly sure who it is I'm angry with. Hayden? Naomi? Myself? Nah. It's the fucking mystery fuck who's behind all of this shit. The *He*. The Devil. Whoever it was that Katie was talking about. When I stumble inside, soaking wet and pissed off, I find a couple of plain clothes cops sitting at the table with Milo. I know they're cops because of the way they sit, the way their eyes swing to me and take it all in, absorbing, cataloguing. Pisses me off even more.

"What the hell do you want?" I ask as I reach for the fridge and grab a beer. Yeah, yeah, yeah, I need a clear head and all, but this crap calls for a little drink. I'm just proud of myself for not slamming any dope.

Milo rises to his feet with a forced smile and tries to soothe my ruffled fur before I tear out any throats.

"Turner, in light of new evidence in the case, these men are hear to ask you a few more questions about Naomi." I look at the two detectives and I don't have anything to say. Maybe they suspect me, maybe not. I don't give a shit. I don't know anything that'll help them.

Sure, I could bring up the foster sister or the key, but I'm not going to. They'll take it away from me, take her into custody, and I won't know shit about what's happening. Fuck, even if they did find Naomi, I probably wouldn't hear about it until it was on the damn news.

"Ask away," I say, intending to get them out of here as fast as possible. I need to get Ronnie and go to check out the RVs. I pop the cap on the edge of the counter and drink up, downing the whole bottle in less than ten seconds. The small smattering of alcohol hits my empty stomach hard and goes straight to my head. I get out a cigarette and try to ignore the fact that my hands are shaking. It has nothing to do with the cops and everything to do with the guitar. That fucker is *expensive.* It's not just an extra, a spare, a mix up. That thing was planted, that's for sure. No doubt in my mind about that.

One of the cops, the one in a brown trench and a white button up, rises to his feet and holds out his hand. He's smiley and young, perky. Exactly the type of guy I hate. He and I are polar opposites on the scale. I bet he grew up in a three bedroom in Suburbia with a dog and 2.5 brothers and sisters. Good for him. I grew up in a trailer park with a sign so faded you couldn't read the *Happy to Have You in Tigard Springs* message that was scrawled across it. Immediately, my guard is up and I'm feeling territorial.

"Hello there, Turner. My name is Jim Pemberton and I'm with the Denver County Sheriff's Department. It really is an honor to meet you. I've been a fan of your music for years now. I was actually at one of your first shows, up in Jersey when Travis was still on bass." I look at his hand and after a moment of debate, I take it and shake hard, letting him know I'm serious here. I watch his blue eyes and his chapped lips and try to decide if he's bringing up my dead friend to piss me off, or to try and win me over.

When the other cop clears his throat and frowns at me, I figure that Jim is the good cop. Whoever's at the table is the bad one. Great. I've played this game before, when I got booked for pissing on that chick. I can handle it.

I slump down in the seat and play my bad boy card, adjusting myself in my pants with one hand and holding my cigarette in the other. Bad Cop watches me play with my balls and doesn't try to hide his disgust.

"You a fan of my music?" I ask as Ronnie enters the room and looks over at me. He knows the RVs are back, too. *Well, of course he does, he's Ronnie freaking McGuire.* Bad Cop continues to stare at me from flat brown eyes, pursing his lips and folding his hands on the table. He's not happy to be here, following our tour around. I bet if he had his way, we'd all be stuck in

Denver until this shit was over.

"My name is Darnell Valentine," he says in a monotone. "And we'd like to ask you a couple of questions." He sits up tall and doesn't try to hide his disappointment. "Before we move this to another department, we'd like to wrap up our end of the investigation."

"FBI?" Ronnie asks, pulling their eyes over to him. They take in his pale skin, the snake tattoos on his neck, and they don't look overly excited to have him in the room. Fortunately for them, they don't say anything.

"Hayden Lee went missing in Colorado and showed up in Texas," Jim says, smiling bright. He doesn't explain further. Instead he sits down next to his partner and proceeds to ask me a bunch of useless questions. *What do you know about Naomi Knox? How are you two involved? Where were you on so-and-so day at so-and-so time?* None of it strikes any chords until they move onto a slightly different subject.

"Have you had the pleasure of meeting Naomi's brother, Eric Rhineback?" Darnell asks. I stop with my cigarette halfway to my mouth. Holy fuck. Have the drugs done that much damage on my brain that I never stopped to think about Eric? Well, shit, he's the obvious suspect here, isn't he? Naomi said he was following the tour, that she spoke with him. But do I tell the cops that?

Or do I search for the fucker myself?

I drum my fingers on the table and try to think. Finally, I decide that this information, at least, is better handled by the fucks in the suits.

"I haven't met him, but Naomi said she spoke with him." The police don't give anything away. If they've heard this information before, they don't let on.

"Did she tell you what they talked about?" Jim asks.

Yeah, I think as Ronnie makes himself a sandwich and eavesdrops on the conversation. Milo sits stiff and rigid nearby, glancing at his watch every now and again. It's *late,* way too fucking late for cops and all this shit. But here they are, and the tour will just have to wait. Ah, the arrogance. And I thought I was bad. *Naomi told me all about her foster parents and how she killed them, how she stabbed a pair of freaking scissors into their throats like some kind of soap opera heroine.*

"He was looking for his sister," I say instead and I notice that Jim's right eye twitches a little. Guess I hit a nerve.

"I see," he says and adjusts himself slightly. He's pretending not to be interested, but I can tell that he is. Bad Cop doesn't move a muscle. I keep my eyes on Darnell and notice that he's wearing a very expensive watch. Guess cops make a lot of money, huh? I wouldn't know. All they ever did for me was show up and drag my

momma away. They never helped me out, never really punished her, never gave me a second chance at *something*. They slapped her wrist and tossed her back, angrier than ever. I close my eyes and try to tone down the simmer of rage in my belly. "And do you know why he might've gone to Naomi for help with that?" I shrug and stab my cigarette out in an ashtray. It's actually my fourth one since I sat down. This is taking longer than I thought. The RVs drift around in the back of my mind. I imagine kicking the door down and finding Naomi, throwing her over my shoulder and rescuing her like a prince in a fucking fairytale.

"How the fuck should I know?" I ask, playing my other card. The fact that Naomi and I aren't connected in any tangible way according to the law is in my advantage right now. "She and I aren't exactly joined at the hip."

"But you're in love with her?" Darnell blurts, leaning forward. His shaggy brows drop low over his eyes and obscure the glare he's tossing my way. My nostrils flare, but I manage to hold back my temper. Good for me. I'm growing in all sorts of fucking ways.

"What's it to you?" I snarl back.

"Darnell ... " Jim begins, but his partner isn't listening.

"We have a whole room full of people that heard you confess your love to her, that heard her deny you back

that same love. That would've pissed me off. Didn't it bother you? To be turned down like that? And so publicly, too?"

I stand up then and knock over the ashtray with my hand.

"The fuck you gettin' at, motherfucker?" I growl as Milo rockets forward and grabs me by the shoulder. Darnell and Jim stand, too, but this time, it's Jim who's frowning and his partner who's smiling.

"Thank you for your time, Mr. Campbell," Jim says, giving me a tight-lipped grin. He moves away and Darnell follows. The sound of the door swinging in the wind seems awfully loud as I stand there staring at a burn mark on the tabletop.

"Turner?" Ronnie asks, and I look up at him. "Take a walk to cool down with me, buddy?" I nod and pull my arm from Milo's grip. My manager doesn't say a thing. Maybe this time, he realizes that it's gone too far.

Nobody questions my love for Naomi. *Nobody.*

CHAPTER 16
&° NAOMI KNOX &°

I hear the voices again. They're arguing this time. I wonder if they're trying to decide what to do with me. I hope that whatever it is they decide, that they let me out of these damn ropes sooner rather than later. I can't feel my hands or my feet anymore, and that scares the shit out of me. I preferred it when they were burning in agony.

The footsteps come towards me, but they don't pull away the curtains. Instead, they move past me for the first time since I got here. The voices don't talk when they're close by, but as soon as they move away, they start up again. Wherever it is that they're standing, they've gotten so muffled that I can't hear anything but mumbling. It's so fucking frustrating, almost enough to

start up the tears again. I thought they'd all dried up those first few days, but maybe I'm wrong. Right now, a good sob feels like it's about to bubble up and take over me.

Stay positive, Naomi, I say, trying to give myself an internal pep talk. Never worked for me before, but there's always a first time for everything, right? *You're going to get out of this a stronger person. And then you're going to go nut shit crazy and blow some fucking heads off. Whoever's responsible for this is going down* hard.

The footsteps come back and this time, there's the customary swish of the curtain, the flash of light. But when I wait for the needle, it doesn't come. This time, the IVs are ripped out of my arm, and I grunt in pain. A second later, I'm being lifted up and tossed over the shoulder of somebody. A man, I think, based on the muscle and the musky smell of aftershave, but I've been wrong before, believe it or not.

The person starts to talk and their voice is still a bit muffled, despite my head resting against their back. That's when I realize it: I'm wearing earplugs. Fucking earplugs. Goddamn it.

"You tell him that the terms haven't changed. And tell him we haven't fucking seen her. If we do, we'll take care of it, okay?" The voice rumbles up from below my cheek as the person carries me forward. My head bobbles as we descend steps and then I gasp against the fabric in my

mouth as cool water hits my skin and brings life back into my numbed limbs. The pain follows shortly after, white hot, like hundreds of needles are stabbing me again and again and again.

I start to struggle and scream as we ascend out of the rain and up another set of steps, into a warm room or bus or whatever the fuck it is. My stomach flip flops and bile rises in my throat as I'm thrown from my captor's shoulder down on a bed and left with bright light blazing into my eyes. I try to turn and bury my head in one of the nearby pillows I can feel against my face, but fingers come down and grab my chin hard, turning me back in the opposite direction.

Nobody speaks again. I suppose it's for fear that I'll recognize them, I don't know, but the silence is eerie. I hear footsteps and shuffles, the crumpling of paper, strange swishing noises I can't place. A few moments later, the cool draft against my back disappears and I hear a door being closed and locked.

The needle pricks my arm again, and I pass out.

CHAPTER 17
TURNER CAMPBELL

The key doesn't work on the fucking RVs. No matter how many times I try, how hard I push, how much I want to scream, it doesn't fucking work.

So Ronnie and I head back to the bus, and I collapse, exhausted, images of guitars and scissors and blood running through my head in a continuous loop. I get that I'm probably going through some sort of withdrawal right now, too, and it's not easy. My mind and my body are both struggling to get through what's probably the hardest week of my fucking life. Falling in love is like catching an incurable disease. Yeah, maybe that doesn't sound so romantic, but it's true. It changes you, inside and out, alters the way you see and feel things, how you perceive

the world. It's incurable and it's contagious as shit. It makes you want to have babies and raise kittens, pet butterfly wings and sleep with your head on somebody else's chest. Love … man, it fucks with everything you are and everything you want to be. I like it and hate it.

I roll over in my sleep and groan, pressing my fingers to the wall beside my bunk. My other hand drifts down below and starts to stroke my cock while images of that blonde fucking beauty fill my head. I feel bad, jacking off to her when she's missing, but somehow, I know she's okay, and I know that I'm going to find her. As soon as I do, I'm putting a ring on her fucking finger, making her mine once and for all, whether she likes it or not. Deep down, I know she still loves me, even if she won't admit it to herself.

So in my half sleep, I run my fingers down my dick and grip myself at the base, squeezing hard, imaging Naomi clenching tight around me, dreaming that I'm filling her with my seed. I bite my lip hard and pump fast and furious, groaning so loud that Jesse ends up throwing something at the curtains and telling me to shut the fuck up. But I can't stop. I'm so wrapped up in that girl that I can't breathe anymore, that I can't see the world without her in it. Love has grabbed me by the balls and it's never letting go. I am so freaking screwed.

I'm going to find you, Knox. You can bet your sweet

ass that I won't rest until you're lying in my arms, sated and sweaty, filled with me while I'm consumed by you.

I squeeze harder and move faster, spilling myself into my pants and wishing it was my lover's sweet pussy. And then I open my eyes and stare at the wall and I know, just *fucking* know that wherever she is, she can feel me wanting her because I can sure as hell feel her wanting me.

Love is a disease, man, and I am fucking chronic.

When I wake up, we're in Austin and the sun is shining just as hard as the rain was falling yesterday. I step out into the front of the bus with droopy eyes and a *bad* attitude. Starting off the day pining for the one you love, filled to the brim with secrets when you *fucking hate* the damn things, is hard to deal with. My personal no secret motto is not holding up right now, and I'm rotten inside, full of those bleeding, reeking monstrosities. I can see how Naomi got so angry at the world. She was carrying some huge fucking tumors of bullshit.

I light up a cig and slump down at the table, across

from Ronnie. He looks better today, less strung out. I'm proud of him. He grins at me and flashes some of the silver fillings in his teeth.

"Have a good time last night?" he asks, and I shrug. I'm not ashamed.

"It'd have been a lot better if I'd had a partner," I say and Ronnie nods, losing his grin to introspection, delving so deep into himself that for a moment, he looks like a corpse. I notice that he's wearing some of those stupid fucking bracelets on his arm. I see that one has red writing that's a bit different from the others. *Mrs. Ronnie McGuire.* He sees me staring and holds up his wrist.

"Your fame is wearing off on us," he says, but he doesn't really look all that excited about it. Instead, he folds himself forward and locks my gaze with his. He's wearing clean clothes today and he's actually got on a shirt that one of his kids sent him. It's a stupid orange color with a bear on the front, and it looks a little ridiculous, but the message is clear. *I love you, Daddy.* I've caught him gazing at it a few times, but he's always shoved it back under his pillow when he's caught somebody looking. My quest, my determination, somehow it's rubbing off on my friend. I like that. Maybe something good can grow out of all this shit like fertilizer? Who knows? "You okay with that?"

"Am I okay with the sensationalism of my girlfriend's

disappearance? Not fucking really, but what am I going to do about it? It's kind of out my hands. Once I've got her back, safe and sound, maybe then I'll smile about it."

"We're making enough money to buy a fucking private island."

"Yeah, well, there's that, too." I watch as Josh moves into the kitchen and starts making himself a cup of coffee. For once in my life, I'm actually awake before noon. Impressive. From the look of the hustle and bustle outside the window, it seems like the crew is actually getting their shit done early for once. The drive from San Antonio to Austin is less than two hours, so my guess is that everybody got what they wanted when we arrived last night – sex, drugs, sleep. The general feeling in camp is one of contentedness, not anger, not fear, not sadness. It's like the murder never even happened. I feel kind of pissed off for Marta. I feel *extra* pissed off for Naomi.

"What's the plan for today?" Ronnie asks me, stretching his arms above his head and leaning back. He scratches at the stubble on his chin. "More gumshoeing?" I take a deep breath, absorbing the warm smell of caffeine. Maybe, instead of having a beer today, I'll start off with some coffee. Sounds like a good change of pace. I knock my tongue ring against my teeth and try to think. Do I mention the guitar to Ronnie? Maybe not

yet. I guess I should go check it out first, see if I can find anything.

"I'm just going to fuck around, and see what I can come up with," I say, and I pretend not to notice the eagerness in my friend's face. He wants to help, and I'm glad. This is the liveliest I've seen him since Asuka died all those years ago, but I don't want that spark in his gaze to turn to suspicion. Hayden, slut that she is, gave me something to think about. Maybe the hostility from Dax and Blair had something to do with that guitar? Maybe everybody's wondering about that? "I'll call you if I find anything," I add, and Ronnie smiles. As I stand up to get a cup of coffee, Josh places one down in front of me.

"For you," he says simply, and I give him a tight-lipped smile.

"Thanks." He nods curtly and we go back to ignoring each other. He's not Travis, he'll never be, but I guess I can forgive him for kissing Naomi. Well, eventually anyway.

I sip the coffee and come up with my plan.

There's a guy named Stack who works for the tour. Technically, he's employed by all the bands, so I feel alright seeking him out. He's got more piercings than a pin cushion, but the women flock to him like he's made out of fucking chocolate. Their lips say they want to eat him up as they flirt and run their tongues over their moist mouths, brush their fingers down his bare arms. I have to wade through a sea of them just to talk to the guy.

"Nah, this is no repair job," he says with a white-toothed smile. I can practically see my reflection in the damn things. I can sure as fuck see myself in his piercings. The six rings on his lip jiggle when he talks. "I saw Naomi's Wolfgang after the show, and it was trash. This is brand spanking new." He spins the guitar around in his long fingers and squints his brown eyes at it like he can decipher where it came from if he stares long enough. "I mean, I could probably track the serial number and tell you where it come from." He looks up at me. "But if I were you, I'd just count my blessings and thank whoever it was that left it for ya." Stack shrugs and hands the guitar back to me before returning to patching up a trashed kit.

"Why's that?" I ask as he settles into his work and his eyes start to get that faraway look in them, proving that he was born for this kind of thing. It's the same look I get when I sing, when Ronnie smashes his drums. The look

of a fucking purist, that artist's eye that blinds you to everything else. It's all fine and dandy and shit. Just wish it wasn't blinding him to me at this moment.

"That guitar is a blessing. Hard to find. Costs more than a car." He looks at me and raises a silver studded brow. "Well, more than my car anyway. I don't like to second guess good luck." Stack smiles and goes back to re-covering a drum. My stomach churns, but I don't know what to say. That this fucking thing is like a curse. I could have him track the serial number, but I have a feeling that whoever left this was careful enough to cover their tracks. I mean, if they're getting away with murder, surely then can outrun little, old me.

I stash the Wolfgang back in the case and pick it up by the handle, moving away before the roadies sneak back in and start hitting up Stack for sex. Guess with me out of the picture, they needed a backup.

"Hey." I turn at the sound of a voice and find Hayden standing close by. Her brunette hair is swept up on top of her head and she's got on a bright pink tank and a pair of white skinny jeans. Spiked bracelets adorn her wrists and a handful of silver necklaces dangle from her neck. When I look at her, all I see is attention whore. There's not really much about her that I find attractive. *Shit, when I banged this chick I must've been seriously fucked up.* She's definitely no Naomi. I wonder if my disgust at

seeing her has anything do with my suspicion. To me, she looks guilty as fuck.

"What?" I ask as I start across the scorching pavement. May as well take this fucking thing back inside. I'm going to need it to play tonight. I pause suddenly, stopping short. Hayden follows my lead as I turn to face her. "Are you singing tonight?" I ask her. She stares at me from cool blue eyes and smiles wickedly.

"Why wouldn't I?" she asks, mouth twisted into an expression that I know must've driven Knox nuts. It would certainly fuck me up if I had to look at it day in and day out. Hayden digs a joint out of her pocket and offers it to me, but I shake my head.

"What about Naomi?" I ask and she gives me a weird look. It's part fear, part confusion. I can't figure out the reason for either, and it makes me even more suspicious. She certainly doesn't seem to be mourning her lost friend. Bitch can play all she wants at being the Queen of Rock, but she has *nothing* on Naomi. It's not my opinion, just simple fact. Naomi writes the music, plays like a Goddess, and has the voice of a fucking angel. Hayden knows how to play up the sex. She's a performer, not a musician. Without Naomi, I don't know if Amatory Riot will survive.

"What about her?" she asks, looking guilty as all get-

out. She glances this way and that, puffing on her joint and not giving two licks about the cops that are passing by not twenty feet from us. Granted, they probably see a lot worse shit around here, but still, pretty ballsy to smoke a fattie out in the open like this. "Am I supposed to stop living just because she's MIA?" Hayden rocks back and forth on her feet as I roll my eyes with disgust and continue towards the door of the venue. Even if she sings, I'll be onstage, making sure everything goes alright, slamming out riffs that are way over my head. The day I stop playing will be the day I give up on Naomi and there is no way in shit that's ever going to happen.

Tonight's venue used to be a church … How inappropriate.

"Turner!" Hayden calls out and I pause, glancing over my shoulder at her. She looks straight at my face and holds tight there, lust and want burning bright in her eyes. Guess she's not as over me as she claims to be. "I want you to know that I never wanted anything to happen to Naomi, not really." And then with that cryptic bullshit, she turns and walks away, leaving me calling after her. But I don't chase. There's only one woman in my world worth chasing after.

CHAPTER 18
⁂ NAOMI KNOX ⁂

I wake up sometime later and am shocked as shit to find out that the blindfold is gone. *What the hell?* Immediately, my gaze snaps around the room, taking in, absorbing. I need to know where I am and what weapons, what escape routes, are at hand if I'm ever getting out of this nightmare.

My arms and legs aren't bound behind my back anymore. Now, I'm lying spread-eagled. Not good. This position only signals bad things, horrible things. I squeeze my eyes shut against the fear and flick them back open.

I'm in a trailer, I think. I mean, it could be a bus, but if it is, it's none of the ones that came on tour with us.

The bed I'm on is part of a pull out sofa. Next to me, there's a slab of run down cabinets with an orange linoleum countertop. To my left, there's a pair of old leather seats, cracked with age, facing the front windshield. We're not moving right now, that much is obvious just from the lack of motion.

I strain against my bindings, but they're just as tight as they were before, if not more so. I wiggle around a bit and am not surprised to hear clinking up above my head. Handcuffs. Fucking handcuffs. The pain makes me gasp which reminds me, a little belatedly that I'm not gagged. I can move my fucking tongue for the first time in days.

"Show me your fucking face, asshole!" I scream. Or I try to. My throat is dry and scratchy, and the best I can get out is a harsh whisper. I try again. "You pussy motherfucker, come and untie me, show me what you've got, bitch." Just a gasping croak.

I start to struggle again, flailing my body around like I'm having a seizure, fighting with every last ounce of strength I have inside to either get a reaction from my captor or find a weak spot in all of this shit. There *has* to be a way out. There just has to be. *Where the fuck are you, Turner?* I think and then realize how foolish I've been. Now, here, with the drugs fading from my system, I realize that Turner might not even be looking for me. I never even considered that before. Don't know when I

became such a bleeding heart romantic. Even if Turner felt all the things he spouted out that night in Denver, that doesn't mean he's going to drop everything and go searching for me. What a crock of crap.

So I kick harder and I keep screaming, willing with each breath for something to happen. Nothing does for a long while, and my voice, instead of getting stronger, gets weaker with each shout, with each whisper of gasping breath.

Fuck. Fuck. And super fuck.

I lay there and stare at the ceiling. It's stained, just riddled with water spots and grease. Based on the musty smell and stench of mildew, it's pretty obvious from scent alone that whoever has me now is residing in a lot less swanky of a place than my previous captors. I adjust myself with a sigh, trying to hold back tears when white hot pain sears my hands and feet. And then I hear a noise. A squeak. It's small, barely noticeable. I yank on my right wrist. Nothing. My left. *Aha.* I pull harder.

I can hear metal sliding on metal followed by an almost imperceptible shriek. Is it a loose bolt? An old part ready snap? I don't know, but it's worth a try. I pull on my wrist so hard that it feels like the bone is about to break in half, sucking in my breath and biting back a scream that's threatening to tear out my throat.

Nothing fucking happens.

I collapse back into the bed with a sob and wonder if this'll be the last place I see. If this room will be my nightmare and my tomb. What will I experience here? All the things I fought to escape when I killed my foster parents? Is this the universe's vengeance on me for taking their lives?

"When the moon hangs low and night is warm, I find my way to you," I whisper as my eyes fill with tears I won't shed. If this is my last moment alone, the last time I'll ever see the world this way, I want to sing. I always played the guitar, it's like a part of my fucking body, an extension of myself, but singing is … it's an extension of my soul. I wish I'd done it more, that I hadn't let Hayden monopolize the lead. *"If life is a question of courage, I've failed, so I hope you'll still hold me. Oh God, please hold me. If you turn me down, I've got nowhere else to go."* I sniffle hard and fight back the wave of crushing depression. *"If you'll pick me back up, I promise I'll stand. I'll find my feet and fight back, nobody will bother me again. Those sticks and stones won't touch my bones, and words will be only weapons I can wield."*

The door creaks, but I don't stop singing. Whoever it is that's fucking with me, I want them to know that I'm a person with feelings, that I'm here, that I matter. I'm not going to be some faceless fuck puppet who screams for their pleasure. I will bend, but I *refuse* to fucking break.

"I'll shed blood if I have to. I'll draw them out while I draw you in. I'll lose them while I find you. Pick me back up, and I promise I'll stand. I promise, swear it, know it, love it, believe it."

The door opens in and I crane my head up to see who it is. Some masked perpetrator? A stranger with wicked intentions?

Instead, the person that ascends the steps is one of the last people I expected to see. I swallow hard and force the word past my dry lips.

"Hayden?"

CHAPTER 10
& TURNER CAMPBELL &

The storm we had in San Antonio rolls right into Austin and slams us all hard, crackling the air with electricity and passing an eerie shadow over the venue. I'm in the back early today, fresh out of ideas and frustrated as fuck. I should've followed Hayden. I watched her, sure, and she went back to Terre Haute's bus, but I should've kept on her. Something isn't right about that girl, never was. For the first time in my life, I feel *wrong* inside for sleeping with someone, like something inside has gotten tweaked in a bad way. Thank fucking God I don't remember that shit.

I stand with my arms crossed and my gaze focused on the stage at Ice and Glass. I don't know much about their music, barely even remember that they exist. They've been opening our shows since we left Seattle and yet, I've never bothered to download a single track. They're alright, but they're not star worthy, not by a long shot. I light up a cigarette and turn away, focusing my gaze on Milo who's speaking with one of the roadies. To be honest, I don't know how any of this works. Milo tells me what to do and where to go, and I follow along. Who does what here, who's in charge, none of that matters to me. It should, maybe, but it doesn't.

I pull out my phone, check for messages, scan my Facebook page, my blog. Nothing. Nobody has anything helpful to fucking say. Bunch of damn trolls. I tuck it back in my pocket and nearly drop my cig when the power flickers off and on. To their credit, Ice and Glass keeps going, not skipping a single beat. The crowd, lukewarm previously, starts to titter and get excited. Good. I need a lively show tonight, something to fuel my blood so I can keep on keepin' on.

The power goes off again, and the emergency lights wink on, bathing both rooms in a red glow that reminds me of dark rooms and perverted serial killers. I don't like it at all. Makes me sick to my stomach. The singer, a guy in his early twenties with a cocky fuck face and an attitude to match, belts out the lyrics to his song, screaming them at the crowd with a music fueled rage.

They love the shit out of that and start to bounce, bathed in the bloody glow of the lights and the distant pounding of drums. When the electricity explodes back into action, they shriek like wailing demons and rush the stage. It's a bit lower than usual, an improvised arena made from an old church dais. Kind of creeps me the fuck out. Either side of the platform is draped in these heavy, red curtains that dangle from the vaulted ceiling like ghosts.

I turn away and close my eyes, breathing in the scent of sweat and pot, wishing like hell I was high. But I know I'm less than useless that way. If I'm not making any headway now, how the fuck do I expect to get shit done with a bunch of screaming voices in my head? Drugs are not an option right now.

"Turner." Just my name, short and clipped. I open my eyes to find Blair dressed in a form fitting red dress, tight and ruched. It looks like it's got a mind of its own as it inches its way up her pale thighs. Her black and blonde hair hangs over her shoulders and teases the edges of her fingers where they're pressed against her chest. Beneath them, I can see something peeking out. A picture maybe?

"What's up?" I ask as I watch her watching me carefully. She's making a lot of judgments right now, and I've got to make sure I'm on the right side of them. There's conflict burning in her eyes, warning me that

something's happened. I don't know what it is, but it's serious. Otherwise, why the hell else would she be here talking to me? Blair closes her eyes and rests her long lashes on her cheeks for a moment.

"You asked me if there was anything of Naomi's that might help you figure things out. Well, I might have something, but I need you to answer a question of mine first." She opens her eyes and cuts me deep. "Where did you get that guitar? We all saw what Naomi did to hers. What the fuck are you trying to pull?" I wet my lips and tap my cigarette ash into a nearby tray. Honesty, my favorite fucking policy. *Finally.*

"It was left on my bus," I say, and then I think about that hard for a minute. The guitar. A piece of Naomi, a symbol. Travis' hat. The same. What. The. Fuck. Is going on here? I get the idea that this whole thing goes beyond Naomi, that it's something bigger, something even more frightening than I thought before. Something that started a long, long time ago. My skin erupts in goose bumps and I find myself wrapping an arm across my chest.

Blair continues to stare at me, taking in the white Amatory Riot shirt with the black and red fist, the dark jeans, the boots. She isn't my biggest fan, but I know before she takes a step forward in her ridiculously high heels that she's going to take a chance on me.

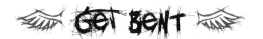

"I found this on the bus, under Naomi's mattress. I found it before the show that night. I was going to ask her after, but … " Blair stops talking and then thrusts the image at my chest. I take it in shaky fingers and unfold it.

Hayden Lee, covered in blood. What a surprise.

CHAPTER 20
❦ NAOMI KNOX ❦

"What the fuck?" I ask as the worst friend, the best enemy, I've ever had slinks in and moves over to the side of the bed, dropping to her knees and hovering her hands over my body like she's casting a spell.

"I wish we didn't have so many secrets," she whispers, sniffling and letting hot, salty tears fall from her eyes and slap the bare skin on my arms. "If we didn't, this might not be happening right now. I'm so sorry, Naomi. I never meant for anything bad to happen to you."

"Hayden," I say, trying to appeal to her soft side. Didn't know she had one until now, but shit, if her weeping face and trembling lips are any indication, she feels guilty. I have to play up on that, take advantage and

get the fuck out of here. The way she's acting, how her eyes are shifting from side to side, I'm willing to bet that this isn't her trailer. She knows who it belongs to, and she's not supposed to be here. That much is obvious. "Hayden, whatever's happened, whatever you did or I did, it doesn't matter. Just get me out of here, and we'll figure it out. We always have, right? Right?" But she's not listening anymore. Her face is in her skinny hands and she's sobbing like I'm already dead, like this is my funeral and I'm as good as buried. I've always hated the bitch, but right now, I *despise* her. "Snap the fuck out of it, bitch!" I scream, and I'm proud to hear my voice actually come out properly. Instead of a wheezing gasp, I sound strong, ready, like I could take on anything. It's all a front, of course. Doubt I could hurt a friggin' fly, but it does draw her eyes upward.

"You've been mean to me, Naomi. Always calling me stupid, whispering cruel words behind my back." Hayden's hand snakes out and grabs me by the hair, pulling tight, squeezing hard. "I should want you here, want you to suffer, but I guess it's just not in me." She lets go and stands up, dashing away tears, glancing at the clock on the stove. She looks so clean and polished right now. Pisses me off. I feel so grubby and disgusting. I would kill for a fucking shower. *Shit.* "I have a show soon," she tells me, confirming my earlier guess that I'm still on the tour. I'm not out in a bunker in the desert. Things are looking up. "*We* have a show soon, and I'd be kidding myself I thought we'd survive without you for long." Hayden turns and gives me a look over her shoulder, reaching up to pull the clip from her hair. Perfectly straight brunette tendrils drip down her back and swing as she whirls around to face me fully. Her nipples are erect and she looks a little too excited for the given situation. "Even with Turner ... " She pauses and licks her lips. I don't like the way she says his name, like she's raping him with words. Jealousy surges through me, both surprising and terrifying. How can I be thinking about that when I'm in a situation like this? *The fuck?* "We'd just be a novelty. I don't want that. I want to be immortalized, Naomi." Hayden moves towards me and purses her lips. "I'll get you out of here. I don't know when or how, but I will. I will." And then she leans down and presses a kiss to my lips.

Admittedly, I want to strangle the bitch, but I can't alienate her now, so I lay there stone still until she pulls away with a sigh.

"Hayden," I say as she backs up and turns away. "Don't leave me here." She ignores me and reaches for the door. "Hayden! Please!" I scream and my voice echoes around the trailer. "Hayden!" Rain and wind pour in through the open door as she descends the steps

and hits the pavement, letting it swing shut behind her. Despair crushes me hard, tightens its grip on my throat and strangles me. I start to scream and thrash, kicking and flailing around, bruising my wrists and ankles and drawing blood.

I'm making such a fuss, I don't even hear the door open a second time.

"Naomi?"

The soft voice is almost inaudible above my shouting, but I hear it. It's a voice I haven't heard in a long, long while. I stop screaming and tilt my chin towards my chest, so I can see. Standing at the end of the bed, barefoot and dressed in rags, stands my foster sister, Katie Rhineback.

CHAPTER 21
❦ TURNER CAMPBELL ❦

Getting through Amatory Riot's set is a fucking chore. Hayden's not a bad singer. In fact, she's better than I want to admit. Thing is, having to stare at her skinny ass as she eats up the crowd's pleasure is like watching a succubus rape a man. He might act like he's enjoying it, but he has no idea that his soul is being ripped out through his cock. I want to smash my guitar into the back of that bitch's head and demand that she tell me where Naomi is. I *know* she knows. And that picture? If Naomi had that, and Hayden wanted to stop her from telling people, it would make sense why she'd go after her. Now, why she'd kill Marta and attack America, I don't fucking know. Maybe bitch is just crazy?

I force my way through the songs, trying my best to match up to Wren, getting nowhere near Naomi. Afterwards, I don't even bother leaving the stage, just step up to the plate so to speak, and snatch the mic from Hayden's hand. The audience hisses at this and cackles as I set the guitar on the ground and slide it away with my foot.

"Howdy," I whisper into the mic, happy to be free of the guitar but feeling a little naked, too, you know? Good thing that's a positive onstage. I tease the edge of my pants and loose a button. The demons below me surge and wail, clawing up at me, worshipping me, having no fucking clue how bad I'm hurting. I want to inflict that pain on Hayden until she gives up her secrets. *As soon as this set is over, bitch better run.* "How are y'all doing this evening?" I lift up my shirt and let 'em get an eyeful while crew members rush around me, breaking like waves when they get close. Nobody touches Turner fucking Campbell. "I'm going to be honest with you right now. I am beyond fucking horny."

Words filter up to me from below. *Pick me. Fuck me. I want you.*

I chuckle softly and kiss the mic, listening to my harsh, angry breath pound through the speakers. I caress my belly with one hand, feeling the hair there, teasing the edge of my denim with my fingers. I sneak over to my

pocket and pull out the shades, sliding 'em up my nose and letting out a deep sigh.

"You're all fuckin' lovely, but there's just one woman that can satisfy me now. Just one woman." I tap my foot on the stage and wait for Ronnie to kick off our first song. *One Woman.* Seems kind of ironic that I wrote it while I was whoring around. Maybe my heart knew something my mind didn't? Maybe it remembered that one woman, the *only* woman, that can match me blow for blow, whose mouth is as filthy as mine? Shit. Damn. And fuck me.

Ronnie slams in sideways and cuts me up through my bones, shaking me hard, bouncing my knee like some sort of old-timey God, like I should be in black and white or some shit, splashed up on a G-rated love story across the silver screen. Trey kicks me in the ass and Jesse follows, dragging Josh along for the ride. I know this is the song he struggles the most with, but I don't care. It's the one I *need* to sing right now.

The power flickers again and kisses me with red, tastes me, eats me up inside while I start the first verse.

"*My one woman, my only woman, the person who is there.*"

"*Who is there,*" filters in softly from Trey's mic.

"*My one woman, the only one who knows me, the person who understands.*"

"*Understands.*"

"*My one woman,*" the softness trails away, the angelic halo around my head shatters and I bend over in a massive scream, sucking in a breath and crushing the eardrums of the crowd with a wailing, breaking shudder of a screech. It rips through them like a hurricane and tears up their souls. "*MYONEWOMAN!*" I suck in a breath, spit it out against the mic. "*She's the ONLY one that understands. That fucking UNDERSTANDS.*" I swing the mic around and spin in a circle, wrapping the cord around my wrist and snatching it in the opposite hand. "*She's the only one that breathes life into this desolate,*" I hiss this last word, grinding it with saliva and sweat against the microphone. When I'm done up here, they're going to have to trash this shit. It's going to have Turner Campbell written all fucking over it. "*Hell hole. This desolate slice of shit. My one woman. My ONLY Goddamn woman.*"

The power flashes again and this time, it stays off for a moment and the emergency lights kick in, kissing my blue-black hair with red, highlighting my tattoos, bathing me in beautiful crimson light. I drop the microphone and tear off my shirt. I'll admit, I'm a little lost in my frenzy, but that's alright. That's what the crowd came here to see, so that's what they're going to get. Me. Bloody, my heart beating outside my chest. They better take a close look because it's the only chance they'll ever get to see it.

"*When she's with me, I am not just a man,*" I slam my fist on my chest and crouch low, shouting my words above the din of the crowd. Ronnie's cymbals ring out bright behind me. Jesse, Trey and Josh keep on strumming it hardcore, even though nobody can hear them, even though it's a serious tonal fuck up. Doesn't matter. Right here, in this moment, the music has transcended amps and speakers and cords and wires. It's all soul in here, baby. All torn up, twisted, fucked up soul. "*I am part of a whole, a LIVING, breathing, FUCKING bit of the universe. And all because of my one woman, my ONLY woman.*" I'm on my knees now and I'm screaming, just shouting this shit out, my voice cracking and breaking like glass, like my balls never dropped and I'm a damn kid again.

The power switches on again and I roll on my back, reaching above my head and using the cord that's wrapped around my wrist to drag the mic back to me. Sweat pours down my face and clings to my lashes, runs my black liner down my face and teases the star tattoos at my hairline.

"*She was there for me when the world was dead.*"

"*When the world died!*" My boys back me up with the lyrics I wrote but never understood. I just sang 'em and I *felt* them. Now, I get it. Might seem stupid. Might even seem like a crock. I don't know much about Naomi,

right? Things could get screwed up between us. But you know what? It doesn't matter. When love takes hold of you and bites down, you may as well just surrender because if you fight it, you're fighting the one thing on this earth that's worth living for.

"She was with me when I was rotten on the inside, when I bled black blood and told white lies. She was with me when the sky fell and the day turned to night, when the seven plagues descended upon me, my one woman was there."

And off it goes again, the power fails and succumbs to nature's infinite power. I hope we have fucking generators or some shit because I think that tonight, she's given all that she'll give. It's our turn to take a step back and reevaluate things.

"And when I go to bed," I growl, hoping that somebody can hear, that there's at least one person in this screaming, shouting mass that's absorbing my voice, my words. *"With my only woman, I taste the sweetness and the shame. My one woman's a fine wine to my caving, aching, suffering pain."* It's so loud in here now that I can't hear the words that are tumbling from my lips, getting caught on my tongue ring and my lip rings, snaking out into the warm air like curses and blessings both. When I lift my chin up, I can see people scrambling around backstage, struggling to get some

sense of order going in here.

I roll around onto my belly and unhook the mic from my wrist.

The song is still inside of me, begging to get out, clawing at my throat with hooked claws, but if there's nobody to hear it, I'm holding it in. I want *someone* to listen to me, to understand what I'm going through.

I push up to my knees and gaze out at the crowd. They're in a full on riot now, shouting my name, calling out to me, cussing, screaming, kicking, biting. It's a madhouse down there and I am King. I swipe my arm across my face and glance over to my right. There's a figure emerging from the darkness of the stage entrance, bathed in dark shadows and bloody red flickers of dying light. I look back over the crowd. They're going to start evacuating this place soon, before this pit of demons turns on itself.

"Turner."

My head snaps to the right. That voice … There is no fucking way. In this craziness, I'm imagining things. I stare hard, squint my eyes and try to focus.

The power flares to blinding brightness for a second, highlighting blonde hair, orange-brown eyes. And then it's gone again and I'm rising to my feet, stumbling towards the figure with my arms outstretched. I can't see *shit.* I trip over one of the lines of tape that keep the

cords down and fall against a heaving chest.

As soon as my hands touch her bare skin, I know who this is. Without a doubt, I know I'm looking at Naomi Knox.

My hands slide up on either side of her wet face as I gasp for breath and try to still my whirling mind.

"Naomi," I whisper as I caress her skin and hot tears slide from my eyes and fall down my face. I can't fucking believe I'm standing up here onstage *crying* like a little bitch. But I can't help it. I can't reign it in and neither can she.

"Turner," she whispers, and I just want to hug the shit out of her, squeeze her so tight that she melds into my skin. I've *got* to fuck her, just so I can feel her body hot and warm around mine, so I can promise myself that she's really here, that she's really okay. She's back. She's back, and I'm the first person she came to. She came to *me*.

Heat and electricity sear through us both where we're touching, and I'm pretty fucking sure that the lightning in the sky must be hitting this church and surging through us

both, filling us up with energy and want and need and hollow friggin' desperation.

I kiss her lips hard, press my hot sweaty ones against her cold wet ones and I taste her, eat her up as my cock rises to meet her, to grind against her soft body. If she's crying, too, I don't know, but she's here, she's just fucking here and I'm never letting go of her again.

Reluctantly, I drop my hands from her face and wrap my arms tight around her, pulling her into me, holding so tight I'm sure I'd break any other woman. But not Naomi. Naomi Knox is unbreakable.

"I missed you so fucking much," I tell her, but she doesn't respond, not right away. She feels cold and a little weak, and parts of her are bruised and bloody. I don't know what happened, but I'm going to find out. I kiss her again, locking my lips tight with hers as the power goes on and off again, killing our night vision, hiding me and my only woman in plain sight. She kisses me back, fierce as fuck, biting at me, nibbling my lips, crashing her teeth against mine. Her nails dig into the bare skin of my back and draw blood as we stumble back and slam into the mass of curtain that hangs down from on high.

The fabric envelopes us, draws us in as I press her back tight to the wall and move against her, feeling her soft breasts through her shirt, her tight ass beneath my

fingers. She holds herself with her arms around my shoulders and pulls away for a moment to take a breath.

"I thought you were going to come save me," she says. "How stupid was that?" With a growl, I lift her up and slam her hard against the wall, too hard maybe, but it's hard to think with all of this adrenaline and power surging through us both. Behind me, the crowd keeps yelling, fighting to get to the stage, rallying against the bouncers. Things are getting dangerous in here, but I don't care. I can't stop. All I can see is Naomi Knox.

"Oh, shit, babe, that's not fucking stupid at all. I've been looking for you since you went missing. I'd have crossed the world for you, walked on fire, crawled across a bed of pins and needles. Fuck, I mean just *fuck,* Naomi." I press my forehead into hers as she digs through my hair and tangles her fingers up, tugging at my scalp with ferocious anger.

"Why?"

It's such a simple word, but there's no simple answer for this. If I could, I'd slice myself open and just spill my insides out on the floor. That mass of glittering entrails would be my answer, that bloody, pulsing mess. I just *exist* for this woman. I can't even believe I ever met her and let her go. I should've held onto her tight and kept her forever. If she'd have me, that is. A woman like Naomi, man, she can't be caged. If she stays, it's because

she wants to. And I want her to want to.

"Naomi Knox, I told you before. I lived crooked, so I see straight. I was blind, so now I fucking see." I kiss her again, but she doesn't return the favor. Instead she drops one hand between us and unbuttons my pants. Thank the fucking gods I don't ever wear underwear.

"That doesn't make any sense," she hisses, grabbing my lower lip between her teeth. She glances up at me and her eyes are just this side of wet, just moist enough that I think something could grow in there, turn that desert into a forest. "You're lucky you sing good."

Her hand strokes my cock, slides down the slick, sweaty shaft and cups my balls. She isn't being gentle when she squeezes them, and I grit my teeth, watching her face, her semi-crooked nose, her lips that remind me of a strawberry, red and round and juicy as shit. I drop her feet to the floor and she uses her other hand to pull off my shades, switching them to her face and sliding them up her nose.

"What happened?" I whisper through the crashing and the grunting and the screeching behind us. Here, wrapped in these curtains, we may as well be in a different world. I let my hand fall between us and go for her jeans. She lets me unbutton them but stops me when she sees the bracelets.

"Mrs. Turner Campbell?" she asks, voice hardening,

coming out of this strange, electrical fog we're both tangled in. I slip one off and pull her hand from my cock, sliding the bracelet over her thin, bruised and bloody wrist. She tries to jerk away, but I pull her back hard and kiss her again, shoving her pants down, pulling her against me and dropping us to our knees. Naomi comes with and lets me lay her there on that stage, lets me pull her acid washed jeans off one leg as I press my half-naked sweaty body against hers.

"There can be only one," I tell her as she groans into my mouth and pulls me inside of her, wrapping her legs around me and forcing my cock where she wants it to go. I glide into her slick pussy so easy it's almost criminal. The ride is smooth and wet, soaking me, drenching me in her as people scream and clamber over one another. As the violence out there gets worse, the heat in here intensifies, burns me up from the inside out, washes over me and threatens to bathe me in flames. Neither of us is thinking clearly. We're just desperate to feel each other, to connect to that other half and walk whole, standing tall on two strong legs.

Naomi lets her head fall back and sucks in a deep breath, clenching tight around me, holding me inside her as I drop my lips to her throat and kiss away the rain.

"Turner!" I hear Trey shouting my name, but I don't respond. Anything outside of this is inconsequential,

blurry and smudged compared to this straight line, this clarity of character and self. I'm so fucking glad that I'm sober right now. I haven't had sober sex in *years*. It's a whole new experience, like I'm getting my cherry popped all over again. Well, you know, metaphorically speaking.

"Why didn't you come for me?" she asks, sounding confused. We probably shouldn't be doing this. I should be holding her, carrying her back to the bus and making her comfortable. I need to get her food and water and find out what the fuck happened, if … if *anything* happened to her.

I slam my hands on either side of her face, looking down at her with a frown. But it's not for her. It's for me. I let her down. I should've done better.

"Naomi," I say, and I mean the words that crawl from my trembling lips. "I will spend the rest of my fucking life trying to make that up to you. I'm a drugged up, fucked up, piece of shit asshole, but when I think about you, I want to be better. I want to make things better."

"Turner!" Trey's still calling out my name, probably terrified that I've been swept up in that writhing mass of hell. Little does he know I'm in fucking heaven right now.

Naomi and I grunt and grind and slam our bodies together in the most wicked of ways. My cock pummels her pussy and my balls slap her ass, creating a kind of

sinful music that's impossible to recreate, no matter how hard we try. And trust me, I do try. With every snarl, every growl, every well-placed riff and slamming melody, we're trying to find this perfect note of love and sex, infuse it into the crowd so they can greedily gobble up a taste.

I savor Naomi's bare body, wondering if it felt this good the night we first met, when I took her virginity without even knowing it. But everyday, my memory gets better, pulled up from the vault of my mind, stored away carefully until I was ready for it. I pound her sweet flesh hard and she covets mine, clamping down around me and taking me prisoner. We rut like animals in heat, fucking and slamming and melting into each other until that pleasure builds up and hits us hard. I grunt and grind into her, spilling my seed and my anger and my pent up frustration, my longing and my misery and my hope, all of it shoots inside of her as she claws at my neck and arches her back. She's the most beautiful fucking thing I've ever seen, stretched out beneath me, filled with me, covered in sweat, soaking my crotch with her hot juices.

People are pounding past us, calling out orders, dragging the equipment back as the first few fans manage to ascend the stage, snatching anything they can find and smashing it against the wall, against Ronnie's kit, tossing it out into the crowd.

The sexual electricity between us clears and more practical bits take over as I slide my cock out and button up my pants, helping Naomi into hers and grabbing her hand to drag her to her feet. I don't know what it is, but I don't want anybody to see her. When she looks at me and raises her shades, I think maybe she's got the same idea in mind.

I shove my way out of the curtains and punch a dude square in the face, knocking him back and snatching my discarded shirt from his hand as he falls flat on his ass. Too dark in here, too messed up for anyone to see. I actually get to deck someone for once and not worry about them pressing charges. I elbow a bitch in the throat when she claws at my hair and yanks my head back. Before I can spin around and push her away, Naomi's there. She pulls a hard knuckled punch out of nowhere and hits the woman under the chin. She drops like a sack of potatoes and grabs my shirt, tying it around her head like a sweaty scarf. In this melee, ain't nobody gonna notice.

I grab my one woman's hand and guide her safely out the back door.

CHAPTER 22
NAOMI KNOX

Turner takes me back to his bus and leads me up the stairs, locking the door behind us and checking around to make sure we're the only ones on it. I think his bodyguard saw me, pretty sure I saw the dude smile, but there's not much I can do about that. As far as his band … I don't know how he plans on keeping me here for long without anyone finding out. As soon as that mess inside is cleared up, they'll all be back.

I collapse at the table and hold back a sob. I don't really know what was going through my mind when I went inside. Katie unlocked my cuffs and let me go without a word, releasing me with a flurry of garbled

words that didn't make any fucking sense. *I'm sorry. Stay away from him. Be careful of the Devil.* So now I'm safe for the moment, filled with confusion and anxiety and fear. I don't know who had me or why, don't know what happened while I was gone. All I know is that I don't see our bus anywhere, that Hayden is obviously fucking insane as well as involved, and that I can't do shit about it. I should go to the police probably. I mean, that's the most logical step isn't it? But I can't. Not with the secrets I'm carrying around with me. If Katie's here, this might all have something to do with that video, with the murders, with all the shit that's gone down around me in the past fucking decade.

I got out and went inside, looking for Turner. I didn't expect his voice to ignite a fire inside of me, to promise that angels really did exist, to make me feel loved and honored and cherished. I didn't know I would hear him singing about me, calling to me, begging. When the lights went out, I knew I had to get to him, so I walked onstage in front of a room full of fucking people.

I drop my head into my hands with a groan. Obviously my judgment at this point is a little compromised. A week in solitary fucking confinement will do that to a person.

"I've been missing for God only knows how long and the first thing I do is fuck bareback onstage?" My heart

is pounding and my body feels sweetly sore. I want to take Turner into the back and fuck him again. How messed up is that?

He comes back from checking the rest of the bus and tilts the slats on the blinds, so it's harder to see in. He's feeding off my energy, but he doesn't know why yet, doesn't know that this tour is a web filled with spiders, just waiting for a little tickle, a flicker of wing, so they can swarm down on me and bite hard. I've got to figure out who the players are in this little game, and I've got to take them out one by one. However that needs to happen, whatever I need to do, I'm going to be the one that comes out of this on top.

"Naomi," Turner says, and his voice is more serious than I've ever heard it. I turn and look at the playboy asswad that left me alone and pregnant, that uses girls up the way he uses condoms, fills 'em and tosses 'em aside. I look at him and his face is *different* somehow. While I was gone, he changed. He doesn't know it yet, I don't think, but it's there. My being missing changed him. For the better.

"Are you sober?" I interrupt before he can say anything else. His eyes are clear, surrounded by sweaty streaks of smeared black liner. His hair is a mess, but his gaze is straight as an arrow.

"Dead sober," he tells me, moving close tentatively,

like he isn't sure I'm really there. His hands come out and touch my face again, pulling my gaze to his and locking brown eyes with me. "God, this is like a fucking dream."

"Try nightmare," I say, pulling away from the molten hot tips of his fingers, fighting my basic biology. I won't admit yet that I'm fighting my heart. I don't love Turner anymore. I don't. I *don't.* "I can't … I just escaped a terrifying possibility and then went and had unprotected sex with you."

"I'm all clean, baby," he says with a stupid smile. Okay, a sexy smile. It's sexy *and* stupid. "I always use balloons and I get my shit checked, you know?" I glare at him.

"That's not what I'm worried about," I say as I stand up and move over to his fridge. He follows me and watches as I open it and scan for food. There isn't much in here, but I manage to wrangle up a pre-made sandwich and some cheese sticks. May as well be filet fucking mignon for all I know. I'm so hungry and yet *not.* Whatever was in the stupid IVs kept me alive, but it wasn't living, you know?

Turner gets me a glass of water *with* ice and brings it to the table, going back over to the window to check on the house of horror we just vacated. I don't know what the hell happened in there, but it was off the charts insane. Too bad I couldn't be a part of it.

"But fuck that," I say, waving my hand around, figuring I'll go get a morning after pill. Or Turner will. I'm not leaving this bus until I figure out a plan. "That's not important. What's important is this." I take a bite of the sandwich and groan in pleasure, drawing his eyes back to me. He moves over and slides onto the bench next to me, rubbing his body along mine and cupping my thigh with his pretty little inked up fingers.

My gaze catches on the bat tattoos on his hard belly and stays there, unwilling to look at his eyes. Right now, there is a tender something or other opening up inside of me like a flower. It scares the crap out of me, makes it harder for me to hate him and wish for his untimely death. Right now, I think I might … *like* Turner Campbell.

"I want you to know everything, just in case."

"Where were you?" he asks, unwrapping the cheese stick for me and setting it back on the granite tabletop. "I had this key … I thought you were in one of the RVs."

"I was in an RV," I tell him, finishing the sandwich, gulping it down like a starving wolf and wiping the crumbs off on my pants. "But it wasn't any of the ones in here. It was parked outside the lot, on the street. The only reason I knew where to go was because I heard the music."

I pick up the cheese and start to peel strings off of it

before I give in and just shove the whole damn thing in my mouth.

After Katie let me go, she bolted and disappeared into the night like she'd never been. I didn't bother going after her, just ended up stumbling out barefoot into the rain and letting the sound of rumbling riffs draw me where I needed to go. Music's never let me down before, so I knew I could trust it. Looks like I was right.

"Fuck," Turner curses, pulling a key out of his pocket and slamming it down on the table. "You were in plain fucking sight, and I missed you." He runs a hand through his blue-black hair and breathes out slowly, flicking his eyes over to mine. A spark passes between us and before I even really know what's happening, he's folding me up in his arms and pulling me onto his lap, pressing me against his sweaty chest. I go stiff at first, but after a moment, I relax. And I hate to say it, but it feels right.

"I have to hide, Turner. There are a lot of layers to this shit that I can't even begin to peel away yet. All I know is that Hayden is involved somehow." Turner's hands squeeze me hard and when he next speaks, I can hear his teeth grit in anger.

"I knew that fucking cunt was a part of this shit. Fucking Christ." I sit up and I look him right in the eye, pulling off the shades, *my* shades, that he was wearing onstage.

"Turner," I begin, keeping my voice low and serious. This is some hardcore shit, and if he's going to be a part of it, I need to know that he's in all the way, that he's ready to jump in the deep end. This isn't a time where a toe in the shallows will do anybody any good. I need someone I can count on. This fucker is telling me he loves me, and in his face, I see dedication unmatched. If I'm honest with myself, it scares the crap out of me. "I need help. I need somebody I can count on. I don't know what this is between you and me, but if you're offering your assistance, I'll take it."

A slamming fist on the door startles us both, and I rise to my feet like a fighter in the ring, ready to defend myself, fists raised.

"Who the fuck is it?" Turner asks, standing up and moving behind me, pressing his heat against the back of me. I can't hold back a shiver, and I know he notices, but I guess that's just the way it is. I blame it all on my fucking crotch.

"It's me. Let me in." I don't recognize the voice, but Turner does. He spins me around gently and looks me straight in the face. His eyes don't waver and his voice is as sharp edged as a sword.

"I love you, Naomi. I don't mince words and I don't sugarcoat shit. I said what I meant, and I meant what I said." He smiles wickedly and brushes his thumb over

my lower lip. "I don't like to keep secrets, but if I have to, for you, I will. I'll hide the world in my throat, and I won't tell a damn soul. As long as I can be honest with you and vice versa, that's all that really matters to me." He pauses and looks up at the door. "So if you'll have me, I'll be your knight in shining fucking armor." Turner looks back at me and lets go of my shoulders. "And if you're willing, I want to bring Ronnie in on this." I start to protest, but he interrupts me. "And Dax." My heart leaps in my throat, and I turn away, running my fingers through my hair. It's matted and greasy and nasty. First thing I need to do is shower. I'll think better that way. *Especially since right now, I've got Turner's fucking cum all over me.* I shiver again and it has nothing to do with the weather.

I have to make a decision right here, right now. Who do I trust? I look back at Turner, shirtless and pretty and fucking dangerous as hell. I let him in before and he screwed me. Can I give him a second chance? Does he even deserve one?

When he steps forward and wraps his hands in my hair, kisses my mouth and sighs against my lips, I decide. I decide and I know then that there is no going back. Whatever happens in my life from this point on, Turner will play a part in it.

"Okay," I say and I can't help but kiss him back.

"You're in. Help me, Turner, and we'll figure this out together."

"Jesus mother and shit," Turner says after I'm finished with my half of the story. Putting what I know together with what he knows hasn't done a damn thing for us. It's all still a big, fucking mystery. And who planted the guitar? Well, when I find the fucker I'll make sure to thank them for replacing my Wolfgang *before* I blow their brains out. "Skinny Bitch has a few screws loose, huh?" he asks, pitching his voice low, so that Ronnie and I can hear him, but the rest of the band can't. I don't know how the two of them plan on hiding me from the rest of the group, but I'll let them work on those logistics. They know their friends better than I do.

A knock at the door hushes us all for a moment.

"We're about to move out, is everything okay in there?" a voice asks.

"Peachy fucking keen," Turner responds, kicking his feet up on the table. We're sitting in the back of the bus, a circular area with a table and a shit ton of ashtrays. There

are windows on all sides but one where the second bathroom sits, door cracked and light off. "You're cleared for takeoff. Now leave us the fuck alone." He takes a drag on his cigarette and offers it to me. I grab a fresh one from the carton on the table and dig the lighter out of his pocket. When I slide the smoke between my lips, I feel like I'm coming home. *Oh God, yes.* My forced separation from nicotine was not exactly pleasant. As the smoke fills my lungs, I sigh with pleasure. *Shit yeah. That's where it's at, baby.*

Ronnie cranks up the stereo to help drown out our conversation. He's a nice guy, I could tell the moment I laid eyes on him. Nice guys are easy to spot because they're so few and far between, like roses in a field of weeds. Even if you've never seen one before, you'll know it when you stumble on one because its presence is like nothing else. Ronnie's the one I should be falling for, but right now, I'm knee-deep in Turner La-la Land. I scowl at nothing in particular and smoke my cigarette. Ronnie watches me and brushes some hair from his face with a pale, skinny hand. He was handsome, once upon a time, but sorrow and longing, drugs and alcohol, all of that has wiped away his pretty and left nothing but sore, sad and fucked. I feel bad for the guy, really. He looks like he needs a hug.

"Why don't we do this the simple way," Turner

suggests, looking at me out of the corner of his eye. He's still trying to pull that masculine machismo bullshit on me, but it isn't working. His heart is bleeding all over his chest. I might be the one with the tattoo, but he's got the real thing, right there above his rock hard fucking pecs. I told him he didn't understand love, but he thinks he does. Whatever I believe about him, all I have to do is look in his eyes to know he truly feels something for me. I guess thinking I was dead pounded it in hard. No way I'm getting rid of this guy so easily this time. I am so stuck with Turner Campbell. Better get used to it. "Let's just corner Hayden and beat the shit out of her until she spills." I roll my eyes.

"This goes so much further than Hayden, Turner. There are other people involved, and if I'm right," I smash my cig in the ashtray. "Then it's not just me they're after. Think about it. Why send you the guitar? The hat? You're involved whether you know it or not. Beating up Hayden might help us scratch the surface, but it won't give us access to the root." I pick up my water bottle and down half in one gulp. It feels *so* good to have liquid pouring down my throat. IV fluid is *not* the same. This shit may as well be ambrosia it tastes so sweet.

"You think somebody's targeting Turner?" Ronnie asks. I notice he likes to repeat things. I think he's committing them to memory. I have a good feeling about

that. Ronnie is the type of man that notices things, little details. He watches and he absorbs, like our own walking, talking guidebook but with zero paper trail.

"I'm almost sure of it," I say as Turner's hand slides up my thigh, brushing softly over the bare skin. I'm not wearing much right now, just a pair of his boxers and one of his tees, so he's got pretty easy access. I just have to make sure he knows his place, where he stands and all that. I asked him to help me, but I didn't say we'd take the romantic route. Maybe I'm the only one in that room that misses the fact that I'm wearing the *Mrs. Turner Campbell* bracelet on my arm still. I push his hand off. "What we need to do is find Katie. She obviously knows more than she's letting on, which is understandable considering her upbringing." I sigh and try not to relive those old memories. I can't help but wonder if all of that has something to do with this, but what are my options? Burying this secret for good is the only thing I can think of. Letting this one fly isn't a good idea. Confessing my bloody past to the world will only make my life worse, not better. Best this shit gets shoveled six feet under, right next to the bastards I shanked.

"So how do we find her?" Turner asks, adjusting himself so that the long line of his thigh brushes against mine. I pretend not to notice. Just because I went missing, just because he mourned me with the angels on

high, doesn't mean that we're suddenly an item. *So, genius, why on earth did you decide to rut with the bastard onstage? And without a condom? Damn, girl, you're in deep.* I ignore my subconscious and start on my next cigarette.

"We don't," I tell him, glancing at him sideways. "We wait. She'll show up eventually." I take a drag and blow smoke rings. I don't miss the rising bulge in Turner's pants. "And we need to find Eric before the cops do. If he's still around, that is." I don't like the idea of the police hovering so close by. Not the FBI either. It's not *impossible* to do things without them knowing, but it sure as shit isn't easy either.

"You trust that slick son of a bitch?" Turner asks me, turning sideways and draping his arm over the back of his seat. He hasn't bothered to put a new shirt on, just sits there with his nipples hard and his muscles gleaming under the bright, yellow light that swings above us when we start to move. Outside, the rain smashes against the windows like a thousand fists, helping shield us from prying ears. But it won't last long. All it'll take is one slip and somebody will see me and everything will just go to shit. I have to make sure I'm in control, that the inevitable downward spiral goes where I tell it to.

"I don't trust anyone," I tell him and then glance across the table at Ronnie. "Not even you."

"Good," Turner's friend says, pressing his palms against the tabletop and rising to his feet. His dark eyes take me in, and he smiles. "You shouldn't. Keep that wariness around and you'll be alright." He groans and sighs, dropping his chin to his chest. "I am fucking beat." He lifts a hand up and gestures absently at the back of the bus. "All of that bullshit in there was too much for this old man. I'm calling it a night. I'll keep my eyes and ears peeled tomorrow for gossip." Ronnie pushes away from the table and reaches for the door handle, glancing over his shoulder at Turner and me. "You want me to bring some blankets and shit back here?"

"Yeah. Tell the guys I'm in a rank fucking mood." Ronnie nods and doesn't question this. I raise an eyebrow.

"And this will what, keep them away?" Turner shrugs like I shouldn't be surprised, gazing at me from half-lidded eyes. He is such a posh fucking prince. Thinks he's all hardcore and shit, but that's a load of bull. He might've survived the trailer park when he was young, but he'd never last now. I watch as he runs his fingers down his abs, playing them like a friggin' washboard and drops them below the hemline of his jeans. He pretends he's just adjusting himself, but I know better. He's trying to get me excited.

I blow smoke in his face.

He just breathes it in with a smile.

"Let's just say, when Turner's on a warpath, people stay out of his way."

"Uh huh." I lean back and wait until Ronnie shows up with blankets and pillows, depositing them on the tabletop and retreating with a little wink. Turner locks the door behind him and settles back into his position across from me. I put my feet up and rest my toes against his legs. "You think you're so tough, but I see right through you."

He leans forward and breathes hot breath against my face.

"Really, Naomi? And what is it that you see?"

"I see a man who thinks he knows what he wants, but doesn't understand it. I see a guy who – "

Turner interrupts me by grabbing my chin and pressing his forehead to mine. I don't move away when he crawls between my legs, keeping those fingers locked tight on my face.

"Naomi, you see a guy who thought he lost the only thing he ever really wanted. The one thing he craved and never even knew about," he whispers, and his voice is soft, like kitty cat fur soft. It's *weird* as shit. This is the same guy who left that roadie half-naked over a PA speaker, that knocked me up and left my pregnant and alone at sixteen, who parties and fucks and sings and

doesn't care whose heart gets broken in the process. This is also the guy who's making my chest tight and my eyes wet, who's created a throbbing pulse between my thighs and slicked my skin with sweat. "You see an asshole with a whole laundry list of faults, who doesn't even know how many chicks he's slept with, but who only wants one."

"What if I said you can't have her?" I tell him, not liking the ache I feel when he pulls away and sits back down across from me. My body is *begging* me to fuck him again, to hold him tight inside of me and make him *mine.* I want to piss all over him and claw up his back and make sure that all of these other bitches know he's off limits. I want them to know that he wants me in ways he's never wanted them, that he craves me in ways he's never felt before. I shiver and snatch a cigarette with angry, shaking hands.

Turner just grins, all cocky and arrogant. It's not a front, not necessarily, but something about it rings fake when he looks at me. I've found a crack in the Campbell shell. And it's me. *I'm* the fucking crack.

"I'd have to say too damn bad. I get what I want, Naomi, and what I want is you. Get used to it." I flip him off.

"Hey, Turner," I say. "Fuck you." He leans forward.

"I just did that." I shake my head and grab the water

bottle, alternating sips with drags.

"I fucked you." He laughs, loud and raucous, like a fucking cheese grater scraped over an old record player. I hate to admit it, but I kind of like it. *Oh God, no. You're not falling for him, are you? What is all of this sappy shit? This isn't you, Naomi. You don't need a man. You need answers and then you need closure and then you need to get back to your career. Your career. The music. Your music that he's been borrowing.* I debate talking about that with him, but I don't know how to broach the subject. It's too sensitive. I pick an easier topic. "When we get to Dallas, I need you to get me a morning after pill, do you understand? Like, before the parking brake is even in place, you're going out to get it." Turner gives me a loaded, cocky ass fucking smile. I want to eat his face off and rape him at the same time. Something is seriously wrong with me. I blame it on my week in captivity.

"Aye, aye, Captain," he growls, taking a nice, long, slow drag on his new smoke. He lets tendrils of gray drift from his nostrils.

"And if I get herpes, I'll fucking kill you." His grin gets bigger, and I notice something different about his face, like he's gotten more handsome all of a sudden. It takes me a minute to figure out what it is. He's *happy.* For the first time since I've met him, I can tell that Turner

fucking Campbell is actually happy. Why? Because of me. I look away.

"I told you, babe, I'm clean. I've used more rubbers than an English school teacher."

"What the fuck is that supposed to mean?" I snarl, grabbing a pillow and fluffing it. Might not seem all that comfortable to sleep on a bench, but to me, it all still feels like heaven. I've got gauze and Neosporin on my wrists and ankles, I'm not drugged, and best of all, I'm *free*. I could probably fall asleep in an alley with a bag of trash as a pillow and diseased rats for bedmates and I'd be alright.

As soon as my head hits the pillow, my eyelids start to droop. There is so much going on in this little room that it makes my head spin. What happened to me, what Turner went through while I was gone, America in the hospital, Katie, Eric, Hayden. *Ugh.* I've had more than enough for one night.

"It means," Turner whispers, grabbing a blanket and laying it over my curled body. "That I'm in love with you, Naomi Knox."

CHAPTER 23
❧ TURNER CAMPBELL ❧

Naomi has no fucking clue how I feel inside. To her, the last week was a nightmare, a trial she had to overcome. To me, it was an aching pit of hope and despair, fear and need and want all mixed into one. I'm not saying I had it worse or anything, but shit. Thinking she might be dead, wanting to believe she wasn't … Right now, staring down at her sleeping face, I want to do a fucking river dance. I want to jump on this table and scream and shout my joy to the world. The high I'm on right now is better than any drug ever invented. I am King today. I am God. I am Happy. Yeah. Happy. That horrible H-word that we spend our lives searching for.

Naomi's asleep, so I figure I can get away with

brushing her hair from her forehead, kissing her cheek, without getting my balls torn off. I touch her arm, press my palm against her shoulder and just breathe. Without even knowing it, I've been holding my breath for days waiting for this girl. Looking at her now, I can't believe I ever touched another woman. I'm repulsed by the idea, fucking sickened by it.

I stand up straight and finish my cigarette.

I don't even know what to do with myself now. I just want to pace back and forth and guard Naomi with my life. I want to snarl at anybody that comes near, and I swear to fuck that I will defend her to the *death*. Truth be told, I don't even care about anything else now. I mean, think about it. I have money, fame, respect, music, and my girl. That's it. What else is there? I've even got friends that'll stick by my side no matter what, and let's just be honest, a hot smokin' body. So now what?

"Now," I tell my cig as I press it in the ashtray. "Now I find the fuckers who are threatening my shit, and I take them down. I destroy them one by one until there's nothing left on this earth to challenge me." I smile and look down at Naomi. "Except for her," I whisper. "Because I know this chick will be challenging me every day for the rest of my Goddamn life."

Morning rolls around, and I haven't slept much. I pretty much sat up and watched Naomi sleep like a fucking stalker. I almost fell asleep a few times, but woke up startled, thinking it was all a dream, that I'd never found her and that she'd showed up dead in a ditch somewhere the next morning. It was kind of a shitty night. And a perfect one. Dichotomous bullshit.

"Get me some fucking orange juice," Naomi whispers when I push her feet off my lap and stand up, rolling my head around and getting a crick out of my neck. "And something to eat." She pauses and then, mouth muffled by the pillow, manages to get out a forced *please.*

I smile and kick open the door, closing it carefully behind me. Ronnie's already up, so I give him a nod and he stands up, moving into the back and slipping inside. I wonder what he and Naomi will talk about when I'm gone.

"Where the fuck's Milo?" I ask Josh who's slumped at the table, cup of coffee clutched between his hands. I snatch a shirt out from the drawer under my bed and slip it on. Just so happens that it's a white one with the words

Breaking Pretty across the front. I touch my fingers to the Indecency logo underneath and stare out the window, following a nod from Josh. The crowd today is fucking insane, taking advantage of the clear, warm weather to pile up outside the gates, shouting and screeching and flailing like a solid mass. This whole camping out shit might be coming to an end soon. Turner Campbell and crew might just have to upgrade.

I stare for a minute as I consider going for a joint. Naomi's back, so it'd be alright, wouldn't it? But then I think about my mind getting cloudy, blurring the edges of her beautiful face. Besides, she needs my help. *I* need my help. The detective work might not be so blindingly urgent, but it's still top priority. I go for a cigarette instead and pass over my morning beer for a cup of black coffee.

"He's dealing with some weird rumors," Josh says, groggy and irritated. Told you, he's a little bitch in the mornings. When he finds out his favorite bathroom is now permanently off limits, he's going to flip the fuck out. "People are saying they saw you having sex onstage last night." I snort and splash coffee into the sink. I imagine that there are cameras zooming in on my face right now and try to keep a wicked smirk plastered on my lips.

"Now that sure is fucking odd," I say, but I don't

respond to the question underneath his words. *Were you?* Josh makes a huffing noise under his breath and downs his cup.

"So now, thanks to that, you're even more popular than you were the night before." He pauses and when I glance over my shoulder, I see him biting his lip. Josh looks so friggin' young to me right now, like a virgin angel or some shit. I can't even imagine how he looks onstage with the rest of us washed up, drugged up motherfuckers. I sip my coffee. I don't want to hate Josh, but it's so easy to. So easy to blame him for not fitting in, for not being Travis, for being too naïve. Life hasn't come and screwed him up the ass with a dry dildo. I should be happy about that, should try to be a guiding hand. Instead, I just get irritated whenever he's around. "How?" he whispers as I turn fully around to face him. "How do you do it?" He sounds perplexed, like he can't imagine why anyone in their right mind would be interested in me. I stare at his pale skin, his blonde hair, the angry tremble in his jaw, and I try to figure out an answer to that question.

See, here's the thing. When I think about myself, I'm arrogant as shit. I can think about all sorts of reasons why people would flock to me, throw themselves at my feet, and beg for more. But when I think about Naomi … I guess I have a harder time imagining why she'd want to

be with me. I screwed her over, betrayed her fantasies and her dreams, seeded her with pain that she's only just now getting over. That makes me want to be a better person, a person that's easy to imagine her with. Maybe that's what the crowds are seeing in me now? Maybe they fell in love with an idea before and they're watching that idea come to fruition?

Or maybe I'm just full of crap.

I take another sip of my coffee, a drag on my cigarette.

"Well kid," I say and watch as Josh purses his lips. "Maybe it's just because I'm the shit?"

I get Naomi her juice and her pill, returning back from the pharmacy just in time to be bombarded with cameras and microphones, raging fans and a mass of cell phones all recording my shocked facial expression when I climbed through the bushes and tried to hop the fence. I got out alright that same way, but I guess the vultures swept in while I was gone. I can see that this frenzied shit is going to get real ugly real fast.

"Almost decked the bitch behind the counter," I tell Naomi when she accepts the plastic bag from me with a frown on her face. Ronnie ducks out right away and says he's going on recon. I assume that means the old whore is off to find a bang and some gossip, but I don't say anything about it. I'm changing, so maybe he is, too? Those in glass houses shouldn't chuck rocks or whatever, right? "She tried to give me some bullshit religious mumbo jumbo speech about contraception. Fuck her."

I give Naomi a once-over as she leans over the tabletop and slides the box from the bag, reading the text on the back of the tiny cardboard packaging. Obviously Ronnie fished through my drawer to get her some clothes because she's decked out in a pair of my black skinny jeans, belted up at the waist with a baggy Amatory Riot tee over the top. No bra and I expect no underwear unless she's wearing some of my briefs. My cock gets rock solid and starts to interrupt signals from my brain to the rest of my body. Tricky little motherfucker.

"Take one pill within seventy-two hours of unprotected sex," she reads as I drop into the seat and do my best to control myself. Not exactly the right time to hit on a chick when she's reading the emergency contraceptive instruction manual. I make sure that I still have some condoms in my pocket for later. "Take the second twelve hours after the first." Naomi pops a white

pill out of the foil and takes it down with a swig of orange juice. "At least it's not friggin' rocket science," she says as she tucks the other away in the back pocket of her jeans. She swipes some blonde hair over her shoulder and glares at me. "And you don't have herpes?"

I unbutton my pants and expose myself, watching as her eyes catch on my dick and hold there.

"Not since I last checked." Naomi rolls her eyes and pretends not to be interested. But I know she can feel the heat between us. Even with the air conditioning running full blast, it's not enough to keep the windows back here from fogging up. I reach back and twist the handle on the blinds to let in a bit of light. The sunshine highlights her perfect cheekbones, her moist lips, her gorgeous eyes. They look orange this morning, not brown. Just orange. Like flames. *I want to be incinerated.*

"Turner," she says and her voice drops low, gets real serious. I button my pants back up, feeling kind of, sort of like a complete tool. I feel awkward around her now. I'm just going to admit it, like she's an angel and I'm … I don't know. A devil? She's become this mystical *thing*, this far off goal I've been reaching for, lamenting at the same time I'm celebrating, and now she's just here. I imagine myself like a nerdy kid in high school, trying to grope his first tit. I feel all wonky right now like I have no clue how to seduce a woman. *I feel like a damn*

virgin. "That can't happen again. I mean, I can't even believe it *happened.* I was in a weird place last night. I feel better today." She sighs and sits down across from me, leaning forward and putting her elbows on her knees. "My experience wasn't so bad, but it could've been worse, Turner. They were gearing up for *bad.* I know it. I could fucking smell it." She touches two fingers to her nose and drops her hand back in her lap. Her eyes dart to the parted blinds, and I know they're making her nervous, so I close them again and drop the room back into shadow.

"So let's find these fuckers and put them out of their misery," I say, leaning back all casual like. Truthfully, I still just want to touch her, feel her skin, make sure she's really here, that she wasn't carted away in that ambulance and slapped on a cold slab, marked like a biological specimen. Instead, I lean over and pull out a drawer that's under the bench seat. When the space is this tight, things get interesting. There are drawers all over this place. Just so happens this one's got some killer shoes in it. "I'll be your eyes and ears, beautiful. You tell me what you want from me and you got it."

"A wig," she says, and I glance up with a smile.

"Kinky." Naomi sighs and puts her hands on her hips.

"I need to be able to go out with you, see things for myself. I'm not going to sit here in the back of your bus like a doormat, waiting for one of your bandmates to find

me here crouched and shivering. I have to take action, Turner. That's what I do. I take charge and I make sure that I'm taken care of. There's nobody else around to do it for me."

"Until me," I say and I toss her a pair of shoes. They're mine, so they're a little big, but they'll have to work for now. Naomi catches the black sneakers and gives me a harsh look. I notice that she doesn't get within three feet of me. Is it because she can feel that passion between us? Because she's afraid to want me? Or because she's disgusted by it. *God, I hope not.*

"I'm not a damsel in distress, Turner," she says, slamming the soles of the shoes on the table. Her ankle tat peeks out at me from the under the jeans and for the first time ever, I get to stare at it while she's distracted. I figure this chance might not come along ever again, so I take it and run with it.

Turner Dakota Campbell is scrawled across her foot just under her ankle bone, where the gauze bandages wrap. Done up in red with two black knives crisscrossed behind my middle name. Guess I was her first in more ways than one. The tattoo's a little amateur, but there's something romantic about the soft lines and blurred coloring. Unconsciously, my hand reaches up and slides over my shoulder. Naomi notices and turns away, blocking my view.

"You might not be a damsel in distress," I tell her, trying to keep my breathing slow and steady. I'm a bit sweaty today, a bit messed up from *not* being messed up if you know what I mean. "But there's no way for you to walk around with me and not get noticed. A wig won't do it, babe."

"Why's that?" she snaps, and I stand up, moving closer to her, brushing against her back just enough that our clothes catch, kiss cotton threads and fuck us hard with the magnetism of our body heat, begging us to clash, to intertwine like we did last night and never let go. Goddamn and *fuck.* I don't want Naomi to take that pill. I want to make little Campbell babies with her and put a ring on her finger and walk her down the aisle, all of that fairytale shit. It's so bad now I'm starting to wonder if I've gone insane. This love at first sight crap isn't easy to deal with. I go from wanting to punch the chick to wanting to marry her? Kind of weird.

I pinch open the blinds, so she can see the mass of reporters. Her eyes get big and her lip curls.

"I thought all of that roaring was a TV or something," she says, sounding horrified. It did just sort of happen overnight. We went from mediocre popularity to all out stardom in a week. As soon as Naomi resurfaces and reveals that she's still alive and well, she's going to be declared a saint. "What in the cock sucking Christ?" I

laugh and the motion of my breath ruffles her hair. She shivers and well, fuck man, but that's all she wrote.

Naomi spins and our mouths clash, our hands grab and we're suddenly pressed together so tight that it'd take a freaking power tool to pry us apart. I breathe her in and she tastes me; I touch her breasts and she cups my crotch. I can't get to her fast enough, can't drink her in deeply enough.

"I'm so confused," she moans as she slides down to the bench and I follow, getting between her legs, tugging at her jeans. She tangles her fingers in my hair as I unbuckle the belt and pull the denim over her hips. Her pussy is right there in my face, blonde hair, swollen and wet. *Fuck.* I kiss it hard and she moans, spreading her knees open for me, letting me in. With one hand, I slip my fingers in her cunt and with the other, I stroke my raging cock.

"Don't be," I whisper against her heat, gritting my teeth with the effort of staying here, on my knees. I've never done this for any other woman. Turner Campbell does not fucking do the knee thing. But Naomi isn't just a woman, she's a rock goddess, a slice of fury, a ball of take no shit rage and beauty. *God. I'm going crazy here.* "Just fucking live it."

"I hate you," she whispers, but I don't know what those words mean right now. They're garbled and full of

confusion, messy and twisted. I want to hear an *I love you* from her, but if it were so easily had, maybe I wouldn't be so willing to work for it? *I love you, Turner Dakota Campbell* rings in my head, an echo of a memory, some ghost from a distant past. One day, I'm going to lie down and remember everything that happened between us that first night, write it all down somewhere or something, prove to her that it's there, buried in me somewhere.

"Hate me all you want," I tell her as I breathe against her swollen clit. It's like a rock now, solid as my dick. "But you're going to moan while you're doing it." And then I kiss her where the sun don't shine. My tongue moves up her wet crack, moistening her even though she doesn't need any help. I lick around my fingers and then slide them out, tasting her as I go. When I grab her hips and press my lips to her clit, my fingertips burn, melting away the whorls and the lines, taking away my identity and mixing it with hers. And even though I know I'm a self-assured, self-centered asshole, it feels good to be this close to another person.

Naomi moans, low and deep, raising her hips to my face, pressing herself against me. It's almost too much to bear. I want to stand up and thrust my cock inside of her, feel her warm and hot around me, grinding her ridges against my shaft. But if I pride myself on anything, it's

on being a good lover, and I haven't exactly shown her my skills. There are *some* pluses to being a dirty fucking whore. Or stud as I prefer to call it.

"You sick son of a bitch!"

The door behind me flings open and in walks Dax, grabbing me by the shirt as I turn around and slamming me into the table. I don't even think, just swing, hitting him in the cheek so hard I hear a *crack.* He stumbles back into Ronnie who's giving me a *shit, I'm sorry* look over his shoulder.

Dax comes back at me quick, taking advantage of my addled state and giving me a good one right in the fucking nose. Blood dribbles from my nostrils before Naomi shouts at us to stop and steps in between us, hands outstretched, pants belted back up around her hips. Me, my erect cock is still hanging out of my pants and my face is wet with Naomi's juices. Great. Perfect time to be interrupted.

"Dude, what the fuck?" I ask, dashing away blood as Dax holds a hand to his cheek and gapes at Naomi. He's actually wearing clean clothes today, another gay emo outfit with skeletons and shit on it. His dark hair hangs over his eyes and obscures some, but not nearly all, of the complete and utter shock he's going through.

"Oh my ... fuck." That's all he can get out. The blood dribbles into my mouth as I watch the play of

emotions between Dax and Naomi. He goes from angry to confused to *enraged* and then straight up to sobbing. He reaches out and she accepts a hug from him. When they part, they're both smiling. I tuck my dick away and try not to get jealous. "I … I … " Dax rubs at his eyes with his black fingerless gloves. The knuckles spell out the words *Lost* and *Love*. I scowl and look away.

"I thought we agreed to bring Dax in, so I took advantage of the empty bus to bring him over here." Ronnie scratches at his head and leans against the wall. He's got on another shirt from one of his kids, a different one this time. I think this one's from his oldest daughter. It says *When times get tough, I get tougher.* Cute. "Didn't expect you two to be pullin' a nooner on me. Shit." Ronnie gets out a smoke.

"I don't … know what to say," Dax whispers, putting his hands over his face and looking at Naomi through teary eyes. *Fucking pussy.* I scowl at him, but he doesn't notice. He's too busy scoping out my woman. "How did you get here? *When* did you get here?" At this, his gray eyes flick to mine for a split second, like Naomi's absence in his life is, at least partially, my fault.

"Fuck." I wipe my hands down my face. My dick is so hard it might as well be made of friggin' stone. I want to grab Naomi and slide myself into her, feel her breath against my ear, her arms around my neck. "Good God," I

groan and Naomi elbows me in the stomach. Miraculously, I don't get angry with her. I'm getting a lot better at controlling my emotions. In the past, getting hit, even jokingly would spike my rage. Not today. Today I'm just horny as shit.

"Don't be a fucking asshole," she whispers as she puts her hands on her hips and looks at the floor. She's gauging how much she wants to tell Dax. Personally, I'd go with nothing and kick his stalker ass off the bus. But then I remind myself that bringing him in was *my* idea. Dax loves Naomi. That much is pretty obvious, so he's a safe bet. He'll do anything for her. I just hope I'm right about him, that it doesn't go any further than that. "Dax, you can't tell anybody about this, do you understand?" Dax drops his hands from his face and nods, sucking in a big breath and shaking his head like he's trying to clear it.

"God, Mi, I can't even believe you're still alive. When I saw the blood and the bodies, I just … something inside of me died that day." He puts a hand to his chest and looks at her with such deep fucking longing. It makes my hackles raise and my stomach hurt. A small speck inside of me feels sorry for the guy while the rest of me just wants to beat the shit out of him.

"Mi?" I ask, getting out my own cig. If I can't suck on Naomi's sweet pussy, I'm going to eat a whole field of friggin' tobacco. Nobody pays me any attention.

"Dax, do you understand what I'm saying? Hayden is a part of this. She can't know I'm here." Dax nods and drops his hands to his hips, mimicking Naomi's pose. He doesn't seem at all surprised to hear her say that.

"I figured she had more going on than she was saying. I mean, her story was true, but it wasn't, you know? I mean, there are parts of it where you can just feel the emotion. The rest seems hollow." Dax lets his eyes trail Naomi's body, up and down and back again. "God, I'm sorry, I'm just … I'm trying to adjust to this. I think I'm in shock. I mean, here you are. You're alive and the only asshole that actually believed you were was this stupid fucker."

I take a step forward but Naomi stops me with a hand on my stomach. Like a lost, little puppy I obey. Good Lord, where did my balls go?

"I need your help to figure this out." Naomi smiles and it lights up her pale face, her sculpted cheeks. I stare at her throat and wish my mouth was pressed there, tasting her pulse and feeling her alive beneath me. Dax isn't the only one that's in shock. Naomi Knox is back. She's alive. Going to take a while to get used to that, I imagine. "You can be my inside guy, yeah?"

"All over that shit." Dax reaches out and takes her hand in his. I watch, but I don't move, just stand there and let smoke curl from my nostrils. "I'm so happy to see you, Naomi. I want you to know that … that I lo-"

"Fuck," Ronnie curses, dropping his cig on the floor and biting his lip. He spins around and gets as close to a jog as I've ever seen him, hitting the door the same time it opens and Milo's blonde head pops in. Naomi steps back into the bathroom and stands out of sight. "Yo, Terrabotti, I need an advance," Ronnie says, pulling Milo's attention from Dax and me. Our manager sighs as he climbs the steps, slow and shaky, like an old man riddled with arthritis. All of this circus shit is hard on him, I guess.

"What for, Ronnie? Acid? Cocaine? Methamphetamine?"

Ronnie laughs and pats Milo hard on the back.

"You're so cute, look at you, Terrabotti. Methamphetamine? It's called dope out on the streets, you know? Ice, clouds, crystal."

Milo takes a massive breath and gets ready to launch into his anti-drugs speech, the one he gives at least three times a week. I grab Dax by the front of his pink emo sweater and yank him into the back, closing the door and locking it behind him. He looks at me long and hard, but doesn't say anything. After a minute, I get the most surprising statement of my life.

"I'm sorry, Turner," he tells me, sounding all genuine and crap. I stare at him like he's crazy. I was just

tonguing the love of his life and he's apologizing to me? Dax wipes at a stray smudge of liner around his eye and runs his tongue over his teeth. "I should've believed you when you said she could be alive. I really … I really fucked stuff up." He looks over at Naomi. "And I'm sorry to you, too. I should've done more."

Naomi steps from the bathroom and pats him on the back. I watch her eyes, but I don't see anything but friendship when she looks at him. What I need to remember is that Dax isn't my competition. *I* am my only competition. Naomi hates me. *Me.* This isn't about getting Dax out of the way. This is about getting Naomi to see that I really do love her. I've got to prove it, and now's my chance. I'll solve these mysteries, get her back onstage. There's nothing more seductive than the power of music. Once she's got that guitar pressed up against her crotch, sweat rolling down her face, a horde of howling devils begging at her feet, she'll realize how she feels about me.

I smile.

"It's not your fault, Dax," she says, sneaking a peek out the blinds again. What she sees makes her purse her lips like she's just bitten a lemon. "There was nothing you could've done anyway." She glances over her shoulder, blonde hair silky and soft around her face. She smells like my shampoo and she's wearing my clothes.

Do you know how seductive that shit is? It's like, the ultimate aphrodisiac. "This is all just one, big clusterfuck." She nibbles at her lower lip and snaps her fingers, eyes twinkling. "A big, tangled web of lies." Naomi turns around abruptly and steps close to me, raising my shirt with her fingers, drawing her nails along my clenched abs. She breathes hot against my mouth as she touches the spiderweb tattoo with rounded whorls. Dax stands by and watches silently, but I can see the envy in his eyes. "All we need to do is trip a thread and the spider will come running."

Naomi grins and a chill rides straight up my spine and into my brain.

Somehow, I've got a bad, fucking feeling about this shit.

CHAPTER 24
& NAOMI KNOX &

When Dax, Turner, and Ronnie leave for the show, I follow after them dressed in a black hoodie and shades. It's dark out and the weather doesn't look too good, so the crowds are much smaller and the shadows much bigger. They don't like my idea, but they're not my fucking keepers. Despite what happened, I'm still in charge. Nothing will ever change that.

I follow them into the venue and flash my backstage pass at the bouncer. He doesn't look happy but Turner waves him away, giving me a look and kicking at a guitar with his foot. He stands over me, keeping watch as I open it, making sure that nobody gets too close a look at this roadie.

I lift the lid and run my fingers over the smooth black and white beauty cradled within.

"Oh God, I missed you," I whisper, knowing full well that this isn't my original guitar. Just the fact that it's the instrument of the dark and unruly gods of rock makes me happy though. It could've been a cheap knock off from Target and I'd be jumping for joy right now. My fingers itch to scratch the strings, fuck them hardcore and smash up the stage. In my throat, my voice coils poised and ready to strike. When I hear the opening band start up their first song, I almost cry. Even a day without music is punishment, but a whole week? No, fucking thank you.

I lift the Wolfgang out with gentle fingers, examining it with careful eyes. I have no idea what I'm looking for – a lipstick stain? a bit of DNA? a fingerprint? Still, I spin it slowly and keep my eyes peeled, nearly exploding from my skin when Hayden's voice sounds from over my shoulder.

"You look good today, Turner," she says as I tilt the guitar and try to get a glimpse of her in the reflection. Doesn't work. I glance surreptitiously over my shoulder and find the psycho bitch dressed in a pair of bootie shorts and a tank with no bra to hold her tiny tits in place. Even those mosquito bites are going to flop when she's jumping around onstage tonight. If I were 'here', I'd make sure she put one on. God. She *knows* I fucking hate that.

Somehow, I feel like she senses I'm close by and is trying to piss me off. She's so getting the cunt punt when I confront her ass. "Different. Something happen?"

Turner shifts his weight and raises his chin. I can't see his face, but I can hear his grin when he speaks next. He's so lucky his balls are out of my reach or I'd crush the fuckers.

"Had a hot fuck last night. Always makes for a good next day, don't you think?"

"Oh yeah," Hayden says with a dirty smile. It doesn't reach her eyes though, just sits there on her thin mouth and looks heavy. *How deep into this is she?* "I can't disagree with that one. Last night, when Dax and I were … " Hayden pauses and puts a hand over her rounded mouth. "Did I say that out loud? God, he is so going to kill me." She fans herself and backs away a step, glancing down at my hunched form. I look away and focus on the Wolfgang. "I am *so* nervous. My second real night back. I hope I can remember how to wow the crowd." She growls this last bit and I can just imagine her tossing Turner a wink before she spins away. The sound of her heels clicking on the floor disappears into the melodic rift that's drifting back to us from the stage.

"Naomi," Turner begins. I cut him off.

"She's full of shit, Turner," I tell him as I look around the guitar case. As far as I can see, there's nothing here.

It's a new case, new guitar, perfect replica to the one I smashed in my confused stage rage. Crouching here, now, with a clear head, all I can wonder is *what the fuck was I thinking?* I smashed my most prized possession because I was messed up about Turner. What a dick. I don't think about the fuck last night or the near fuck this morning. "She obviously said that on purpose. She must've seen Dax get on the bus or something, and she's screwing with you." I snap the case closed and stand up.

When I turn around, Dax is coming across the room towards us. Turner doesn't waste any time, and in his fucking *way* just blurts out the question.

"You fuck Hayden last night?" he asks and I cringe. Dax looks a little perplexed and then whispers the one word that I did not expect to hear.

"Yes."

"Ah, shit!" Turner shouts and people scatter. Somebody even tries to hand him a water bottle. Once a diva, always a diva. Turner grabs his head and turns away, but I keep my gaze firmly focused on Dax's face. He's never screwed me before, but there's always a first time for everything. If he wants to mess with me now, he's got a golden opportunity. He looks apologetic and regretful, like he's just been caught cheating. But I don't hold it against him. I mean, look at me. I've got this … dirty *thing* going on with Turner. I can't even touch the

guy or my wiring gets all fucked and I can't think straight. "Should've known not to trust this motherfucker."

"I thought you were dead," Dax whispers and I take a breath, look him square in the eye. People part around us and take no notice of another extra in a sweatshirt. I might as well be invisible right now. I think of that poor girl, Marta, that Turner told me about. She died so somebody could get a laugh out of fucking with my friends, my fans. When he told me they cut off the skin on her chest, belly, and ankle, just so they'd think it was me, that made my stomach twist painfully. I feel like that girl's blood is on my hands. I've already got enough of that, thank you very much. The bad blood already burns like acid; I can't even imagine what it would be like to have the blood of anyone of a lesser evil splattered there. How could you live with yourself? "I was drunk, high, depressed. And Hayden … if she's involved, it's on a minor level. She's not a monster, not really. She's just –"

"Seriously off her Goddamn rocker," Turner says, turning around and giving Dax a disgusted once-over, like he's diseased or something, carrying the black plague under his silver fingernails. It makes me so pissed, I just want to deck his ass.

"Turner," I hiss, trying to keep my voice pitched so that the music from onstage covers it up. "*You messed with me and now you're done. I will finish you. Finish*

you fast and bleed you dry." I listen to the lyrics as I stare Turner's dark eyes down.

"Don't get on his ass because he scooped up some of your soggy leftovers." Turner leans back like he can't believe I just said that to him. "You fucked her, too, once. Obviously, she has some kind of pull." *Is that … jealously in my voice? Am I jealous? This is ridiculous.*

"She's confused. I think she's trying to figure out how to be a better person, but just doesn't get it yet." I look at Dax and decide if I should tell him about Hayden's crazy rant in the trailer. I mean, she said she'd try to help me out, right? I want to give her the benefit of the doubt, but she's kind of been holding me ransom for years, so you know, it doesn't come easy. "Let me talk to her." Before either Turner or I can interrupt, he holds up his hands and continues. "I won't tell her about you. Just … let me see if I can get anything out." Dax squares his shoulders and locks his gray eyes on me. "I love you," he declares, and I can tell he wants to say my name, spill it in the air like a fragrant curse. But he can't, not back here.

"Dax," I whisper, stepping close. I'm not trying to be mean, but shit, I can't handle all of this at once. Things are tough enough as it is. "I'm not looking for love right now." He stays stone still and doesn't respond. "But if you could talk to Hayden, I'd like that. Don't do it because you think it'll win me over, do it because you

want to, okay? If not, I understand." I step back and watch him watching me for a moment. After a few seconds, he nods and moves away. This isn't going to be easy. He's not going to take *no* for an answer anymore. My temporary death has caused quite a few hearts to rip open and bleed all over the place. I need to stitch them up and move on.

I glance over at Turner.

"You're not looking for love," he says, taking a drag on his cigarette. "But what if it bit you in the ass?" I stare at his strong face, the star tattoos at his hairline, his lip rings, the single nick on his throat where a razor left its mark. He's pretty, but it's a dangerous kind of pretty, the kind that kills souls. Not going to happen. I start to say something, but he interrupts me. Typical. "Just let it simmer up there in your gray matter for a bit, babe." I narrow my eyes at him. He takes a step forward and grasps my shoulders. Even through the thick fabric, I can feel his heat. My head drops back and when he presses his mouth to mine, I don't fight. I kiss him back until I realize how fucking stupid we're being.

I stumble back and cover my mouth with my gloved hands. All around me, twitters and cruel giggles ring out. Other girls watching Turner put the moves on a new roadie. Huh.

"Hey," he says as I move around him and start

towards the door. "Don't forget to watch me onstage, beautiful." I look back at him, making sure to keep my head down in case anyone tries to scope me out. They don't. But I do feel an almost audible sigh of relief backstage, like the crew can finally rest easy. If Turner Campbell has stopped shouting his true love bullshit, then he's over Naomi. *We* can be over Naomi. It isn't a good feeling to be forgotten so easily.

I turn and reach for the handle of the door, realizing as I do that the one person that was keeping me alive while I was gone was that fucking asshole chuckling wickedly behind me.

I wish America was here.

I could feed her all of the bits and pieces, like typing information into a computer program. Give her a few minutes and she'd print out an entire dossier on the subject, who did what and when and why. She'd know everything. I think about calling her, but I don't know what I'd say. *Sorry I got you fucked up. They were after me, but you got in the way?* Or maybe that's not even

true. Maybe they wanted her dead? How should I know? Dax said she's okay now, out of intensive care, but that she was pretty bad when they first got to her, that she'd have died from the bleeding. Hearing him and Turner talk about the blood on the bus makes me so sick. The suffering the two of them alone went through is enough for an ass kicking to take place. Add my shit and America's shit and Marta's death, and these motherfuckers have it coming.

I step outside, and flash my pass at the security guard before I start to walk the perimeter. In my front pocket, I've got a knife and a can of mace. Ain't nobody getting the jump on this chick again. I make sure to stick to the lighted areas and avoid the shadows. There are guards posted here and there, so it's not like I'm all alone. I'm safe enough for now. Still, it's kind of hard to shake the feeling of shock and amazement at this whole set up. I mean, we've always had the chain-link fences, but not this type of security, these locks, the spotlights. This is a big thing now. *And I have to sit on the sidelines. I bet that crowd is like a pulsing heartbeat.* I sigh and pull out a smoke, fingering Hayden's picture when I reach into my pocket. Turner gave it back to me, but we didn't show Dax. Not Ronnie either. So I guess Blair, Turner, and I are the only ones that know about Hayden's secret. Guess if worse comes to worse, we can always use this to blackmail her. I'd rather not, but hey, payback's a bitch.

I make it around most of the camp before I spot the champagne colored car from before.

"Katie," I whisper. I move up to the gate and show the guard my badge. He glances at it and then looks up at me with an irritated expression, rolling his eyes as he unlocks the bolt and unwraps the chain. Lucky for me, she's idling up on the side of the overpass outside the south entrance. Easy out, easy in.

"You people have no work ethic, you know that?" the man says as I move past him. "You come and go as you please, smoke like chimneys, screw like rabbits. I mean, get a grip for God's sake." I ignore his rant and hop the small stone wall at the edge of the lot, using the hardy shrubs that dot the highway as handles to climb the steep hill. When I reach the top, I climb over and hit the moist pavement just as the sky overhead crackles. Looks like the storm's following us. Raindrops splatter my face as I check the window and find that I was right. Inside the car, is Katie Rhineback. She rolls the window down.

I put my hand in my sweater pocket and clutch the knife. I imagine that if Turner found out I was up here, that he'd be pissed. But he's not my keeper, nobody is. If I want to do dangerous shit, I'll do dangerous shit.

"Get in before he sees you," she whispers, and I can't help but glancing around. I figure she's probably talking

about Eric, but who the hell knows? "Hurry," she urges, eyes wide and forehead drenched with sweat. I check and double check, making sure the new cell Turner's manager got him is still in my pocket. If I need to make a call, he's got Ronnie's on him. Strangely enough, there's no doubt in my mind that he'd come running.

I open the door and slide in, leaving my shades on and hood up.

"How'd you know I'd be here?" I ask her as she eases onto the highway and gets in the fast lane. "Were you waiting for me?"

"I was looking for *him*," she says, keeping her eyes forward and her hands steady. Her head is shaved and her cheeks are hollow. I don't like the look of her, like something else has managed to come in and screw with her since we last talked. Her sorrow hasn't lessened, only gotten deeper. What the fuck? What did I do all that for? I *want* Katie to have a good life. She deserves it. Even if she is obsessed with me. I shiver, but I tell myself that she was never a threat. She kind of stalked me for awhile, called me her hero, but nobody ever knew why. Nobody but her. She knows I killed her parents and for the longest time, she worshipped me for it in the worst ways. I stare at her hard and try to get a feel from her, some sense that I'm in danger. I get nothing. If she really was trying to screw me, she wouldn't have let me go.

"Eric?" I ask and she shudders, her pain almost palpable, hunching over the wheel and swerving the car dangerously. I reach over and grab the wheel, but she recovers quick.

"No. Not Eric. Eric is gone. The Devil. I'm looking for *him*." I raise my eyebrows. Okay, here we go. More of the crazy talk. Great. Just great. I watch Katie's lower lip tremble and then let my eyes fall to the plastic purse in her lap, the dirty dress. She looks like a character from a dystopian novel, wild and frightened yet somehow fierce, crazy but focused and determined, too. It's scary as shit.

"You sent the video, didn't you?" I ask and her eyes fill with tears. *Bingo.* I knew it. One mystery solved, a thousand more to go. "Why?"

"You needed to know who your friends were," she whispers. I lean against the door and watch her face, the play of emotions under pale skin lined with blue veins. In the background, I hear a bit of jazz on the radio.

"You really put me in an awkward position, Katie. Not fucking cool." I pause and wait for her to explain herself further. She doesn't. Figures. "Are you stalking me again?" I ask as calmly and politely as possible. I can't imagine Katie as a murderer, but maybe she's responsible for the other stuff, the dead birds and the doll head, the hat and the guitar. Maybe there are two stories here intertwining? That would explain the convoluted

shit hole I'm now swimming in.

"Naomi, I wanted you to know who you could trust because he's after you. They all are."

"Who?" I grind out, desperate for answers. My head is spinning with all of this crap. On the outside, I'm okay, but inside, I'm confused. Lost. Empty and bursting both. Things are changing around me faster than I can blink. My secrets are being spilled from my soul, taking away that reeking rot I've been carrying around for so long. But what do I fill those spaces with? Love? It's never worked out for me before, never been that healing balm that poets promise and authors employ for giggling fangirls. I've hated Turner from afar for so long and now … he's in reach and I'm not sure if I even want him. I press my hands to my face and try to breathe.

"The demons," Katie whispers, her voice almost lost in the rush of wind and water outside the window. I've always loved the rain, but for once in my life, I wish it was sunny outside. The weather is thick and heavy, bearing down on my already burdened shoulders. I press my fingers to my temples. Eric was right about at least one thing: Katie has gotten worse. But why. That's what I want to know.

"Did you steal the scissors?" I ask her, figuring I already know the answer to that question.

"Satan did. So he could bind you under his dark

graces." I drop my hands to my lap and push up my shades, so I can see her better. I'm probably fifty shades of fucked for getting in this car with this crazy woman.

"And the dead birds, the message in blood, did you write that?" Katie bites her lip so hard it starts to bleed. She takes the next exit and goes under the overpass, getting us back on the freeway in the opposite direction. "What have you done?" I ask her, not wanting to give much more away, just in case. "Other than the video, what else are you responsible for, Katie?" She doesn't answer, just sits there and stares out the windshield with glassy eyes. I slam my fist against the dashboard, and she whimpers. "Goddamn it, Katie. I've never asked you for anything, but please, *please*, whatever it is that you know, tell me."

"This is big," she says to me. "Much bigger than you and I. We're just fish, caught in a net. I sent the video, Naomi, but only so you would know who to trust. They kept your secret, didn't they?"

"Who else did you send it to?" I whisper, thinking of Turner and America. She's right though. Even though they didn't have to, even though they should've gone screaming to the police with it, they didn't. Says a lot, doesn't it?

"Dakota and America," she whispers as she pulls into the parking lot of the venue. It's *packed*, but she manages

to find a spot in the back and turns the car off, leaving us buried in silence. "That's it, I swear it, Naomi. I would never hurt you." She turns and looks at me, eyes wide as marbles, lips quaking and chapped. Her whole body screams *pain, pain, pain.* She's cut so deep that she's bleeding inside and there's not a surgeon in the world that can save her from that. I hate to say it, but I don't think Katie will ever recover. I used to think so, but right now, I'm not so sure. "You're my sister, Naomi."

I give her a tight-lipped smile and reach for the door.

"Foster sister," I say, and then climb out into the eye of the storm.

I head straight back inside the gated area and around to the back, moving in the door and crouching in the shadows, so I can listen to Turner sing.

He is so on tonight that I get chills over my entire body when I hear his voice, can practically feel him crawling inside of me and splitting me apart, the most delicious kind of torture. He's singing that stupid *One Woman* song again. It's enough to make the audience

swoon and flutter like a cluster of butterflies, desperate for a taste of his nectar. The word *mine* pops into my head and is dismissed immediately. I will *not* think that way. I told Turner no before. I have to stick to my guns.

But then I watch him rip the stage up and destroy it. I see that passion in him that I admired before raging bright, that happiness and joy spilling out into the crowd and promising them that you can have everything if you just try hard enough. It's fucking mesmerizing. And it's all because of me? Or just the idea of me? The thought that he'd found love and then lost it? I have no clue.

What I do know is that when Turner walks offstage, smelling like sweat and cigarettes, I almost jump him.

Instead, I wait stone still in my spot while I listen to the sounds around me dying down, fading away to whispers. Just as I'm about to go after him, get out before the last of the crew leaves me alone and in a vulnerable place, he comes up behind me and whispers in my ear.

"Boo." I jump, a little, and then chastise myself for not paying better attention, turning around to find him grinning like a Cheshire cat. I frown.

"I almost shanked you," I promise, which is true. At least my reflexes aren't complete shit right now. It's not easy staying away from the good stuff, the booze and the coke and the dope, especially not in a situation like this. But it's necessary, life or death crucial even. Turner just

reaches out and tries to touch my lower lip. I push his hand away. I've seen that move pulled on a dozen or more girls since we started this tour. I'm not going to play that game. "And stop smiling so much. Don't you think people will find it odd if you go from mourning and pissed to happy and carefree in a day? Can you tone it down a little?" He reaches a hand in my hood, inked fingers tangling in a stray strand of hair.

"Not if I pick up a new roadie girlfriend. That's more my MO anyway. Besides, I always thought you might be jealous of that chick." I raise my eyebrows and take a step back.

"The one you left with her panties down around her ankles, crying on the PA speaker?" Turner wrinkles his nose.

"She was crying?" I shake my head and sigh. He's a rich, rock star, piece of shit, asshole cock sucker. He will never change. I have to keep that in mind when making my decisions. I look around and decide I don't like how quickly this place is emptying out.

"Look, just forget about that. I don't want to be rammed over a speaker, alright?" I pull the morning after pill out of my pocket, pop it from the foil and swallow it. Turner watches silently, but for once, has nothing smart-alecky to say about it. "Let's just get the fuck out of here and get on the bus, so we can talk." I start to move past

him, and he grabs my arm. Again, I get *this* close to shanking his ass. "What?" I snap.

"Dax left with Hayden, right after their set."

I shrug.

"So?"

"So," he says, sounding annoyed. "You didn't let me finish. They left, but they didn't go back to the bus. They went out front. I followed them during the set change." I don't like where this is going, Turner looks guilty as fuck. Why, I don't know. Maybe because he suggested we bring Dax in on this? I don't blame him for it. I said it was alright. Besides, we needed someone from Amatory Riot to check shit out for us. I'm starting to wonder if we should've picked Blair. "I didn't have time to chase them down, but I waited until they were almost at the end of the lot, near the street. It might not mean anything, but it could mean fucking everything. Thought you should know." Turner gets a weird look on his face, two parts irritated, one part hopeful. He probably wants Dax to be a bad guy, so he's out of the picture for good.

I turn away and breathe in deep.

I want to end this shit, find out whose hands are in the cookie jar, but I don't want to lose all my friends and band members doing it.

"Thanks, Turner," I say instead. Since there's no way to know where they went, we'll just have to wait this one

out, maybe send Ronnie over to Terre Haute's bus to see if they're back. Until then, I'm not making any assumptions. "This shit just gets weirder and weirder," I mumble under my breath, moving out the door and across the rain soaked pavement. Turner keeps pace with me and doesn't let me get even a foot ahead of him. Inch for inch, we walk as equals.

CHAPTER 25
TURNER CAMPBELL

Dax and Hayden don't show up until right before we're about to leave, so we don't learn a damn thing. We don't bother to call him. It's hard enough to get privacy on our bus, let alone one with twice as many fucking people.

"Must be fucking hell in the bathrooms over there," I tell Naomi who's sitting half-naked in one of my shirts. Ronnie rolls a joint at the table between us. I don't know why he gets to sit closer to her than I do, but that's how she wants it. I have a bad feeling I'm not getting lucky tonight.

"I don't want to make small talk," she tells me, mulling over the information again. I want to kick her ass for getting into that car with Katie, but I settled for

yelling. Didn't exactly go over well. Naomi is not the type of chick that likes to be bossed around. Good thing, though. I've been with some of those. The sex isn't nearly as much fun. She looks up from painting her nails and smiles meanly. "With you. I want to hear about Ronnie." Naomi turns to my friend and continues coating her nails with black polish. It'll actually help her blend in better here, and believe it or not, actually makes her more androgynous. Half the fucking guys in the tour have black nails. Kinda comes with the territory.

Ronnie smiles and pinches his joint between two fingers, leaning back into the cushions and scratching at the snake tattoos on his neck with his other hand.

"I'll tell you all about Ronnie," I say, giving him a look that says *get the fuck out, so I can have some alone time with this girl.* He sees it, registers it, and ignores it. He's not interested in her, thankfully, or I'd have to kick his ass, but I think he does like her. So he's going to play cock blocker and stick around. Fine. I sigh and watch his joint with hungry eyes. I can smell it. Naomi can, too, but neither of us accepts it when he offers. "He's a hopeless romantic turned whore. He loves to drop acid and he has like sixty kids. We've been friends for over a decade and he still doesn't remember my middle name."

"First of all," Ronnie says, taking a hit and holding the smoke in his chest as he continues. "I have four kids."

He blows the smoke out with a sigh. "From four different mothers. I'd rather be a hopeless romantic than a hopeful cynic, and I'm pretty sure your middle name is a state. Arkansas? Nebraska?"

"Fuck you."

"Oh, it's a curse word. My bad." Ronnie throws the joint at me, and it hits me in the chest. "It's Dakota, you fuckin' asshole." Naomi laughs and smiles. But not at me. At Ronnie. Guess she's still pissed about my freak-out. I mean, come on though, anybody could've been in that car. Or waiting outside those gates. Or shit, for all we know, Katie is almost completely and utterly responsible for all this shit. Naomi said at least one guy was involved, but he could be working for Katie. What do we really know about this chick?

"Tell me about your kids," Naomi says, watching as I toss the joint in the ashtray and pretend I'm not trying to breathe in as much secondhand smoke as humanly possible. Ronnie rubs his chest and shakes his head, dark hair falling into his face as he stares at the tabletop. That melancholy is back again, flitting briefly behind his eyes. I don't know where it's been going lately, but I hope it stays gone. This whole murder mystery thing is working for him, giving him a purpose. That, and I think he's sort of living vicariously through me, falling in love all over again. I hope this cures him, or at least helps. Marta's

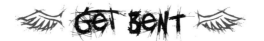

death will have saved Ronnie's life in that case. "Convince me why I should or shouldn't have any."

Ronnie looks guilty as fuck and plants his elbows on the table, reaching tentative fingers for the abandoned joint.

"I couldn't say either way really," he tells Naomi honestly. She doesn't blink, just sits there and stares at him while her nails dry. I wonder if she's thinking of our almost-kid, imagining what he or she would've been like. I know that I fucking am. And as soon as I have a kid, I know I'll be a better father than Ronnie. I sit and listen anyway, wishing it was just me and Naomi and a can of fucking whip cream in this room. I could show her some fun stuff. "I've only met three of the four. The youngest was just born a few months back. The mother doesn't want anything to do with me, so what am I gonna do? Take it to court? I don't stand a fucking chance." Ronnie looks down at the tabletop and starts to fade away into that ghostly otherworld where he's spent the majority of his adult life. "I'm not saying I don't want to know them. I just … haven't found anything in myself worth knowing. I don't want to saddle them with this shit." Ronnie looks up sharply and slices me with his gaze. I know some deep shit is coming. When he looks like that, it always cuts hard and fast. I get ready to bleed. "What I do know, but that nobody tells you, is that I wish I'd had my kids with a woman I loved. I mean, I imagine that it would make a world of difference. I'm no good to them as I am. I should be a rock, but I'm just a stone, sinking faster than I can blink." Ronnie takes a hit and drums his knuckles on the table. "I wish I'd treasured Asuka more when she was alive, and I wish I'd died right along with her." Naomi gives me a look that I return. She doesn't know all the lurid details of Ronnie's past, but she will. I'm going to tell her everything I know about everything. No secrets. No fucking secrets. "But since that's not an option, all I can do is wander and hope I find somebody half as good. I want to fall in love again. There, I said it." Ronnie takes a deep breath and stands up, giving me a look that plainly says *move*. I glare back at him, but he's not in a place to be messed with. I could punch his skinny ass out if I wanted, but it's not worth screwing with him when he's this fragile. I swallow my pride and get out of his way, so he can make a quick exit. "I know you didn't ask for it, but I said it." He moves to the door and pauses with his fingers outstretched and reaching. I imagine that's a position he's metaphorically been in for a long time and hasn't even known it.

"The first step to recovery is admitting you have a problem," I say, scooting back into the seat and watching his shoulders shake with the revelation. Might not mean much to anybody else, but this has been a long time

coming. I swallow my arrogance and my cocky bullshit and my need to show off for Naomi, attract her like a posturing animal in the throes of heat. "Hey," I say and he throws me a glance over his shoulder. "I'm proud of you, man."

Ronnie smiles, grins, flashes us some of his silver fillings and winks mischievously.

"Thanks," he says. "I owe you both one, even if you don't know it. Whatever shit you two have got going on, it's toxic and it's contagious. Keep spreading the disease."

"And you'd know all about that," I laugh as he opens the door a crack and slips out, making sure I lock it behind him, pressing my back to the flimsy, folding wood. Naomi is staring at me with a frown. The room heats up a degree or two. *We're alone.*

"And what is it?" she asks, poking one of her nails with a cautious finger. Satisfied that it's dry, she grabs for a pillow and wraps her legs around it, resting her chin on the top. If I thought she was hot onstage, it's nothing like this vulnerable softness I see in her now. *So fucking cute, Knox. I could eat you with a friggin' spoon.* "This thing that we have."

I stare at her. Answer's easy for me, maybe not so easy for her.

"Love."

Plain, simple, easy.

I cross my arms over my chest and stare her down. She doesn't respond.

"You said you loved me before, why can't we start over again? Everybody deserves a second chance?" More silence. I look at her face, her arched brows, her porcelain skin, the way she runs her tongue over her lower lip when she's thinking. I try to think up something intelligent to say, something meaningful, something that'll light up her eyes and bring her running onto my arms. Instead, I break down and hit old habits hard. I say, "You want to pick up where we left off this morning?" She just keeps staring at me. The silence is getting eerie. I shift forward and plant my hands on the tabletop. "I could show you exactly what you're missing out on, maybe change your mind about things?"

"Do you think, maybe, that Katie is telling the truth? That all she did was send the videos?" I roll my eyes and stand up straight. I know if I reached out and touched Naomi right now, that we'd both explode into a million pieces. My cock is responding to the pull, rising to the challenge so to speak. I can't even look at the woman without getting a rager and coming inside my damn pants. This love shit is tough.

"Can we put that on pause for a second and figure out this other thing?" Naomi's pale lashes flutter slightly, like

trees in a breeze or some shit. Sorry, I'm not very poetic.

"What's there to figure out, Turner? Relationships are not puzzles. They are not mystery whodunnits. There is no right answer, no clues to string together. Either we'll fall in love or we won't. That's it."

"I'm already in love. You mean, if you'll admit to yourself that you're still in love with me." She gives me a mean look, orange eyes flashing so bright they could blind.

"I fucking hate you," she says, and I know that's true. Honesty drips from every syllable.

"Yeah, but love-hate is the best kind. It's passionate and it defies logic and it just fucks with your mind on a daily basis. So, that's what I am for you. A mind fuck. And baby," I whisper, leaning down, brushing our lips when I speak. Flames roar higher than Hades. "I'm gonna make you come all over."

Naomi laughs, but she doesn't kiss me back. Somehow, someway, she resists the pull between us and scoots back. I want to freakin' choke her. Anybody else, anybody, man or woman giving me a look like that and I'd knock their fucking teeth in. I want respect and Naomi does *not* respect me. Not even a little. Not yet. I imagine that if I'd saved her, if I'd ridden to the rescue that it might've changed things. But I didn't. I tried and failed. Time to find a new tactic.

I take a step back.

"I've got to find Eric," Naomi says, grabbing a smoke from the carton on the table and lighting up. She doesn't look at me again.

"I'm going to go jack off," I tell her, gesturing at the bathroom door. "Any chance you'd care to join me?"

"Knock yourself out, cowboy," she says, cig dangling from her lips as she opens the notebook I got out for her earlier. I have no fucking clue what she wants it for, but there it is.

"Fine."

I spin away and squeeze myself in the closet sized bathroom. What Naomi doesn't know is that as I'm closing the door behind me, I see her slide her hand under the waistband of her borrowed underwear. Oh yeah. This shit is going to get good.

Oklahoma City, Oklahoma.

We get there pretty quick, even with the dragging entourage of buses and RVs. Naomi spends the rest of the drive scribbling in that notebook, pressing the pen to

the page so hard I'm afraid it's going to break and splatter black across that beautiful fucking face of hers. She probably doesn't realize it, but when she's bent over like that, golden hair falling over her shoulder and kissing the page, she's that kind of breaking pretty, the one that men war over. Just looking at her is driving me friggin' nuts.

Soon as we come to a stop, I stand up and watch as her eyes follow me.

"I'll have Ronnie come keep you company while I hunt down Dax." Naomi stares at me, dressed in my T-shirt and not a whole lot else. If I don't get out of this room, I'm going to go insane. I glance at her notebook page and grab glimpses of gravestones and broken hearts, knives and pistols, books with torn pages, angel wings. There are words there, too, but they're so small and cramped that I can't read any of them.

"Be careful," she says, and that's it. She goes back to her writing.

I unlock the door and end up running chest to chest into Trey. Without a moment's hesitation, I shove him in the chest and knock him back. He stares at me with wide eyes and doesn't bother to keep his voice down when he speaks.

"I knew it. I knew it was true. You're keeping a woman in there, you sick son of a bitch." *God fucking damn it.* "I know you're missing Naomi, but shit, man.

You took a girl from the concert?" I don't know what to say to that. How do I correct him without giving anything away? Milo, Jesse, and Josh are starting to stare. Our driver turns up her music. "Was she willing?"

"Oh for shit's sake, Trey. Fuck you. What kind of question is that?" My friend holds up his hands and then drops one to his hair, so he can rake his fingers through it like a neurotic nut bag. "You ever ask me something like that again, and I'll deck you." I see Milo coming down the hall towards us. Great. Just great. Now what?

"Turner," he starts, adjusting the lapel on his suit and licking his lips nervously. "You brought a woman on the bus?" I lean against the wall with my arm up. I've got to deal with this shit right or it's going to fuck not only me but Naomi, too.

"You got a fucking problem with that? It's in my name, isn't it? If I want to bring a tagalong chick with me, what's the issue?" I raise my chin and give them both my most arrogant look. *See me, Turner fucking Campbell. I am God right now, so you better bow down before me.* This sort of shit's never been hard for me to pull off. I mean, I've never even had to try for it. It's just the way I was. Right now, it sort of feels like bullshit.

"She … is she over eighteen?" I roll my eyes and slump against the wall, keeping the door between my legs, one foot in, one out.

"Oh Christ, Milo," I say, looking up at the ceiling. "Really? Since when have I ever gone after jailbait?" As soon as the words leave my mouth, I blanch. Milo notices and looks closely at me. After a moment, he waves Trey away. My friend grumbles and cusses him out, but he listens, tossing me dirty looks as he goes. I'm never going to be able to explain this shit to him. He wouldn't understand.

Naomi was sixteen when we first fucked. God. What was I thinking? I am completely and utterly going to screw this shit up.

"Are you alright?" Milo asks me, looking concerned. I wish I could trust him, tell him everything and let him deal with it. That's what I've always done. But not this. I can't tell anybody else about this, especially not when Dax might be fucking with us.

"Everything's fine, Milo. She just doesn't want to be sensationalized. Don't worry about it. She's not a prisoner back here, are you, babe?" I look in at Naomi who's sitting there staring at me with wide, wide eyes. I have no clue what's going on inside them, but whatever it is, it's scaring the shit out of me.

"I'm doing fine, cupcake," she trills, mimicking Skinny Bitch's voice. She's pretty good at it, too. "Just hanging ten with my honey bear." I give her a look, but she's not really in the mood to patronize me. "We're in love. Everything's going to be just peachy." I roll my eyes back to Milo who looks, admittedly, a little terrified.

"Is this another stalker?" he whispers, and I snort. I've actually had a few of those. You'd be surprised at what some of these chicks are capable of. I thought only dudes did that sort of shit. Not true.

"It's fine," I tell Milo, but I have a pretty good feeling he's not going to leave this alone without seeing her. I try to cook up something good, but he interrupts me.

"Turner," he says softly, putting a hand on my arm. I tense, but I don't shove him away. He *knows* I hate being fucking touched, but he's willing to go for it. Why? "I've known you for a long time now, and I've only seen you this beat up once before, when I pulled you from that hotel room. Since then, this is the first time I've really *seen* you look at the world with a different set of eyes. Naomi was special to you, don't just jump on the first girl that comes along because you miss her. You can't stop hoping that she's still out there somewhere." I just stand there and stare into Milo's blue eyes. There is no way in fuck I'm looking back at Naomi. There is so much wrong with what he just said that I don't even know where to begin.

"The hotel room?" I ask, but I already know. We all do. What. The. Fuck.

"I came and got you before … you know, things got

bad." Milo leans in close to me. "Please tell me this one isn't underage, too?" I almost throw up in my mouth, right then and there. "Stick with Naomi, with the hope of Naomi. She's the best choice you've ever made."

"You pulled me from a hotel room?" I whisper. The bus is dead silent right now, ringing with revelations. *No.*

"The girl was sixteen, Turner," Milo says, and I'm hoping to hell he's really as innocent as he sounds, that he doesn't know anything beyond what he's saying. If so, he's a dead man. "You were devastated for weeks after that." He leans back and gives me a strange look. "You don't remember?" I think back to that night, past all my recently recovered memories, and all I can come up with are weeks of drinking and slamming and smoking. Was I mourning the loss of a girl I didn't even remember? Jesus H. Christ. My heart slams in my chest and my head feels light and fuzzy.

"She's not underage, she's willing, and she's not going anywhere. Leave her the fuck alone, alright? I'm going out."

I shove past Milo and slam the door behind me. They'll keep out or I'll kill them. They know it; I know it. I storm down the hall and out the door, refusing to make eye contact with anyone, not stopping until I'm swimming through the warm dark on my way to Terre Haute's bus. My pulse pounds in my head and my

eyelids flutter closed as I bend over and put my hands on my knees.

And the plot thickens.

Fuck.

I put together a loose timeline for myself: *I see Naomi at the concert getting roughed up, I help her out, we have fun, get tats, go up to a hotel room. She blows me in the elevator, I fuck her good, she falls asleep. Milo shows up and 'rescues' me from getting my ass thrown in jail and slammed with a sex offender charge. I don't remember shit and I mourn a friggin' feeling, like some chick flick hero in a world of autumn. I fuck myself up and forget all about it. And now here I am, getting rammed up the ass with revelations. Great. Just fucking fantastic.*

"Hey."

I snap to attention and see Dax standing a few feet in front of me, arms bare, ghost tattoos bright under the moonlight. He's wiped off most of his makeup, so for the first time ever, I can actually read what's tattooed on the backs of his eyelids. The silver light from above makes the two words pop straight out at me when he blinks. *Born Wrong.* One word on the right eye, one on the left.

"What the fuck, man?" I ask, taking my anger and my frustration out on him. Either he's an enemy, a lying, backstabbing cock sucker, or he's a rival in love. So yeah, I get pissy with him, and I don't feel bad about it.

"Where the fuck have you been? Running off to that trailer with Hayden to scope out the crime scene? Try and figure out how to keep Naomi from escaping next time?"

Dax just stands there and watches me rant. After a minute, I get pissed and shove him hard in the chest. He stumbles back and grits his teeth, but that's about it.

"Hayden was showing me where she was kept while she was held captive. She said the trailer was where Naomi was being held, tried to get me to come up with a plan to get her out."

"Bullshit." I point at him with an accusatory finger. "You're fucking in on this, aren't you?" Dax wrinkles his nose in anger and scowls.

"First of all, keep your voice down, you stupid fuck. Second, I would *never* do anything to hurt Naomi. I love her. More than you could ever understand. You say you do, but what do you know? You're a playboy partier with a bad attitude and too much money. You don't deserve her, Turner, and you've already won, do you know that? I'm no idiot. It's over for me. I knew that the second I heard her tell you about the abortion, but it's taken me this long to figure it out. There's not going to be a contest for me. I don't even get a *chance.* So shut your mouth and listen to me." Dax takes a deep breath and I drop my hand to my side. *Shit.* "Hayden was a part of this, but she bargained her way out. She doesn't feel good about it, but she's not ready to crack yet. She doesn't know everything, but she knows at least one person who's involved." He licks his lips.

"Is it Katie, Naomi's foster sister?" I ask, but Dax just shrugs.

"She won't say yet. She's still scared about something." Dax glances over his shoulder and gets in close. "There's a picture," he begins, and I interrupt him.

"Naomi has it." Dax pauses, nods, sighs.

"Okay, good. Let me see if I can talk Hayden into telling me something. If I can't, I think your best bet is to bring Naomi out into the open." I take a step forward, and he holds up his hands, which are actually bare for once, gives me a look. "Hear me out. If she's hidden, she can be captured again and nobody would know but us. I know she doesn't want to deal with the FBI or whatever, but sooner or later, they're going to figure it out, if they haven't already. She might be on their radar now for all the fuck we know. I mean, think about it, man. They're cops; we're musicians. They have the upper hand when it comes to this shit."

I know that what Dax is saying makes sense, but I don't feel ready to share Naomi yet. I want to keep her all to myself. Is that fucked? Besides, I'm worried. Terrified maybe. Now that I've suffered through her

dying once, I don't think I can handle it again. If something really were to happen to her, I would just flip shit and die. It's that bad. The love has sunk that deep into me and taken over. I am thoroughly and utterly poisoned, baby.

"Hayden will break," Dax says with a contemplative note in his voice, like maybe he isn't sure he even wants her to. "Give her time to repent before you go after her, alright?" I get out a smoke and try not to imagine the conversation Naomi and I might be having when I get back to the bus. *The hotel. Milo. Fuck.* My hands shake as I light up.

"I could use a hit right now," I tell Dax, but he doesn't respond to that. Pretty, little, emo drummer boy can play pussy face all day long, but I know he's full of shit. I saw him score acid off Jason, our roadie, not too long back. The dude wears a skirt, so he's not hard to miss. Doesn't exactly make him the world's most inconspicuous drug dealer. *Idiot.*

There's a long, awkward silence while gray smoke drifts in the air between us.

"You into that chick?" I ask him.

"Her name is Hayden and no, I'm in love with Naomi." I blow smoke in his face, but he doesn't react. "Just because I can't have her doesn't mean I'll stop, that my feelings will just go away. I'll do whatever I can for

her, the same way I would if she were with me. Love's kind of fucked that way, isn't it?"

Dax turns and starts to walk away, and I have no clue what to say back to that. Maybe there's nothing to say at all? Guess, I should just turn and accept my supposed victory with grace. Thing is, it doesn't feel like a victory at all. If Naomi stays true to her roots, thick headed and stubborn as shit, nothing will ever come of this. I'll help her solve her mystery and she'll take the stage like the goddess she is. But I won't be by her side for it.

"Fuck." I throw my cigarette down and crush the burning ember with my boot, hoping this whole thing with Milo doesn't do the same to the growing attraction between Naomi and me. *Time to be a man and deal with this shit once and for all. Talk it out. Get it over with.* I ascend the steps and move quickly through the bus before anyone can start asking me stupid questions.

I pause outside the door to collect my breath and push my way in, finding Naomi already asleep on the bench. Ronnie sits across from her, eyes droopy and face in a crooked half-smile.

"What?" I ask, feeling frustrated. When my friend looks up and over at me, his smile turns into a grin.

"You and this girl," he says, rising to his feet with a groan and putting a hand on my shoulder. I brush it off irritably and listen to him chuckle. "You two have got a

future together."

And with that cryptic message, Ronnie turns and leaves me with nothing but my thoughts for company.

CHAPTER 26
❧ NAOMI KNOX ❧

When I wake up the next morning, I can see that Turner is desperate to address what happened yesterday. What he doesn't get is that I don't care. I don't care that his manager came and got him, that he was too fucked up too remember but somehow, upset with himself that he didn't. That doesn't change things. He still screwed me, I still got pregnant, and my life still sucked. The what and why and who doesn't even really matter anymore. Now that he knows, that everyone knows, that secret is done and buried for me. Who's to say that when March 15ᵗʰ of next year rolls around that I won't get upset, that I won't lie in a dark room and write terrible poetry? But for now, I have to deal with this crap. I feel like if I do, I can even

put the murders behind me, really and truly start over.

Hayden won't have anything to hold over my head anymore, and I can be free. For real this time. I drum my fingers on the table while I wait for Turner to get dressed. He's either so arrogant that he doesn't mind me seeing him naked or thinks that because we fucked, we're like a couple or some shit, and just changes right there in front of me, dick flopping around as he shimmies into his stupid pants.

I watch as he tucks his cock into the denim and zips it tight. Looks pretty uncomfortable from where I'm sitting, but what do I know?

"The sad part about those fucking things is that, other than in the waist, they cup me like a second skin. Don't you think you should at least buy a size up?" Turner sniffles and ignores me, stretching his arms above his head and flashing me the long, lean lines of his body. He's muscular, just friggin' perfect, filled out in all the right places with grooves and valleys and rock hard fucking perfection. I think I actually start to salivate and for sure know there's at least one spot on my body that's getting even wetter. I cross and uncross my legs.

Turner turns around and cups his ass with both hands. I watch his inked fingers curl around his butt and try not to let it get to me. It's just my lack of sex talking. I mean, all that captivity time and then the few days prior

where I was dealing with Turner … I'm averaging about once a week here. Not cool. I glance away and rest my chin on my hand.

"Then I wouldn't get these contours, babe," he says, and I ignore him. I have no clue what goes on inside that idiot's head, but I hope he makes more sense to himself than he does to the rest of the world. I lean forward and peep out the blinds while he slips on a shirt. There's no show tonight, so the crowds are much less concentrated, but it's kind of like watching a tidal wave gather before a storm. It's going to get worse and it's going to crash down around us and there's nothing we can do, so we better get used to it. That's how it feels anyway. "So we're trusting Dax?" Turner asks for the hundredth time. I nod absently, trying to piece things together in my mind. I don't have enough pieces yet to make these parts into a whole, but I will. Eventually, I'll get there. Good thing about Turner Campbell is that he's as stubborn as I am, unwilling to fail. Between us, we'll make things right. Funny how the enemy of my enemy turned out to be my friend, right?

"I want you to find Spencer, see if she's still with the tour. If you can track her down, ask her if she saw whoever it was that delivered that stupid plastic doll head. Dax said she was the one that gave it to him, so maybe she can give us a clue where to start." I look back

at Turner and watch him watching me. His eyes have a look that I can't decipher. No, that I *won't* decipher. I know what he wants, but I refuse to give it to him. He can't just wipe away the history with a sexy, tattooed hand.

I rip a page from my notebook and scribble down Spencer's name and a rough description. Turner takes it and stuffs it in his pocket without even looking at the words.

"I don't like you going off by yourself. I don't trust this Eric fuck."

I stand up and grab the hoodie that's draped across the table. Maybe it's not smart for me to go out by myself, but if I don't look for Eric, if I hide here all damn day, I won't learn anything. Dax might be right about me going public, but then there'll be other players in this already crowded game. Besides, as soon as I reveal myself, whoever's responsible will know they're being hunted. I don't want them to know that I've switched up the roles, that I'm the one with the poisoned needle and the ropes. My turn to fuck with them.

"And I don't care. I know what I need to do and I'm gonna do it. Get over yourself." I check to make sure the knife's still tucked inside next to the mace then slip the sweater on, slide my shades into place and hit the parking lot.

Today's an off day, so half the crew and most of the musicians are gone, exploring the city, making complete asses out of themselves. That was never my scene. I'd rather stay in the bus and nurse a beer, write up some new lyrics, but right now, this works in my advantage.

I do what I did before and scout the perimeter, noticing that there are more cops here than usual. Maybe the FBI really is getting involved? I don't see any conspicuous folks in dark suits and glasses, but who knows, they could be anywhere. I don't doubt the power of the police, but what I do know is this: first, red tape sucks and they can't always do what they need to do. Second, the underbelly of the world operates under different principles than the rest of this Godforsaken shit box. I can find things out that they'd never dream. It's all about knowing where to look.

After a couple rounds, the guards start to get weird with me and I abandon that post, poking around the buses until I spot Turner leaning against a bus and talking to Spencer Harmon. She's gazing up at him with wonder sparkling in her brown eyes. Every now and then, he pauses to run his fingers down the smooth skin of her shoulder, teasing her coffee and cream complexion with stars and paw prints. He's using flirtation to get his way with the starstruck roadie. It kind of makes me want to take this knife and chop his balls off. *But only because*

you're jealous, my mind whispers as I spin away and start off towards the gate. There are reporters galore, but I figure if I grab a trash bag and follow the other crew members out to the dumpster, they'll leave me alone.

While I'm walking, I hum that tune I was working on before, the one without an ending. It's not over yet, but it feels like it could be, like I could wrap it up with a pretty bow and a kiss. *Yeah, by getting with Turner Campbell. And that's too easy, babe. You can't do that. You just freaking can't.* I get out a cigarette and snap it between my lips as I reach for one of the massive bags of trash. *But, come on, let's be honest, the man can pash hardcore. Best oral sex* ever. *And that was just a tiny taste. I bet he's got all other sorts of nasty.* I try to argue with myself, brain versus pussy. Pussy usually wins, but at least I'm trying here. *Yeah, because he learned it fucking half the girls on the West Coast and a quarter on the East. Do you really want a piece of cake that's been passed around the entire bakery?*

I flash my ID badge and slip out the gate without any eyes on me. I'm just another mindless, nameless tagalong with dreams of fame. Or drugs. Yeah, more likely it's about the drugs. I dump the bag, get screamed at by a shift leader about how I fucked up the garbage and the recyclables or some shit and then drift off in a group headed for the local bars. At eleven in the morning. See

what I mean? Drugs, alcohol, same difference.

I break off from them at the parking lot, wondering all the while if I'm just doing this to prove to myself that I *can.* That I'm not weak. That getting kidnapped does make me a victim. I was wronged, yeah, but that doesn't show a kink in my character. Right? I hate that I'm even asking myself this question. And I hate that I know going out here alone is a stupid idea. I'm trying to prove something while putting myself in harm's way.

I pause with my arms crossed over my chest and nearly stab someone when a voice sounds from behind me.

"Thought it might be you."

I spin around and there she is. Hayden fuckin' Lee. Nice. Really. Am I that obvious?

"Huh?" I ask, trying to pitch my voice low, sound strung out. Hayden looks at me and sighs. I hate to admit it, but I think she's *relieved* to see me. How interesting.

"I can read Dax like a book," she whispers, popping her hip out and flipping her hair. We're in the corner of the lot, shielded from the media by a van and a large pickup, but it's still just a matter of time until someone sees her and she gets swarmed. I notice she's got on some Mrs. Turner Campbell bracelets. Hmm. "Been chasing after him for enough time that I can see it. He's

all lit up like a Christmas tree, Mi."

"Don't call me Mi," I whisper to her, narrowing my eyes behind the shades, eyeing her hot pink pants and sparkly halter with distaste. "And stop dressing to piss me off. I don't like it. You look like a fucking hooker." Hayden doesn't laugh, doesn't smile, doesn't even look angry with me.

"I was going to get you out." I laugh, harsh and bitter. It echoes off the pavement and sounds like a flock of angry birds.

"Before or after I was gang raped?" I ask with a wink she can't see. I reach in my pocket and finger the knife, just in case. I almost wish she'd attack me, so I could put her down. She's been traumatizing me for years, treating me like a slave. *Never again.* "Thanks but no thanks."

"Katie's going to suffer for that, you know?" she tells me with a little sniffle. She's obviously spent her morning being productive, snortin' some high quality coke. I tell myself I'm not envious at all. Turner and me, I know we're both due for a little withdrawal, some shakes, night sweats, cravings for days. I shift on my feet and glance around, making sure we're still alone out here in the hot as shit sun. It's *March* for God's sake and this place feels like it's on the face of the sun. If you open your mouth a little and taste the air, you can feel the storm waiting. I'm just hoping we don't get any

tornadoes. Hate tornadoes.

"How's that?" Hayden's turn to look around, eyes flickering from side to side.

"Naomi, you and I have both done bad things in the past." She sniffles again and focuses her blue eyes on the pavement at her feet. Her voice is much softer now, a little scratchy. There's a hint of that rock goddess in there somewhere. She really does have a beautiful voice. It's just hard to hear sometimes with all the bullshit clogging my ears. "But we did it because we had to, for a greater good." I have no clue where she's going with this, so I wait. "You understand why I didn't let you go, right?"

"No, Hayden. I don't. Why don't you explain it to me in small words." She looks up quickly and stares straight at me, eyes wide and swimming with decisions. Hayden Lee's never really been all that good at making them.

And then it happens so fast, hands grabbing me from behind, Hayden coming at me from the front. An arm wraps my throat and presses against my windpipe, closing my trachea and blocking off my air supply. My hands come up and I throw a quick punch at Hayden's face, hitting her tiny nose with a crunching satisfaction. She stumbles back with a scream and blood spurts out in a bright red fountain, staining her shirt and turning the fabric beneath the sequins see-through with wetness. Her nipples stand at attention.

My next move is aimed behind me as I smash my borrowed boot down on my attacker's instep. The man grunts, but he doesn't let go. *Shit.* I try to make as much noise as possible, flail around and elbow back, trying to either get the guy to let go or try to attract the attention of the mass media and the fangirls and boys that are flitting around the gates. We're placed just so here, near a stand of well manicured trees, obviously not native to this area, big flowering suckers placed for aesthetic purposes. They keep us nice and shaded, hidden in beautiful darkness.

"I am so done with this shit," Hayden whimpers from where she's collapsed on the ground. I notice she doesn't try to get up and help. Either she doesn't care what happens back here or she's supremely confident in my attacker's skills.

I decide that enough is enough and reach for the knife, slamming it back into the side of the man behind me. He grunts again, but this time, he lets go and I stumble forward, spinning to face him with hot red dripping from the end of the blade.

My face blanches and I drop the knife.

Oh. Shit.

I just stabbed a fuckin' cop.

"Oh my … God," I whisper as the man turns and starts to run. He doesn't let his wound slow him down, just takes off into the trees with red trailing behind him in tiny dots. My knees feel weak, but I maintain my footing, trying not to be sick. A split second later, I hear Turner's voice behind me.

"I don't think so, princess," he says, breathing hard. I turn to find him holding Hayden back, arms wrapped around her like a lover's embrace. "She tried to hit you in the back of the head."

"You don't fucking understand," she growls, but she doesn't try to fight him, just stands there with hazelnut hair dripping around her wild face. "I don't want to do this, but I *have* to. If I don't, I'm as fucked as all the rest of you are." I look over my shoulder for the cop but don't see him. He was young, probably early twenties, with white blonde hair and pale eyes, skin ruddy with an old sunburn. I'd probably recognize him if I saw him again.

"What are you even going on about you crazy bitch?" I ask her, staring at the knife in terror. I can't go to prison. I can't. And if this gets traced back to me, it's not

hard to connect the dots. Stabbed foster parents, stabbed a rabid fan, stabbed a cop. *Fuck. Fuck.* And …

"FUCK!" I shout so loud that some of the crowd does glance this way. I duck down.

"This shit is *big* and *old* and it's not even our faults, but we're suffering for it. That's it, Naomi. That's all I know. If you want to learn more, ask your crazy incest foster fucks."

I just stare at the crown of her head while she hangs limp in Turner's arms and lets her chin fall to her chest. He, on the other hand, glares at me over her shoulder, dark eyes sparkling with *I told you so* and loads and loads of machismo. His blue-black hair shimmers like a raven's feathers.

"What did you just say?" I ask, removing the can of mace and stuffing it in my back pocket. The knife goes in the sweater and my mind belatedly wonders how the shit I've gotten away with carrying this crap around. The guards might be there, but they certainly haven't stopped me to see if I'm packing. "What the *fuck* do you mean by that?" I snarl, getting in close and grabbing her hair the same way she grabbed mine the other day. Admittedly, that feels pretty good.

"Eric and Katie," Hayden says and my blood chills. "She's fucking pregnant with his baby. Told me herself." My stomach lurches painfully. *No.* "Crazy incest screw up *freaks*. I don't want to be a part of this, but if I stop, they blow my cover and take me down with you. I don't want that, Naomi. I want to sing forever."

"Just shut up!" I whisper fiercely. I look at Turner, but he's just wrinkling his face in horror. Fat load of help he is. I look back in the direction the cop ran and have no clue what to do about that. My mind is on overload right now, about to crack in half and spill my crazy out into the eerily still air of the afternoon. Hayden has no idea what she's just implied. If Katie really is pregnant with Eric's baby, it's not by choice. *The apple doesn't fall far from the tree.* I throw up in my mouth and swallow it back down.

"We should take this somewhere else," Turner says, glancing over his shoulder. There's a large group of people heading straight towards us.

"I stabbed a cop," I say. Turner releases Hayden with a shove and puts a boot to her ass. She goes down hard and kisses the pavement. I notice she doesn't try to get up.

"No, you didn't," he tells me, looking into my face, studying me, desperate to see what I'm up to behind the shades. "That's bullshit. You weren't even here."

"Where was I then?"

Turner looks down at Hayden.

"You're missing, remember?" He pokes at Hayden's

ass with his foot and I'm happy to see that it jiggles. *Flabby ass little cunt.*

"Why is a cop involved?" I ask her as she drags herself to her knees. I really, really hope there isn't some sort of inside police corruption bull going on here. This better just be a surface scratch.

"He's a friend of Eric's. Your brother has money, you know? Lots of it. Money makes people do crazy things. That's all I know, really. I'm an outsider who made a terrible mistake and I'm paying for it everyday."

"You're more full of shit than a Porta-Potty," Turner growls, kicking aside the cigarette I dropped from my lips without even realizing it. "You're going to tell us what's going on here. Everything. From floor to fucking ceiling, and you're going to smile while you're doing it."

"Or what?" Hayden asks, getting snippy and rising to her feet with a smirk plastered on her bloody face. "You'll make me suffer through another horrible fuck? First time was bad enough, thanks." Turner laughs, harsh and echoing. People are definitely noticing him now. Not good.

"Baby," he says, cruelty lacing his every word. "I don't even *remember* your ass. You're too damn skinny and you have a bad fucking attitude. Thanks but no thanks. You can banish that little fantasy." I watch curious faces start to move down the hill. The group

approaching us already has their cell phones at the ready. "You're going to tell us or we're going to plaster that picture of you across the web."

Hayden doesn't stop smirking. She just gets a nastier look and shoves past us, moving around the side of the chain link fence toward the back gate. The crowd really gets a good look at her now, covered in blood, tits bouncing as she starts into a jog. They follow and we run.

"I feel strangely violated," I say, panting and pulling off the hood of my sweater. The knife comes out next and goes straight into the sink. I start searching in the cabinets for cleaning supplies, but either a mythical cleaning fairy visits here regularly or Indecency hires that shit out. "This murder/kidnapping thing is doing wonders for our careers." I grab some dish soap and cover the blade in it, scrubbing at the metal with quivering fingers.

Hayden slumps down in a chair and lets Dax clean her up with paper towels, once again refusing to lift a damn

finger for herself. He's too nice. I have no clue why he does it. Ronnie leans against the door after locking it and shakes his head.

"I want to hear all about this shit," he says with a massive sigh. "And I've got to give you the latest gossip." He points at Hayden. "First off though, who invited this girl?"

"She's our hostage," Turner says, grabbing towels from the back and throwing them on the table. He watches as I pull of the sweater and throw it in the sink, filling it with soapy water and hitting that bitch like it owes me money. "Until she explains why she tried to attack Naomi. With the help of a cop."

"Aw, man," Ronnie groans, hand to his face. "The cops are involved? This is not going to turn out well for us."

I glance over my shoulder and watch as Dax stands up and backs away from Hayden like he's never seen her before. She's been carrying a torch for him for years, so I imagine that's gotta hurt. I shake the soap bubbles from my hands and rinse my arms under the cool tap, turning away and letting the fabric soak.

"I don't have a choice," she repeats for the hundredth fucking time.

"We always have a fucking choice," Turner growls, moving to the fridge and grabbing a beer. When he hands

me one, I don't protest.

"But they're not always good," Hayden whispers, looking at Dax with a resigned sigh. She peels her shirt over her head and slaps the bloody monstrosity on the table. She gets up and wets one of the towels, scrubbing at her tits and not caring who's looking. In fact, I think she likes the attention. "Sometimes, you get shit held over your head and your choices are so limited, you make the wrong ones, okay?"

"No sympathy bullshit. Doesn't kick in for like, seventy-two hours. Make this count." Turner sips his beer and I take a step closer to him. It's unconscious, but there it is. He may not be the best knight in shining armor, but he's trying. That's what counts. I don't need anybody to save me anyway. *Naomi,* my mind warns. *Don't let him trap you. Men like this are bad news.* I take a conscious step away.

"You want the play by play?" she asks, but nobody answers, so she starts off on her rant, scrubbing at her bloody nipple with angry motions. "After that stupid bloody bird *thing,* I get some weird messages from this girl who says she knows more than just Naomi's dirt. She tells me to meet her, so I do when we're in Denver." Hayden stops attacking her boob and runs her tongue along the inside of her cheek. "I get there and they fucking knock me out. I don't see who does it. Then I

wake up in a room, tied and drugged. A few days pass and Eric shows up. He takes my blindfold off and tells me that he's sorry, but that he needs my help." Hayden sniffles again. I want to shake the shit out of her, watch the pieces of this story fall to the floor and shatter, open up and reveal themselves. Instead, I just stand there and clench my fists tight. Behind me, Turner moves and ends up pressing against my back. I pretend that my cunt doesn't moisten as fast as a flick of the tongue across the lips. Not exactly the most appropriate time for a screw.

"He tells me that he'll make me a deal." Hayden swallows. "He only wants two things, he says. Katie and Naomi." Hayden takes a massive breath and her ribs poke out of her skin. She really is anorexic, I think. Despite my constant insults, I never really believed it was true. Right now though, she looks all skin and bones. *Eric.* I knew, somehow, that he was behind all of this shit. I knew it, knew it, knew it, but I didn't want to believe it. What happened to the kid I shared flasks with under the stars? He turned into his parents? How? Why? When? My head fucking hurts. "But he said there were other people involved and that if I wanted to walk out of there alive, I'd play along and they'd leave me alone. He said I was one of their targets, but that he could get them off my back if I helped out. So I did. And I am. I. Don't. Know. Shit. Don't ask me who the other

parties involved are or what they want. So, I'm sorry for what I did. I really wanted to save Naomi, okay? I was going to figure out a way to help her without putting my ass on the line. Right now, Eric is pissed, and I'm afraid of him." She grabs the countertop and curls her fingers around the edge. "I said it. There. I'm *terrified* right now, and you all should be, too." Finally. Some fucking honesty from her.

"Why?" Ronnie asks, moving up the steps and pausing with his eyes on Hayden. Dax stays silent and Turner growls low in his throat, like he can feel the storm brewing in the sky and even worse, here on the ground.

"Because," Hayden whispers, keeping her eyes on the pink water in the sink. "Eric said the other targets," she pauses and looks around the room. "Are all of you."

CHAPTER 27

& TURNER CAMPBELL &

Night falls on the camp and the weather gets real weird, real fast. Hail storms from the sky like a torrent of tiny soldiers, pummeling the metal of the bus and pinging off the sides. It coats the ground in ice and traps us on the bus with our thoughts.

Naomi and I sit together alone in the back, quietly playing a game of cards and nursing some beers. We've been talking for hours, her and me and Ronnie and Dax. Indecency and Amatory Riot. We're the targets. Not just Naomi, but *all* of us. I think about the baseball cap and wonder who sent it. Eric? Or somebody else?

"At least we know where the guitar came from," Naomi says as she slams an ace down on the tabletop.

"From Eric. My foster brother and own, personal stalker. Wonder if he sent the doll head, too?"

I don't respond, but I do watch the way Naomi's lips move when she talks, how they form syllables with rolling motions that remind me of much dirtier things. After a few moments of silence, she sighs and drops her hand to the table.

"God, I'm exhausted," she moans, running her fingers up her throat, bringing my cock to attention without even realizing she's doing it. *Shit, this girl is toxic.* I want to get poisoned and die between her beautiful thighs. "I can't even begin to untangle this shit. There's too much. Eric's paying cops off with money from God knows where, blackmailing people, *fucking* his little sister. Shit." Naomi drops her arms to the table and lays her head on them. "Let's talk about something else for awhile, anything else."

"We could leave the talk out and go for something deeper," I tell her, knowing that I sound like an asshole, but unable to hold it back. I'm not going to lie, the information we got from Hayden, from Ronnie, from that girl, Spencer. It's a lot. It needs to be mulled over, but it's hard to focus on that when I'm tired as fuck and twice as horny.

Naomi ignores me.

"Turn out the light and tell me a fucking story."

"I don't like being bossed around, Knox," I tell her, but I'm only half-serious. We shared a joint earlier, so I'm calm. Enough. I spin in the bench and use my boot to knock down the switch, plunging that tiny room in shuttered darkness. I lean back and let my head smack against the cushions with a sigh. For awhile, the only sound is the violent crash of ice cascading from the dreary sky.

"Were you born an asshole?" Naomi asks me. Sounds like a legit question, so I think about it for a second. Instead of getting pissed like might've done before, I just answer her.

"No, I was made one," I say, kicking off my boots, peeling off the socks underneath. I sit up just enough to rip my shirt over my head and toss it to the floor. The air in the cabin prickles my skin like needles, shoots me up with electricity and brings goose bumps up across my skin. When I'm in the same room as Naomi, I just stop thinking clearly. Shit. What am I saying? I don't even have to be in the same room as her to go nuts. I am now inexorably tied up in this chick's guitar strings. "My momma made sure that there wasn't much worse in the world beyond her free hands. My step-dads liked to join in, just to pound home the point. So maybe I am an asshole, but I've been waiting my whole life for respect, and I'm not letting anybody take that away from me." I

pause and try to listen to Naomi's breathing, see if she's still awake. Can't hear a fucking thing above the clattering hail. "And I don't like to be hit. By anybody. I won't take that shit ever again."

"I'm sorry," Naomi says which blows my friggin' mind. Sorry? For what? I shift onto my side and try to snag a glimpse of her under the table. It's too dark to see my hand in front of my face. "Remember what I said about crumbling foundations? I have one, too. It's hard to build a solid life when the one you were born into fucked you."

"I think you're doing pretty alright for yourself," I say, wishing I could see her desert eyes, find out if they're still holding a drop of that glistening wetness. One day, it'd be nice to see them moist all the time, open, swimming like the ocean under the sun. Bright, free, ready for everything. "You play guitar like a goddess, and you're the hottest lay I've ever had." Naomi laughs at me and it's only tinged with bitter. For the most part, it's just fun.

"I doubt that. We haven't exactly had the most opportune moments to show off our skills. Please tell me that's not true because I can do better." She pauses, and I can almost see her licking her lips, wetting them for me, spreading them over my cock … I shake my head and put the palms of my hands against my forehead. I want Naomi to be more than sex to me. I just don't have any

other point of reference to deal with my feelings.

"It's not about the actual act with you, babe," I tell her, praying to God that nobody's on the other side of that door listening. If I'm going to open my rib cage and let Naomi see my bloody heart, I have to make sure we're in private. Turner Campbell is not vulnerable or soft or tender. Not for anyone else. Never for fucking anyone else. And this is all new to me. I'm going to have to learn as I go.

"And why's that?" Naomi asks. Her voice sounds a little too harsh to me, like she's trying too hard to be tough. I told you when I first looked at her that she was vulnerable. But in the same way as me. Not weak but ready to show somebody her hidden side. I get it.

"You've been on my mind constantly since you thrust my jacket at my chest, even when I thought you were just another conquest." I swallow hard and hope this doesn't just piss her off more. "Even when I thought I disliked you, I was drawn to you. And I like you because you *don't* like me. It shows you have a good judge of character." I try to smile, but I don't know how it's supposed to come across in that dark ass room. I dig a cigarette out of the pocket of my jeans and light up, using the crackling cherry as a point of reference to stare at. "I love you, Naomi, and I'll say it a million times if you need me to. Every day until the day I die. Even if you don't believe me, even if you don't accept it, I'll say it forever. I'm twenty-eight years old. I know what I want at this point on my life." I roll back on my side and pass the cigarette under the table to her. Surprisingly, she takes it. I grab her wrist in time with a crack of lightning outside the window, and I swear to fuck that I can *feel* it. It travels into the ground, up the tires, into my spine and through my arm straight to Naomi's heart. She shivers violently, but she doesn't pull her arm away. "And what I want is you."

"Fuck you," she whispers, but her voice isn't as powerful as it was before. I'm getting in there, climbing into that crack I left before.

"Any time you want. I am on call for that shit."

"Your manager, Milo, coming to get you," Naomi begins and I freeze, fucking still as a Greek statue, chiseled abs and all. "That doesn't make you blameless. It doesn't free you of the responsibility."

"I know," I start to say, but she isn't done. She lets me keep holding onto her wrist though.

"But it does help," she starts. "You were still too trashed to remember me later, but you didn't choose to leave. That doesn't mean everything, but it's a start." She pauses and my throat gets tight. I want to kiss her so bad it hurts. "Now let go of my fucking wrist. I want to know what Spencer said to you again. Someone from Ice

and Glass got the doll head package delivered to their bus by accident?"

"Naomi," I begin, keeping my hold tight, my fingers tense.

"Let go of me, Turner."

"No."

I roll to the floor and drop to my knees, pulling her down with me and snagging the cig from her other hand. I smash it into the floor and drag her against me, wrapping my fingers in her blonde hair and kissing her mouth so hard it hurts. At first, she resists, but only until my tongue ring clicks against her teeth. It's like a bell, calling her to arms.

Naomi flips her arm around and looses my grip, grabbing onto my wrists instead. She takes both and slams them against the seat of the bench behind my head. My body gets hot with adrenaline and it takes everything in me not to fight her back.

"I don't like to be controlled," I tell her, but she shushes me with an angry nibble on my lower lip. Thunder rumbles and rattles the windows above us. The storm is picking up energy, feeding it into the two of us, igniting the toxic cloud of lust and longing we're carrying around. And this time, I really hope there's an explosion.

"Turner, if you want to stand a chance with me, and I mean a *chance,* not a guarantee, you will shut your

fucking mouth and do as I say." I start to protest and then stop. Lightning flashes outside and I catch a glimpse of Naomi's pretty face, rimmed in shadows, wet with tears. My walls come crashing down fast, and I relax into her, lean back and let the softness of her body brush against the hardness of mine.

I don't know why she's crying. All I know is that I want her to stop. Not because it bothers me or because I'm overwhelmed, nothing like that. I want her to stop because I can't stand to see her sad.

"You better not be fucking with me again or things will end bad for you, you know that?" she says, and I wonder what she's getting at. Is she going to give us a chance? Is that what this is about? "When I said I'd cut off your prized bits, I wasn't joking."

"I believe it," I tell her. Which I do. But I'm not afraid. I'm not afraid of anything but losing this girl. I've found what I want in my life and I'm going to have it, the rest of the world be damned. I'm going to find Eric and smash his face, drag the rest of the information from his bloody body and finish this. I *will* be that knight in shining armor for her. No matter what it fucking takes. I have a lot of baggage to make up for. Here's to hoping it'll be enough.

"I don't want to be a passing fancy or a one week girlfriend. I'm not a toy to be played with Turner, and I

know you like to party hard. Do you understand that what you did to me before hurt? Do you know hard I ached after that? How much I wished things could've been different?"

"I do," I say as she straddles my lap and rubs her heat against my jeans. I can practically *feel* her pussy wrapping my cock. I stay still, sweat pouring down my face, skin burning at her touch. This is fucking torture, man. I want to grab her and touch her, kiss her face and remind myself that she's alright, that she's still alive. I want to feel her and breathe her in, absorb her scent and make her mine. Or give myself to her. Maybe that's the part I'm missing? Maybe that's what I'm getting wrong here? I can't *make* Knox do anything, but I have full control over myself.

"And you do know I have blood on my hands?"

"Watched the video myself," I say as she releases my wrists and reaches her fingers under the hem of her baggy shirt, tentatively.

"And?"

"And I don't hold it against you. You did what you thought you had to do. It took some serious balls, and I respect the hell out of you for it."

The shirt comes off; Naomi's mouth smashes into mine, destroying words, tasting the truth in my mouth, the conviction. I bet there'll be a lot of people out there

who will think I'm full of shit, that a playboy can't change, but that's only because they're still searching for something to live for. I found my purpose and I'm going to grab life by the balls and hold on tight. I saw dark, so I recognize light. I ate a whole heaping truckload of *shit,* so when I first tasted something good, I knew it right away. I actually imagine that if I'd been surrounded by love my whole life, kindness, joy, that it would've made this harder. How would I have known the difference? But I've got contrast which is a lot easier to distinguish than subtle shades.

"Condom?" Naomi asks, and I pull one out of my pocket, flashing the Indecency logo at her with two fingers. I want to be inside her bare, feel her wetness, her slick ridges, fill her with my seed. I want to make babies with this chick, be a dad to a kid I already love even though it doesn't exist. But she's not ready for that, and I don't press the point.

She sits back on my knees and unzips my pants slowly, teasing me with the rush of warmth that swirls around the room, escapes from her lips and fogs the windows. Her feet are forward, close to my hands. I reach out and brush my fingers across the scabbed surface of her tattoo. It's hard to distinguish which of the rough surfaces is the knife wound she gave herself and which came from the rope and handcuffs, but I'm sorry

just the same. For all of it. Every last wound.

I brush my fingertips on the colored words, wondering if we laughed at each other in the tattoo parlor, shared stories, smiled at one another. Out of the whole night, that's the part I remember the least. I'll get it eventually, I know I will. For now, I just touch her skin with soft whispers and suck in a rush of air between my teeth when her hand frees me from my pants.

"*Struggling to understand why this pain feels different from what I've felt before,*" Naomi sings, low and off-key, eyes tracing the lines of my pecs, my belly, traveling down my cock. She leans forward and presses her lips against my nipple, kissing the hardened point and trailing her mouth down. This song she's singing, I know it's about me. I feel like it wouldn't be right if I didn't feed it back to her, nourish her with her own words.

"*Waking up to the sound of your voice, playing in my head, always running in my head.*" I sound so much smaller here, under this table, no heaving crowd, no microphone. It feels … it feels fucking great. I'm smaller, but I mean so much more. Does that make sense? Sure as shit does to me.

Naomi licks my belly, running her tongue down the space between my abs, where the muscles cave before giving rise to others. She licks the sweat and the electricity from my body, drops my head back with a

single kiss of her warm lips. I stare up at the ceiling with half-lidded eyes.

When a knock sounds at the door, we both ignore it.

"Tornado watch has been issued, asshole," Trey says, sounding tired. "Milo's talking to the rest of the crew and the other managers, trying to decide what we should do." He pauses and listens, but Naomi and I make no noises he can hear, protected from outsiders by the rush of rain that's just started up, replacing the hail. "And I know you don't give a shit and will continue to do whatever you want, Mother Nature be damned. Fuck me." Trey pauses again and then presses his face against the door, rattling the folded wood design. "Man, I'm sorry. I'm sorry about the shit I gave you before. I know you're not easily fooled or fucked with. If you say you love, Naomi, I get it. Don't throw her away for whoever that is in there. It's not worth it, okay? Shit. I sound like a fag." Trey stops talking, and a small chuckle escapes my throat, warming my belly and my chest as Naomi pauses her breath against the inked up perfection that is my cock. Yeah, alright, I'm a little full of myself, but I call that confidence. It's a good thing, right? "Just, forget it. Never mind. Just don't blame me when you die mid-fuck in the middle of a tornado."

"Your friend is annoying as shit," Naomi says, but she doesn't sound irritated, more … contemplative. I've

never had a thoughtful blow job before. This should be fun. "Have you ever made love before, Turner?"

"Nope."

"Me either."

Naomi wraps her fingers around me and tastes me with hot lips. I groan and grab onto the red leather cushions, feeling that electricity snake through my crotch and straight up to my brain. This is better than any dope, better than a wild acid trip. Naomi Knox is just … fucking hardcore. I let go of the sofa and bring my hands down, cup them under her chin and pull her face to mine. When we kiss, I taste my own sweat on her tongue and it drives me friggin' nuts.

"You're turning down a BJ?" she asks as I bring my arms down and wrap one around her bare waist, feeling the beauty of her perfect skin, the gentle curve of her spine. My other hand finds the slit in her borrowed boxer shorts and strokes down the hair there, diving deep and finding that molten spot between her thighs.

"Postponing it," I whisper as I dip inside, watching her face in another flash of lightning as she tightens around my hand, washing me in juices and bringing a growl into my throat. I can't help it. I feel like a fucking animal around her. Naomi has got me stripped primal, baby.

"You disgust me, Turner," she says as she rides my

hand, grinding herself against my knuckles, getting me in there nice and deep. "But you turn me on, too. I don't get it." I try not to smirk. I don't think smirking would be appropriate here. One slips out anyway.

"I thought we were supposed to be making love here?"

"I didn't say that, asshole," she groans against my forehead. Somehow, even in the dark, she manages to seek out all the star tats that are partially buried in my hair and licks the skin with long, slow strokes, hot as fucking fire. More thunder rattles the windows, but it's not a biggie. I could die in here with Naomi, leave a beautiful corpse, wrapped up inside of her. Man, I'd die happy.

"Aren't you supposed to be telling me you love me and shit?" Naomi pauses the grinding rhythm of her hips and looks me straight in the face. She's serious as a heart attack when she next speaks.

"Don't expect that out of me, Turner. If you go into this with that expectation, you might be disappointed." I feel her body cooling, her spirit drawing back. I don't want her to dive into herself. I want her to burst free, drench me with that fiery devil-angel she tries to keep hidden. But I see it. I see it clear as fucking day.

With a slow, wicked motion, I pull my hand away from Naomi's pulsing pussy and slide my wet fingers

down my cock, making sure she sees, that she's watching my teeth when I bite my lip, that she knows I'm going to be covered in her, condom or no.

"Put it on," I whisper, and she throws the package at my face.

"You put it on," she growls back. "I don't like being told what to do." Push and pull, back and forth. Neither of us knows how to be vulnerable without being an asshole right after. I don't let her bother me, just grab the square and rip it with my teeth. The condom rolls over me, nice and tight, fighting the straining hardness of my dick.

"Ah, don't get pissy, beautiful. I'm just starting out."

"I don't want generic pussycat nicknames. Call me by my real name."

"Alright, *Knox,* just relax and I'll show you what I can do." Without waiting for a response, I push her back and climb on top, sliding my tongue down her throat, pausing at her full breasts to nip and lick, hit her hardened nipples with my tongue ring. The warm metal teases the pink flesh into painful points, actually getting a rise out of my Rock Goddess. She groans a beautiful ugly groan, a growl that's pure music to my ears, tangling her fingers in my hair and pulling hard enough to hurt. I run my fingers down her sides and push her thighs up, sliding down her belly with hard kisses and nips. When I hit her hot cunt, I

dive straight in.

One hand wraps my cock and the other cups her firm ass while I pick up where we left off before, worshipping her with my body, giving myself up in a way I've never done before. I stroke my shaft and warm myself up for her body, making sure I won't disappoint, that I can take her to the end of the universe and back.

I'm not going to lie. I've never really cared about pleasuring a woman before. Whatever I did, it was all for my own enjoyment. If I fingered a girl, it was for fun. It wasn't to make her feel good. And I didn't do it because I'm a bad guy or because I hate women. I fucking *love* women. I did what I did because I didn't care. I was living for, *striving* for, respect, but I wasn't dishing it out. I'm not saying I'm suddenly cured, that I'll start saying please and thank you and shit. I'm still going to mark the stage up, piss on it and make it mine. I'm going to get angry at people for fucking with me, and I'm going to hit back. But I'm going to try. I'm going to try because I want Naomi to see me as a better person. That's it. Plain and simple.

Now here I am, and for, like, what is probably the first time ever, I care how she feels, what's going through her mind, what she thinks of me.

"I love your ass hardcore, Naomi," I whisper, spreading her wide, not afraid to get my face wet. She

doesn't respond, but her moans echo in time with another roll of thunder, a snarl from the sky that swears to fuck that we are *not* the most important things on this earth. Doesn't matter to me right now. All I know is that Naomi is *my* most important thing, and that's that. End of discussion. Mother Nature can suck my dick.

I whisper words against Naomi as I taste her, the words to her song. When I said they gave her life, I wasn't kidding. These are slices of her soul, floating in space, poisoning crowds with hope and starry-eyed, glassy snippets of love songs long lost. *Shit. Shit. Shit.* I really do love this woman.

"*When I walk, I stumble. When I run, I fall.*"

"Turner," she says, but I'm not sure if she likes it or wants me to stop or what. Her voice gets lost in another moan as I nip her clit, brush my lip rings over it and tease it to wild attention. I stop stroking myself and slip my fingers inside of her, feeling how ready she is for me, her pulses getting hotter and quicker and faster. It's more than I can take, so I slide up over her, pressing my abs against hers, rubbing our bodies together and grinding my hard-on against her pussy. "I hate your fucking guts," she tells me, right before I find her opening and slide in, one, slow, cruel inch at a time.

Naomi writhes beneath me as I grit my teeth and tense my muscles, holding myself in check, forcing my body to

wait. It wants to explode inside of her, release a rush of manic heat, but I won't let it. I'm in fucking control.

I press my mouth to her neck, kiss her exposed throat with tenderness, no teeth, no tongue, just lips and love.

"'Cause it's the same mistake that will fool us all. I fell in love."

"Fuck you," she says as I hit her pelvis hard with mine, brushing her cervix, filling her up. And right there, I know it inside and out. I am right where I'm meant to be.

"Fuck you right back," I say and then I start to thrust, planting my hands on either side of her face, looking down at her physically but looking up metaphorically. I curl my fingers tight, my knuckles tense as I hold myself up and move my hips, engaging my stomach in ways that are going to make me hurt sore as shit for days after this. I melt into Naomi, listening to the wet sound of our bodies sliding together play against the rushing screams of the rain and wind.

"Die and rot," she whispers. "Fucking die and rot in hell." I let her curse me out, and I just smile. I smile and then I drop my mouth to hers and kiss her again. My cock struggles to move inside of her tightening body, sweat pouring down my flesh and dripping across hers. She holds me hostage and squeezes, clenching muscles owning me. I have never been owned by another woman

like this. I never want to be. "Fuck!" she screams against my lips, clawing at my back, bloodying me, digging at the tattoo of her name across my skin.

I keep smiling, and I fuck her hard.

Pleasure crests and breaks and Naomi lets out a scream I'm proud to be a part of. My mind seizures and the intensity in my body smacks hard against my brain, dragging out a growl of my own, a whimper, then a scream.

Naomi's body spasms around mine and I come hard, hitting her flesh with a wild ferocity, forgetting where I am and what I'm doing. I spill my seed inside the condom, orgasm buried inside of her, and then I collapse.

We lay there quietly for awhile, panting and breathing in time with one another. Her chest rises, mine falls. We go back and forth for a few minutes before she slowly, softly, tentatively, wraps her arms around me and holds me tight.

CHAPTER 28
NAOMI KNOX

I don't have awkward morning afters. That would imply having some sort of emotion or feeling pertaining to the sex the night before. Whether it was embarrassment or shame or … whatever else. I don't have sex with emotion. Or I didn't. Not until Turner.

Now I'm sitting here with his shirt draped over my shoulders, legs up against my chest, and I have no clue what to say or do. I feel asleep feeling pretty good last night and woke up with a massive panic attack in my chest. I feel … *off.* I don't know what it is, but when I look at him, I get … weird. My heart is fluttering and I feel like a fucking fangirl, gazing up at my idol with starstruck eyes. But I won't play that apart again. We're equals, both rock stars now. He can suck my clit. *Oh,*

but that's right. He did that last night and it was fucking ah-maz-ing. So now what?

"Show tonight," Turner says, standing naked and proud in the bathroom, washing his face with his hands and showing off his fucking tight perfect ass. He wants me to look at him, but I refuse to give him the satisfaction.

"Hope we don't get a tornado," I say randomly. There hasn't been an official warning, but when I gazed out at the sky this morning, I saw it was just a wall of solid gray clouds and icy wind. Even our fans are wary. The crowd is half the size today it was yesterday, but twice as hardcore. I can hear their screams from here. Guess only the ultra loonies will show up in the middle of a massive storm. Turner doesn't respond right away, and I wonder if he's suffering from any of the same feelings I am. The confusion, the fear, the trepidation. I don't have a clue what I'm doing, not with him, not with Hayden, Eric, whoever. "I'm going to reveal myself tonight," I blurt.

Turner wipes off his face with a towel and turns to look at me with a wild grin on his face.

"Hell to the fuck yeah," he says, tilting his head to the side and moving forward on soft feet. His fingers find my chin and lift my face to his. Disgusted with myself, I actually let him. I look into his brown eyes and watch him lick his lips. "Make it epic, Knox. Kill that fucking

crowd and come roaring back with a vengeance. We'll destroy these cock suckers either way. I'm not afraid."

"But you should be," I tell him as I pull my face away and he steps back. "Obviously, there are a couple of screws loose here. Don't let your guard down, alright?" I rise to my feet and he takes another step back. Still, we're close enough to touch. Our toes brush and the temperature in the room skyrockets. He's acting weird now, too. It's *not* just me. Good.

I step around him and reach for the door.

"What are you doing?" he asks as I slide it open and find myself face to face with his friend. Treyjan I think it is? His brown hair is spiked and pretty and he's wearing a shredded shirt collar and bow tie, leaving his chest and stomach bare. He stares at me like I'm a ghost.

"You tell anyone about me before tonight and I will fuck you up. Is the shower free?"

"I … uh. Fuck." I push past the guy and open the second bathroom door, banging my fist on the frosted glass. My awkwardness is pushing me forward, making me bold. Or maybe it's the odd feeling of my crumbled foundation being repaired, slathered with fresh concrete, drilled through with steel support beams. How, why, I don't know. Because of some hot sex?

"Fuck you, Turner, I'm … " The door opens and another one of Turner's friends peeks out at me, halting

his angry retort and standing there naked and dripping wet. I don't know this one's name, but I don't care. I tell him the same thing I told the other guy.

"Naomi Knox. Pleasure to meet you. Can you keep a fucking secret?" I slide my finger across my lips. "Don't tell anybody you've seen me." I start to turn away, glancing over my shoulder briefly to give him another look. "But hurry with the shower, would you?"

Ronnie winks at me when I march into the kitchen, and that blonde kid, the one I made out with to screw with Turner, stands up and gawps. I move over to the door and lock it, glad the driver isn't onboard. She and Kash have a thing going on that I don't want him to know I'm here yet.

"When you commit to something, you go all the way, don't you?" Ronnie asks. I smile at him and turn to face Milo, their manager. He's a short man with blonde hair and a face creased with worry, but I could see how someone might find him handsome. It's the kindness in his eyes, I guess. This is a guy that doesn't fuck around, that's easy to understand. Not like Turner Campbell whose moods flip-flop like a fish out of water.

"Can you call the cops for me?" I ask him. "I'm ready to talk."

I don't feel ballsy talking to the police, just … unsure. At least I'm freshly showered and dressed in another set of Turner's clothes. My tits are starting to ache like hell, desperate for a fucking bra. Unlike Hayden, I'm packing a bit more than mosquito bites around. I hold my arm under my breasts and keep them pushed up while a pair of detectives from Denver ask me a bunch of questions while another man watches silently. I think he might be from the FBI, but I don't ask. He's wearing a suit, not a uniform, and his eyes take in everything with careful, frightening precision. From the look on his face, I can guess he'd like to tear this bus apart. I bet there's at least a half dozen misdemeanors and a few felonies floating around here. When Turner was getting socks this morning, I saw him finger an eight ball of coke in buried in a weird drawer. But he didn't snort any and that says something.

Turner stands close behind me, teasing my bare neck with his warm fingers. I kind of want to punch him in the face, but then I'd probably get arrested for assault and that wouldn't look very good. I think he did it on purpose

though, gave me a T-shirt that said *Mrs. Turner Campbell* across the front of that.

"So you didn't see anyone at all?" Jim asks, sounding perplexed. I fed him the exact same story that Hayden gave the cops, about waking up on the ground outside the venue. I told them all I could remember about getting hit on the head, waking up in the darkness, the needle pricks, the rope. I told them as much as I could about the trailer, too. And Eric. Not that I know he was involved, but that he sought me out, asked me questions about Katie and the scissors. I told them I didn't know anything about it and had asked him to leave, that he'd gotten enraged and stormed off. It looks like they're buying most, if not all, of it. After all, people believe what they want to and they already think Eric's guilty as charged. It's just a matter of time until they lock him up. And that's good for me in so many ways. Of course, if he knows my secret, which it seems like he does, he could talk. But I'm done running from this. I'm going to try this plan, trip the web and call the spider, and if it doesn't work, so be it. I need to be empty and free. That's it. That fucking simple.

"I'm sorry, sir," I respond lamely. I smoke a cigarette and blow the white tendrils into the detectives' faces. The Darnell guy wrinkles his nose at me, but I don't even give him the satisfaction of a smile. I just sit there and stare with blank eyes, tired eyes, eyes that say *I'm just an*

innocent bystander caught up in all of this.

"So, let me just reconfirm your previous statement," Mr. Valentine says, peering at some notes he's made on a pad of paper. This guy's super old school, doesn't use his iPhone to write shit down. These are the kind of cops that get stuff done, that don't believe old fashioned detective work should be thrown by the wayside for technology, that the two should work in harmony with one another. I make sure he doesn't catch my gaze directly. "You waited to talk to us until now because you were scared. Of what? Hayden Lee spoke with us right away, and she's doing just fine." I shrug and reach my hand up to tangle my fingers with Turner. It's an act, but he doesn't know that. He steps closer to me and borrows the cigarette from my fingers.

"I just didn't know who to trust, officer. I think it's this weather. It's making me paranoid." As if on cue, some golf ball sized hail pelts the side of the bus. Jim jumps, but neither Darnell or that FBI dude make a sound. They stay frozen, like mannequins.

"Could have a tornado on our hands," Darnell says, closing his notebook with a grudging finality that tells me he knows I've given him all I'm going to.

"Yes, sir," I tell him, hiking my knee up to my chest and dropping my shades from my hair to my face. I pause and pull them off, examining the label. I haven't

thought about this before, but … my shades are gone, thrown against the wall of that bathroom and shattered. These must be another gift from my stalker. I look at the for a moment and then set them aside. I look good in sunglasses, but I don't need them to hide behind. Not anymore. "I grew up in Tulsa, so I've seen a few myself. They always start just like this: wild fury, then unnerving stillness, and then devastation." I hold up my hand and Turner places the smoke between my fingers.

"And after devastation, there's room for rebirth, space to push aside the old and start anew." Darnell smiles at me. If I'm not mistaken, I think he may actually like me. "Build something fresh." The big man rises to his feet and holds out his hand to shake mine. I take it and squeeze hard. "Stay safe, Naomi. And if you need us, we'll be around. Weather permitting, we'll be at the show tonight, too. Just to make sure everything goes smoothly."

"Thank you," I say, but I don't rise to meet him. I watch as the two detectives shake hands with Milo. He's just like America when it comes to Indecency, sweeping in, smoothing cracks, smiling when nobody else will. America. I want to call her next. She might be in the hospital, but I doubt she'll be sitting idle for long. As soon as she's able, she'll be Tweeting and posting status updates with an IV in her arm and a nurse checking her

vitals.

The bus remains silent while the three men leave. As soon as they're gone and the door is locked behind them, Milo starts to talk.

"We need to get a few select crew members together and plan this out, make sure it's as organized as possible. I'll get some extra security on the stage as well, someone to follow you around."

"Nah, fuck that," Turner says, coming around to sit across from me. "Let's just do this our way, crazy fuck break that stage to shit. Let's just beat it down and make the crowd ours." I look across at him and run my hand down the front of my T-shirt. Turner sees me playing with it and smirks. "And make sure that Jason knows I don't want any of that *Mrs.* shit sold at the merch tables anymore. Forgot we even carried that crap."

"Yeah, because you haven't helped us set up the table in years. Right after we sold our 100th album, your arrogance went off the charts," Treyjan says to his friend, leaning against the counter and crossing his arms over his chest. Ronnie steps forward and slips a baseball cap over his head. From the looks on his friends' faces, I make the connection that this is the one they got delivered to the bus, Travis' cap. We sure are getting a lot of presents from Eric or whoever else it is he's working with. Someone, I imagine that my foster brother doesn't give a

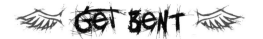

shit about Indecency's old bassist. Or any of the rest of these assholes. If he's in on this, it's as a pawn in a bigger game. I rub the space between my eyebrows in small circles.

"Why don't we let Naomi decide what she wants to do?" Ronnie says and I smile. I really do that like that guy. I look at Turner, watch him rub at some of the paw print tattoos on his neck. He's staring at me with an intensity that's almost frightening. All of that passion I observed him before is now fully focused on me. I don't know how I feel about that.

We haven't told anybody else about what Hayden said. Why let them know they're targets in a plot we don't even understand? I think hard about the what we learned last night. The sex with Turner is clogging my mind with candy clouds and smiling kittens which is freaking me the fuck out, but I force myself past it and try to analyze things carefully. Spencer said the package with the doll head was brought to her by the drummer from Ice and Glass, our opening act. It had been delivered along with a bunch of other packages, the name on the top abbreviated simply as NK. And Ronnie had dished out the camp gossip: everyone was afraid of Hayden. She'd been acting off lately, enough so that it was obvious to the roadies and crew members. And she'd been meeting with a blonde guy that nobody recognized. Ding, ding,

ding.

Bitch is full of shit.

No surprise there.

I try to figure out if I want to confront her, knock her teeth out along with a few more nibbles of information. But maybe I don't need to? Maybe I'm starting to put things together.

I look over at Turner and my chest stirs strangely. I'm not willing to admit what I'm feeling now – what I've felt all along. It's going to take something big to force my brain to accept what my heart already knows. I hope to hell it isn't something tragic.

"I want to talk to America," I tell them, looking at Turner, at Ronnie. "Can you bring Dax over here?" I notice the asshole's lip twitch at the mention of my bandmate. He's afraid of Dax, even if he doesn't know it. Maybe he's afraid of every guy? After all, there's nobody like him in the world, nobody who has this much baggage with me. He should be scared. There's a lot I have to get over to make this work. *If I'm even willing to try.*

"Yeah, Naomi," Turner says, rising to his feet. "I'll get him."

Dax looks tired when he ascends the steps, walking over and scooting in beside me. Ronnie's cooked up some some tacos which gives me a nice change from all the instant crap Turner's been feeding me. I scoot the plate over to my friend. We've known each other a long, long time. And I trust him. Even if he is kind of stalkerish sometimes. I've been working over the clues in my mind since I hit the shower this morning, and I can't imagine why or how Dax would be involved. I mean, nothing is certain, but I'm willing to take this chance. If he is fucking with me, if it was his crotch pressed to my face, or his hand holding the needle, I will figure it out and I'll cut his damn dick off. For now, I just reach out my hand and ask for my cell phone.

He blinks his eyes at me. They're covered in liner and shadow and he's got his hair all spiked in the back. He looks good today, Dax does. Even his shaking hands and sweaty forehead are a good sign. I don't think he's hit the drugs today. I'm kind of surprised I'm not going through withdrawals, Turner either. Maybe it's the magic of love or some shit?

But I do smoke a joint. Just a little. I take a hit and hand it up to Turner who's standing beside the table glaring.

"America's a little out of it, but she can talk. And complain. I have a feeling she'll be back before we know it, bearing down on us twice as hard." Dax searches for a number in his contacts and passes the phone to me, licking his bottom lip and letting his fingers brush against mine. He hasn't given up, not completely. I think he's hoping Turner falls on his ass and fails. I don't know what to hope for right now. I just want to find Eric and figure out what this is all about. If I show up tonight, he'll come to me. I know he will.

"Did she see anything?" I ask Dax, but he's already shaking his head, adjusting the purple gloves on his hands and glancing around the bus at the other members of Indecency. He doesn't ask why I'm sitting out here in front of them all. I figure that Turner probably filled him in. He smiles at me and if he senses that something happened between me and the self-proclaimed King of Rock, then he doesn't let on.

"She doesn't remember anything yet. She told the cops she remembers walking out of the venue and finding some roadies smoking pot, but that's it."

"How's Hayden?" I whisper, leaning close, hoping he'll tell me something, anything. Dax is too nice, too

fucking trusting. I pray to God that he doesn't let this fucking get to him. When I destroy Hayden, he's going to be there to watch.

"Not so good," he replies, pursing his lips. I know he feels guilty for sleeping with her, but he shouldn't. He doesn't owe me shit.

"That fucking cunt is lying through her teeth," he says, putting his boot up on the seat and retying his laces. "She's probably got some cult shit going on with that Eric fuck. I bet he wanted to, like, fucking keep Naomi and his sister as sex slaves or some crap. And I think that Hayden." Turner slams his boot down on the floor and inhales some THC into his chest. "Hayden wants her own, personal cock garden."

"What?" Dax asks, looking at Trey and Ronnie and Milo with pinched brows.

"I think maybe we could be of better use elsewhere?" Trey suggests, poking his dark haired friend in the bicep. "Like, somewhere other than here? Rook has some good shit on his bus. Let's go score some." He starts to move towards the door and pauses, looking at Turner with a twitching lip. He cares about his friend, that much is obvious. They're macho fucking tough guys, so they don't show it much, but it's there. I decide I like their dynamic. "Just be careful, alright? Whatever's going on, I don't want to know. Just remember that there's a

murderer on the loose and a tornado watch in effect, okay?"

"Yes, mother," Turner says, looking back at his friend with a wicked grin. "Now get the fuck out."

Trey leaves and takes the blonde kid and other dude with him while Milo hovers near the sink looking alarmed.

"It's fine, Terrabotti," Turner says, looking at his manager and blowing out some smoke. "I'll take care of this shit, and we'll make platinum." He pauses and Milo opens his mouth, pauses, snaps it closed.

"Alright. Just don't take anymore photographs of your genitals." Turner laughs, loud and raucous and kicks his manager out into the pouring rain with a gentle shove. He locks the door and comes back up the steps. Dax and I both give him looks, but he doesn't acknowledge them, and we don't ask. I, for one, don't want to know. I imagine that someone as full of themselves as Turner Campbell takes a lot of crotch shots.

"Okay, Knox. What's the plan? I want to figure this crap out before anybody else gets hurt. If I lose one of my friends because of this fuckwad, I will *kill* him myself. I'd rather not spend twenty years in jail, so why don't we see what we can do?"

"I'm going to call America," I tell him, tapping the screen and trying to decide exactly what it is I want to

say. I trust her, but I don't want to put her in any danger either. I stare down at the screen, at the picture of stars that Dax has posted as his background and I think about Eric and the brief period where we dated. He was detached maybe, but I never thought he was cruel. I look up again and hope I'm making the right decisions here. Apparently, my people judging skills aren't exactly up to par. I should've seen bad things coming when I met with him before, but I didn't. I still can't figure out why he didn't take me before. He had plenty of opportunities. "And then I'm going to figure out what to do about my outfit. This shit isn't going to fly onstage. I'd kind of prefer it if my tits didn't steal the show." Turner grins and opens his mouth, ready to blurt some shit that'll force me to kick his ass, so I keep going.

"You think Hayden's still into this?" Dax asks as I hit the button to dial. Neither Turner or I respond to his statement and he leans back with a sigh.

"Dax, thank the fucking stars. I need to get out of this redneck shit hole before I blow my brains out of my skull." Nice to know she's retained some of the slang we've been feeding her along the way.

"It's not Dax," I say and the phone goes completely silent.

"Naomi," she says after a moment. "Good. You're alive." Those few words might as well be a shouting,

sobbing cry of relief. This is all I'm going to get out of my manager. "Now listen to me. Don't speak. Don't respond. Don't ask questions." I wait as America sucks in a gasping breath. It sounds wet which scares the crap out of me. If she dies, our band is done for. Fucked. Screwed six ways to Sunday. We need her. "The night of the concert here in Denver, when we were attacked, there were six people that came onto that bus. None of the bouncers stopped them, nobody noticed. Six people in masks." I stay silent, just as she'd asked. "They were there for you and me specifically. That pothead girl was an accident. They meant to kill me, and they meant to keep you." She takes another gasping breath, and I hear a voice in the background. "Can't you see I'm on a call for business right now, you addle headed bimbo? Get out." America pauses and snarls under her breath. "There's no privacy here. It's ridiculous. You'd think *I* was the one that committed the crime." She sighs. "I need the details, but I don't want them over the phone. Give me a few days, and I'll meet you guys in Wichita. Are you singing tonight? Don't say anything to that. I think you should. Just be careful and watch your ass. This isn't over yet, and I don't imagine it coming to a close for awhile. If the police manage to learn anything, I'll be shocked. Now, hang up and go do your thing. I don't want this little snafu ruining our careers." Only America

would be ballsy enough to call a violent assault/homicide/kidnapping a snafu. I take the joint back from Turner and pull calmness into my lungs. "And Naomi," she says before I hang up. "If you speak to any of the cops there, tell them I want my wedding band out of the evidence locker. They won't listen to me anymore."

And then she hangs up.

I put the phone face down on the table and try to breathe.

"Well?" Turner asks, hands on his hips, looking sexy as fuck in a pair of ripped jeans and a plain black tee that pulls tight over his muscles. "What did she say?"

"She says," I explain to him, looking around at Dax and Ronnie. "That were six people on the bus that night."

"Six?" Turner asks. "How the fuck did they get past security?" I think of the cop that I stabbed. An incident like that should've had the whole place buzzing with activity. They take assault on an officer pretty fucking seriously, and yet, there's been nothing. No words. My blood chills and goose bumps spring up across my skin.

"I was putting together a theory, but it's kind of gone to shit." I sigh and run my hands down my face. "Your weird sex cult idea doesn't sound so ridiculous after all. With all of this crap going down, who knows?" I slam

my hands down on the table top. "You know what. Fuck this. I just want to sing. Maybe when whoever's involved sees me, their true colors will start to show?" I look straight into Turner's face and just hold my gaze there. He returns the favor and doesn't waver. I hope that when push comes to shove, that he'll really stick around like he says he will. I could use an ally right now.

"Let's knock 'em dead," Turner says with a slight grin, and I pray to the fucking gods of rock that that sentence remains metaphorical.

CHAPTER 29
& TURNER CAMPBELL &

We get Naomi all decked out and she goes from hot to fucking delicious. My dick ends up playing hotdog with my pants as the damn bun. Not very comfortable. I reach in and adjust myself while she gives me a look and eyes the shades with distaste.

"You think he sent them?" she asks, and I figure she's talking about her foster brother. Dax stands in my bathroom, slipping compacts and lip liners into a plastic bag. I'm not a big fan of the guy since he is an emo bitch, but I have to admit, he did kind of come through for us. He jacked a bra, panties, and makeup from Blair without her even knowing it. And now Naomi is standing before me, full tits ripe and perky, lifted and swollen into an epic

line of cleavage in her mangled Turner Campbell shirt. She sliced and diced that baby until it was unrecognizable, leaving a stripe of pink over her bra and tendrils of torn fabric hanging around her soft belly. The silver skull ring in her belly button winks at me as I scope out her *Real Ugly* tattoo with the angel wings and pretend I'm staring at the broken heart tattoo, so I can check out her breasts.

"Who the fuck knows? Does it matter?" She narrows her smoky eyes at me and I have to wonder if Dax is really a fag or not. I mean, damn, the guy knows how to do makeup. "You're going to use the new Wolfgang tonight, aren't you? Might as well accept the shades, too."

"Even if an incestuous rapist stalker might've sent them to me?" she asks as Dax flicks off the light and joins us in the kitchen area. Ronnie's out scopin' around the venue looking for more gossip, so it's just the three of us in here with a gray sky and raging rain out the window. I hope there's still a crowd tonight. Tornado watch or no, I can see rage and riffs and blood boiling in Naomi's eyes. She's going to take her anger out onstage and it's going to be killer. It's worth the risk.

"Fucker spent his money on some nice shit. Why? To freak us out?" I reach out to grab the glasses from her hand, and she tightens her fingers around them. I want to

snatch her wrist and drag her against me, kiss the fuck out
of her moistened lips, but I doubt she'd let that fly. As
much as I want to be an item, rock god to her goddess, I
don't think she's ready. But I'll wait. She'll come around,
eventually. I smile. I sound like a fucking chick. I wait
with my fingers resting on hers until she relinquishes the
shades to me and slip them on her face. "Screw 'em.
We're going to nail them either way, might as well get
some free shit out of it."

Naomi sighs and leaves them on, sweeping her blonde
hair over her shoulder and picking up the new hoodie I
got for her. It's a bright red Indecency sweater with our
logo slapped on the front in white. She pulls it over her
head and makes sure the hood is in place.

I don't ask her her plans for the stage. I don't need to
know them. I'm going to do what I feel is fucking right,
whatever strikes me at the moment. I don't imagine this
night ending without me joining her onstage though.

The air is charged as shit tonight, filled with the wild
energy of the storm. It's going to churn this crowd up, no
matter how big or small it is.

"What do you want to do about Hayden?" Dax asks,
tucking the makeup bag under his arm. He looks
nervous. He should be. Something's going to happen
tonight. I don't know what it is or if I'm going to get all
the answers, but shit is going to go down, and I'm going

to be ready. Nobody, and I mean *nobody* is touching my woman tonight.

"Let me deal with her," Naomi says, taking a breath. "She's going to give up the spotlight tonight. Willingly. And then tomorrow, when everybody knows I'm back, we'll figure this shit out." She shakes out her wrists and takes a deep breath. "My fingers are itching for my baby. If I don't slam some strings tonight, I'm going to go fucking insane." Naomi moves forward and pushes open the door, and at that same moment, the rain just … stops. I hear her mutter something about tornadoes under her breath, but I grew up in California. I don't know shit about tornadoes.

I jump down the steps after her and Dax follows, keeping close but feeling so far away. I know he can feel it, this thing between Naomi and me. Shit man, anybody could see it. The water beneath our feet evaporates away with the heat. She tries not to look at me too hard or for too long, but I know last night meant something to her. I'm changing her mind one slow, sweet fuck at a time.

"You know," she says, voice pitched low. She knows Dax can hear, but whatever it is she wants to say, she wants to say it now. "If I hadn't been kidnapped … if I wasn't being stalked and betrayed and screwed with at every turn, I'd be thinking a lot more about this … *thing* with you." I stop walking and get out a cigarette. Dax

glares at me, and despite his earlier proclamation that he didn't stand a chance against me, he doesn't exactly look like he's ready to give up. I wonder how this will all play out. "I spent years with … " Naomi grabs at her sweater and twists her fist in the fabric. "With you as my saddest secret. Now that it's out, that you know about the baby and," Naomi pauses and sighs, slapping her hands against the legs of her borrowed jeans. "And everything else. I'm having trouble figuring out where to place myself, how to react. I have one more secret, one more." Naomi bites her lower lip, looks down at the ground and then up at me. "One more and then I'm free and I don't know what I'm going to do."

"Hit diamond with Amatory's next album, I imagine. Sit right next to us," I say and she smiles. I think that it might be the first real smile I've ever pulled from her stubborn lips. My body gets tight and I find it hard to swallow. *What the fuck? You sixteen years old, Turner? Gonna start stuttering and blushing now, too?*

"I just wanted you to know that I'm surprised by you." I wait for her to elaborate. I'll admit, I'm a little slow. I don't get where she's going with this. "For sticking around, for not running off and forgetting me the second I was gone. You might not have actually unlocked those handcuffs, but you tried. You sang my songs, and somehow, I heard you. I didn't realize it until now, but

that was one of the things that kept me sane." Naomi huffs and for a split second, I can see her breath outlined in the still air. It's deathly quiet out here right now, no crowds, no musicians, no crew members. There are a few cops and security guards, but they, too, are few and far between on this gloomy day. "I guess what I'm trying to say is, thank you. And ... " A big gasp of breath, a shake of her head. "I respect your passion and your commitment, Turner Campbell."

And then she turns and walks away. Dax moves after her and takes up residence by her side. I hear them talking, but I don't register the words. I hear one thing, just one thing only playing round and round inside my thick skull.

Respect.

Naomi Isabelle Knox respects me.

My soul screams a ballad of joy and my heart explodes inside my chest.

CHAPTER 30
❧ NAOMI KNOX ❧

I push open the doors and step backstage, reveling in the wild heat and frenzy of it all. I missed it so fucking much, enough so that I realize suddenly that I would never survive doing anything else. I was built for this, mind, body and soul. Dax reaches down and squeezes my hand, and I don't care who's looking or wondering or contemplating my identity. They can guess, but they won't be sure, not until I reveal myself. Let them stare and whisper. My turn for a little mystery.

The venue here is a big, brick building with a massive auditorium and a rounded roof soaring above our head in steel beams and bright, blue paint. It's industrial and old and probably a terrible place to be during a storm. All

around the room, phones and tablets crackle with weather updates and reporters in heavy, winter coats, braving the worst of the weather for a good story. *Fucking idiots.* First sign of the sirens and I'm out of here. I'll lay down in the ditch outside the chain-link, and I'll make sure I take everybody that matters with me.

Police are everywhere in here, but whether it's because of the storm or the murder or even me, I have no clue. I ignore them all and focus on the bitch that's moving across the room towards me in gold heels and a white top. With no bra. What the fuck is wrong with this cunt?

"Even tiny tits sag," I tell Hayden when she gets close and tries to smile at Dax. He can't even look at her. I wonder what happened between them last night, if anything. Maybe he's just disgusted with her after what Ronnie told us? Bitch stormed out after her story and didn't bother to stay to explain her actions, and now we're left with this. A big, fat fucking elephant in the room.

"Thanks for the *tip*," she hisses and the word falls right off the end of her tongue like a slap. Her makeup is too much, too loud, too raunchy. She's trying too hard, and her skin is ashen. Something isn't right with her. That's pretty fucking obvious. I stare at her tiny, upturned nose and her massive nostrils, and I try to stay calm when I say this.

"You're a fucking liar," I tell her and she opens her

mouth to protest. "No. Shut your fucking mouth and listen to me. I have no clue what's really going on. I'll be honest about that because I'm tired of keeping secrets, but I know you're blowing smoke in my face. Whatever it is that you're doing for Eric, for whoever, it's not going to work. Your best bet is to tell me the truth right now. Just admit to it all and find out how far my mercy goes."

She just stands there and stares at me with wide, blue eyes and drooping lips. She's not smirking anymore.

"Hayden, please," Dax says. He wants to save her, but he can't. Nobody can. Only she can save herself. I give her a chance, one last chance to give me something other than a bullshit sob story. She doesn't.

"I don't know what you're talking about." She tries to reach for Dax's arm, but he slaps her off.

"Don't. Touch. Me," he whispers, voice low and harsh. "If you don't want to tell us why you're still meeting with Eric, then don't even bother." Hayden's face falls even lower. Didn't think that was possible. She looks like a fucking Shar-Pei.

"I *have* to," she whispers, looking down at the floor. The metal bars overhead quiver and vibrate with sound as Ice and Glass opens up their set. The crowd cheers, but the sound is a little subdued by fear. This weather just fucking sucks. "I'm sorry."

"That's it?" Dax asks, shaking his head and licking his

lower lip angrily. "That's all you have to say? Why can't you just tell us? Why keep lying? We can protect you, Hayden." I think of the picture she gave me, the way she acted that night and I wonder if it was all an act. It means something to her, sure, but what? So many questions, so few answers.

"Because I don't need any fucking protecting. I just … I'm a little confused right now." Hayden touches her fingers to either side of her face, pressing her long nails against her temples. "And I'm starting to wonder why exactly it is that you're here. Aren't you in hiding or something?" I start to smile, slow and sinful. Wicked.

"Does that matter if you're feeding information to Eric? He already knows I'm here, right?" Hayden grins, but it's not a pretty smile. In fact, she looks kind of crazy. I can't even believe we used to be friends. I guess I should've thought something was wrong with the bitch when she watched me murder my foster parents. She *wanted* to be there. When I shared my feelings with her, she encouraged me. Why has that never bothered me before? Because I was too wrapped up with guilt and fear? Because I wanted an alibi? I have no fucking clue.

"It's not just Eric you have to worry about, *sweetie*. He's kind of … extra. Like a perk or something, you know? He's inconsequential, really. And he knows. He knows *everything*." She laughs and I realize I have to get

Dax out of here before she spills it. I don't want Dax to look at me different. He might not understand, not everybody will. That's why I reserve the right to tell who I want *when* I want. That's my freedom.

"Can we have a minute please?" I ask him, and he starts to protest. Absently, I realize that Turner isn't in the building yet. That freaks me out. A lot. "Can you please go see what Turner's doing outside?" Dax stares me down with his gray eyes. "Please." He waits another moment and then sighs.

"Alright. Okay." He glances around the room, scopes it out. It's dark and crowded back here, but it's not possible for anybody to sneak up on me. I'm as safe as I can be for the moment. I notice Blair giving the three of us a queer look from across the room. She's going to figure this out pretty quick I think.

I wait till Dax moves away and I feel a rush of cold air from behind me.

"You told him, didn't you?" I ask her, and she pouts out her lips. "When?" Hayden shrugs.

"He pretty much figured it out by himself. Katie's too much of a fuck up to do anything that calculated, so who else? I just confirmed what he already knew. But he helped you out, ever wonder why?" I don't respond. "He's always loved you, Naomi." I shake my head. I will not stand here and listen to crazy talk.

"I'm taking the stage tonight and you're not getting on it. If you behave, if you redeem yourself to me, maybe I'll change my mind. Until then, watch your fucking ass. I will figure out what you're up to and if it's bad enough, I'll chop off your fucking clit." Hayden laughs, giggles actually. It's creepy as fuck.

"Seriously? How about, no? You think you can do shit? You got *kidnapped* Naomi, and it took that balding psychopath to get you out. Think about it, what will you do when he finally finds her? Hmm? Once Eric gets Katie back, he's never letting her go. She escaped once. It won't happen again. He wants her almost as much as he wants you." My turn to laugh, to shake my head and look at the floor. It's rough cement speckled with bright splatters of paint. Artsy, twisted, weird. I like it.

"I can't even believe this shit. Is that what this is about?" Hayden just keeps smiling that weird smile.

"Um, let's think about this. She stole the scissors from Eric and sent them to the police. She killed fucking birds and wrote in *blood* on our trailer. She hopped the fence and got to Turner, screwing up the plans we had for him. She stole his keys, nearly got us caught when she sent Turner snooping around. She set you free. Need I go on? Without her, you're screwed, Naomi."

"The doll head?" I ask. "The baseball cap?" I figure if she's going to tell me shit, I might as well know all of

it. Hayden shrugs.

"I don't know, Naomi. I really don't. I know what they want with you, with Katie." She bites her lip. "Turner, Dax." And then she snaps her gaze up to mine and slashes right through me. "Think you're done being my bitch? Not a chance. Not ever. I will *never* let you go completely. Never. And you can't. Have. Them. Both." She steps closer to me, and I finger the knife I have in my back pocket. "Where's the picture?"

"On a cloud drive waiting to be uploaded at noon tomorrow if you don't tell me everything." I smile, even though inside I'm a mess, sliding jigsaw pieces across a massive tabletop. I'm starting to see part of the picture, but I don't have the box. It's taking me longer than I want.

"You're a liar."

"Not as big a one as you are."

"I'm singing tonight."

"You're not."

Hayden stares me down and then she sighs and glances away at the floor. I can't tell if she's actually crazy or playing a game, if she's in this because she wants to be or because she feels like she has no other choice. I don't care.

"Fine," she whispers. "Upload it." She backs away a step and scoops hair behind her ear. "Tell the world I'm a

monster and they'll love me harder for it. I'll survive."
Hayden smiles. "But I am singing tonight."

"If you get on that stage, I will kill you."

I keep very still when I say this. She needs to know
I'm serious.

"If my words fall from your lips, you will die and it
will not be pleasant. Don't force my hand, Hayden. The
death of that girl, Marta, that's on you. I don't know what
else you're capable of, but if you fail to see how serious I
am right now, I will know without a shadow of a doubt
that you're not stable." Hayden ignores me. She doesn't
think I'm a threat, doesn't mind giving me all the behind
the scenes bullshit. I don't matter to her right now. She
knows that I'm being forced into a corner. I can't ask the
police for help because of what I've done. My secret is
wrapped around my throat. I'm about to slip free, but if
I'm not careful, the noose may tighten around my neck.

But I'm serious about what I said. She better not test
me tonight.

A rush of cold air hits my back and Turner's arms slide
around my waist, bringing a small gasp to my lips. He
presses his face into the crook of my neck and tears prick
my eyes. I don't expect it, but something just wells up
inside me, making my heart stop, my lungs contract. My
hands rise to his and brush against them. Dax scoots by
us and intercepts Blair on her way over to us. I don't

know why he does it, but he keeps her back. I guess he doesn't want to sabotage Turner. That's not how he wants to win my attention. Good for him. I like Dax a little more.

"Why'd you have to go and say that to me right before a show?"

"Huh?" I ask, trying my best to keep the jiggling tears behind my shades. If they hit my cheeks and fall, I'm done for. I keep my eyes on Hayden's back, but she's just doing her usual before show bitching. She doesn't sneak off and talk to a person bathed in shadows, doesn't try to find Eric. There's already a plan in play and it doesn't matter what I do.

"Say you loved me."

"But I didn't."

"Close enough," he whispers, releasing me and spinning me around, crushing his lips to mine, cupping my face with his inked fingers. "You're going to turn my tiger into a pussycat."

"Hayden ... admitted a lot of shit, Turner. I think we're in trouble." I touch his chest. "I think this, we, us, whatever this is, is in trouble." He grasps my hands, pulls me to him. Roadies and crew members, musicians and managers, even a few cops, watch us with disbelief. Here he is, this asshole, this playboy, this guy who breaks hearts in his wake, smashing them like a storm, not even aware that he's doing it. And he's kissing this mystery girl in a hoodie with the sweetest lips the world has ever fucking seen. My heart starts to pump frantically.

"We got this. Fuck the fucking fuckers." He starts to pull me towards the bathroom door, but I plant my feet firmly on the colorful concrete.

"We can't do that right now, Turner. There's serious shit going on here." He grins at me and pulls at my Mrs. Turner Campbell bracelet with a snap. *Why the fuck am I still wearing this thing?*

"I don't know what your dirty fucking mind is up to. I thought you had something to tell me that required privacy."

"Uh huh."

"Come on." He pulls on my arm again, and I follow, feeling like the world is crashing down around me, making waves. Some of them are good, some bad. I don't know. I'm all sorts of messed up right now.

"I want a bump," I tell him. "I miss coke." He laughs, but he doesn't respond. Instead, I get whisked into the tiny bathroom with the silver toilet, slammed against the wall and kissed so hard I can't breathe. Turner sits me on the sink and presses his erection against my jeans. "Turner, seriously?" I ask, but I don't sound as bitchy as I want to. Instead, I sound kind of … happy. *Gross. Fucking disgusting.* "Hayden's got a plan in

place. Eric knows I'm here."

"What's new?" he asks between kisses to my throat.

"If this your idea of talking, you suck at it." He pauses and puts his hands on either side of my hips.

"Naomi," he begins, pushing himself back and reaching for my belt. Despite my protests, I don't try to stop him. I also refuse to look at the used syringes on the floor or the walls covered in wet toilet paper. I don't like to make a habit out of fucking in nasty ass bathrooms, but here we are again. When it's the most inappropriate, awkward moment of all. "You can't say something like that to me and not expect to get fucked." I raise my brow as he tugs my pants down and leaves them dangling from one leg, cupping my bare ass in his hands.

"What the fuck are you babbling about?" I ask him as he fumbles to get his pants undone and slap a condom on his dick. But if Turner Campbell's an expert at anything besides singing, it's sex. He manages.

"Respect, Naomi. You can't tell me you respect me and not thoroughly just … fuck with my head. I might have a bit of an inflated ego right now."

"Right now?"

"Are you going to shut up and let me fuck you? Frankly, I don't care about any of this other shit. I'll deal with it when it comes."

"I fucking hate your ass," I tell him as he jerks me

against him, fills my body with his and spreads my hips wide. I'm not going to sugarcoat what happens next. We just screw. We slam together hard and fast, slapping sweaty warm skin against one another and grunting like a bunch of ancient cave fucks. It's ugly. Real ugly. And disgusting. But then, it's beautiful, too. It's a slice of wild nature happening right here in this bathroom, bringing us close, stopping our hearts and starting them again in unison. It's quick, it's messy and then it's done.

He comes; I come.

And then we just sit there while electric guitars and drums vibrate the walls around us. I drape myself against his chest and just try to breathe.

"I don't know what I'm doing here," I whisper and he gives me an answer. The man I hate, that fucked my life up, that shouldn't have anything nice or constructive to say, gives me a solid, reasonable step to stand on. What the fuck?

"You're learning to love."

Pure. Simple. True.

And from the mouth of Turner Campbell. The world is full of surprises.

Just not all of them are good.

The stage is set.

The players are all thoroughly entrenched in the game.

Me, I'm standing on the edge of the stage with my eyes closed and hot blood pumping through my veins. I *feel* Turner Campbell standing behind me, and I feel better because of it. I don't want to love him, but I think I do. Or I might. One day, when I stop hating him so much maybe.

The crowd is quiet, almost deadly silent, as they wait in nervous anticipation. The problem is that they're still thinking about the storm. I'm going to kill that fear. When I get onstage, they're only going to be thinking about me.

Dax sits down behind his drums and gives me a gentle nod of his chin.

Without waiting another second, I move forward, out onto the open stage in front of a couple thousand people. I wish there were more, but I'll make do. The word will spread and soon, everyone will know.

Whispers and rumors spread like fire, catching on people and flaming bright and suspicious in the dull light.

I ignore them and focus only on Hayden who's coming out the opposite side, walking straight towards me. She doesn't look angry or nervous. She smiles at me when we get close and pauses, leaning forward and putting her lips to my ear.

"I won't ever say I'm sorry, but I'll tell you this. If you think I'm a good performer, let me be onstage with you. You can borrow the spotlight … for now. I won't help tonight, but I won't hurt either. If you survive, we can talk about it."

She leans back and we look at each other for a long, long moment. Time stretches thin and brittle. I stare at her and then I shift my eyes back to the crowd, a subtle cue. It only takes me about ten seconds to see them both. Eric and Katie. He stands on the left side of the room and she, the right. I don't know if either knows the other is there, but they both see me. That's for fucking sure. *Everybody* sees me right now. There is no retreating inside of myself, diving deep and hiding in plain sight. Tonight, I'm going to have to come out and show them everything I've got.

Turner moves out beside me and steals Wren's mic. He doesn't protest, but he looks confused. He's not the only one. The crowd starts to get restless. I take a deep breath and hold it in my lungs before bringing my hands up to my shades. I touch the nosepiece and wait.

Seconds tick by and the wind outside howls so loud we can hear it through the brick. It's roaring like a fucking freight train. I know then that we're going to get a tornado. I don't hear the sirens yet, but I will. Soon. Right now, I will use the force of my will to make Mother Nature wait. She will not fuck me here. Not tonight.

I pull the glasses off and there are some gasps near the front of the room. I toss them to the floor near my feet and reach for the bottom of the sweater, digging my fingers under the fabric and pausing. Turner's voice slithers into the microphone like liquid sex.

"Good evening, Oklahoma City, Oklahoma." He chuckles and wraps both hands around his mic. "We're having a bit of weather tonight, aren't we? But that just makes you lucky. You're going to get a show that not many will see in person but that everyone will be talking about come tomorrow. You're like fucking pioneers, forging their way into new territory, and believe me when I say you've never seen anything like this."

I lift the sweater up and pull it over my head. Blonde hair cascades down around my shoulders as I face the crowd, eyes blazing, lips already pulling up into a small smile.

For one second, one split, tiny second, the purest of silences hits the room and nobody moves, no one speaks. I drop the sweater; I grab my guitar.

Explosion.

The roar of the wind is nothing compared to the screeching of the crowd as I slam my fingers on the strings and worship a god that's older and stronger and wiser than me, using my music as a prayer, my voice as a sail to carry my ship to the mouth of heaven and the depths of hell.

Dax slams in next, pounding his music down through the stage and up into my bones, breaking my tibias, shattering my femurs, and it feels *so* damn good. They thought I was dead and now here I am, ready to tear their shit apart.

"*Get fucking READY,*" Turner screams, voice breaking as he bends over, releasing every last drop of breath in his lungs into the mic. He springs back to life like a fucking daisy, spinning in a circle and slamming his boot on the ground.

The people in here give their souls up to us, leaping and punching, flailing and sobbing as they bounce to the beat and record us with phones, cameras, tablets. We become immortalized in an instant, spread across the web for all to see. Idiots singing in the eye of a storm, uniting as a front against a hidden enemy.

I couldn't be happier.

"*Don't ever be afraid of me. I cannot see.*"

"*Cannot FUCKING see!*" Turner screeches for me in

full on devil mode. There are no angels here. We are all full of sin and it is beautiful.

"*I can't see, and I'm blinded by your love,*" Hayden sings as I bring my voice over hers, relegating her to the background, taking the spotlight. I fuck my guitar like a long lost lover, forgiving it entirely for coming from the hands of corruption. I don't care who bought it or sent it, only that it's here, pressed tight against me, singing my soul into the air with frantic twangs and gurgles of devilish delight.

"*That day you walked away from me, I went down hard and I could not see. I could not see, and baby, you're fucking bullshit is killing me.*"

"*Tear us apart with your LIES and taste my HEARTBEAT with your cries,*" Turner growls, coming up close to me, wrapping the cord of his mic around my hips, just under my guitar, pulling me against his body as we start to sweat and grind and bleed.

"*I cannot see because the visions you showed me brought me pain instead of pleasure, left me numb and got me bent for forever.*" We sing together and my eyes close of their own volition, loosing me into the crowd, stabbing them all through the skull with Kash's bass, Blair's keys, Wren's guitar.

My solo hits and that's just all she friggin' wrote. Turner drops to his knees, and I step over his cord,

moving to the front of the stage and strumming my baby like my life, like the world depends on it. I grind my pelvis into my instrument, pretending it's Turner's body, so I know they're feeling how I felt, how I want to feel for the rest of my fucking life. I don't want to love. I don't. But I do.

"I wish I didn't love you. Things would be easier that way." My voice alone moves though the sky in time with my guitar, melds us into a single entity that breathes then lives then dies. It's simple, but it has to count. I have to make the middle worth the end. That's the way it has to be.

I play like I've never played before, and I hardly notice when the rest of my band joins in, so lost am I in the music.

"Easier to breathe," Hayden sings, giving me that special blend of eighties and pop and nails on a chalkboard heartless beauty that makes it hard for me to hate her.

"Easier to bleed," Turner coos and I loose my shit. I hit the floor on my knees and my head moves in time with the music. I forget to sing because he's there and his voice is the only one I want to hear. *"Easier to need the truth."* I feel him behind me and lean my head back into his throbbing cock, pressing my hair against that bulge of denim. I look up at him, and he gazes down at me. *"I*

cannot see because the visions you showed me brought me pain instead of pleasure, so take me in and make me yours forever."

He leans down quick and kisses my lips, sears me and burns me, cauterizes old wounds and leaves me with a scar that I hope never heals.

CHAPTER 31
❧ TURNER CAMPBELL ❧

As soon as I pull away from Naomi's hot mouth, feel my heart slamming against my ribcage and my hormones flowing like rapids, we hear the siren. It sounds so old school, a blaring cry of danger that shakes the building with its intensity, sounding off at the very edge of the parking lot. *This is not a joke,* it says with its crying fear. *This is life or death. Get your asses moving.*

The music dies off at the end of the song and stays quiet. Instruments drop and people start to panic. The police milling around immediately start directing people out the doors. I'm glad to see their lack of hesitation. It gives me hope for the human race. Not much, but there it is.

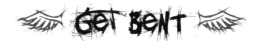

There's still excitement in the air, still that sweating, crying, breathing monster of rock nipping at our heels and drawing devilish grins, but the fear is coming quick, rising up over us and bathing the room in shadow. The crowd, though relatively small for a show this size, is thick, and when folks get panicked, they do weird shit.

I watch crew members scrambling and nervous faces peering up at me from various positions below. It was selfish bringing them in here with the threat of danger looming, but it had to be done. This was a fucking necessity for us, for Naomi, and nobody was forced to be here. They chose. Hey, at least if anything happens, we've all got the hot heat of music pulsing in our veins. I could die happy right now. Though I'd rather fucking not. There's a whole host of positions from A to Z that Naomi and I haven't tried yet. I intend on mastering every single one. Oh, and marrying her ass. I want to be buried next to this chick on a hill under a fucking tree. And I'm not ashamed to admit that.

I get out a smoke. I guess I don't realize how serious this shit is yet. I told you, I'm from Cali-fucking-fornia.

"Why are they making them go outside?" I ask Naomi as she slips the Wolfgang off regretfully and I help her to her feet. Her eyes immediately rise to the ceiling, and she licks her lips nervously. I look around and I can make a pretty easy guess about who's a local and who's

not. Some people are walking, others are sprinting like their life depends on it. Huh.

"This is not the sort of place you want to be if the shit goes down. A wide roof is bad news, and this artistic well of sin has no designated shelter." She smiles with tight lips and grips my hand tight. "We'd be better off in that ditch next to the parking lot. Let's go."

Naomi turns to face her band. Hayden is already gone, but the rest of them are there, staring at her with stunned disbelief. Guess this is a lot to take in.

"You can all kiss my ass and praise my resurrection skills later. We have to get the fuck out of here." Naomi doesn't wait for them to respond. She's a natural leader, born and bred. She just moves and expects them to follow.

Thing is, they do.

"I'm so glad you're back," Blair says, moving across the stage with Dax. "Really. I … I missed you, bitch." Naomi smiles at her, but she doesn't stop walking. Instead, she keeps gathering people until we have a friggin' entourage – Ronnie, Trey, Jesse, Josh, Milo, her bassist dude, her backup guitarist. She pulls them to her like a magnetic force, calming some of the panic and guiding us through the already empty backstage area and past a shouting cop. It all happens so fast that my head starts to spin. Why is it that crises always seem to go so

quick? To exist in a place that is out of this fucking world, like a whole other dimension or some shit.

"I knew it," she said, but she's almost smiling. Her confidence gives me hope. But then, I don't know crap about tornadoes. "But at least I got my song. That's all I really wanted." I take a step forward and press my back against the door, opening it for my friends, her friends, but mostly for her. Naomi steps up beside me as people filter out, draining past us in slow, ambling steps, like they're not really nervous even though they should be. "Get in the ditch!" she shouts as she notices some idiots heading towards the buses. Fans are getting in the back gate and harassing people. Some see us and come our way. Folks are just fucking shameless, taking advantage of a crisis to what, meet some people that'll never remember their names?

"Fucking assholes," I growl as chaos just breaks loose around us, unraveling human society and practiced order in less time than it takes me to blink. A cloud of debris swirls, dropping bizarre shit on our heads: boxes, trash can lids, a dead squirrel. That's right. A dead fucking animal falls not three feet away from where I'm standing. *The fuck?* "God, fuck this weird Midwest shit. Give me earthquakes any damn day." Naomi ignores me as the last of the people exit this side of the building. A cop checks around inside and gives me an all clear before

telling me to get the fuck out of here. He doesn't wait around long enough to see if I do.

Dax stands and waits, proving his devotion while the rest of the group is lead away by Milo, taking charge of the flock even though he's the shortest damn sheep in it. People are screaming from the area of the parking lot, but there are still fans back here, rushing towards us, eager to get in a fuckin' meet and greet. That is, until they turn around and see what the commotion is about. Our friends crest the edge of the building at about the same time and stop short.

The air goes completely still. And I don't just mean the breeze dies down. No, I mean it feels like the life has been sucked out of the air, pulled away and left bare and dead. A roaring scream sounds in the distance beyond the crying sirens.

I turn around and drop the door back into place. It clicks shut, but the noise is lost in the eerie silence, sucked away like water up a straw.

"Oh. Shit."

On the horizon, like a fucking movie nightmare swirls the biggest damn dust cloud I have ever seen. It looks angry, alive, whipping across the landscape and tearing a scar that'll take a long time to heal. It doesn't discriminate, doesn't judge. It does what it came here to do, destroying with a gleeful twirl and a rush of

helplessness. It's like a mighty Titan, ascending Mount Olympus to kill the gods. It's a part of the earth; it can do whatever it wants.

The screaming starts up again, the running. The rest of the fans abandon their frantic rush towards us at about the same moment I hear a telling click.

Man, I don't know what the fuck comes over me, but when I hear that sound, I go all karate and shit. My primal instincts take over, and even though I know I don't know shit about combat, that I'm just an asshole with a good right hook, I react. After all, I'm an asshole in love.

I turn, spinning sharp and letting my fist fly without much thought. It cracks Eric 'the fuck up' Rhineback right in his pale jaw and spills a rush of blood from his mouth like a Halloween prop. But he doesn't drop the gun. Instead, he lowers his aim and fires.

CHAPTER 32
NAOMI KNOX

"Turner!" His name barely escapes my lips before he buckles, blood spraying out his thigh and soaking his stupid girl jeans. I don't know if I've ever been as afraid as I am in that moment, my heart beating in slow motion inside my tightened chest. His other hand comes up and grabs Eric's wrist hard, biceps squeezing, using that practiced pretty strength to drop the gun from my foster brother's grip and send it skidding across the pavement.

Behind me, the monster screams and stops, closing in on us and the buses start to shake in the currents of wind and the trees whimper. Lawn chairs go flying and the debris that was dumped on us lifts back up as if by magic. The gunshot is going to kill Turner, but the tornado is

going to kill us all.

I move forward as the man I hated more than anyone else in the world, the one person I thought that could never redeem himself, collapses in a puddle of his own blood with a grunt. But he never screams. Not once. He won't give Eric the satisfaction, stubborn even in his pain.

"Not right now, Eric!" I scream, watching his face, watching his eyes as they move to the sky and fill with fear. Whatever he says, whatever he thinks, he isn't really prepared for this. "Get to the ditch and we'll deal with this later! Go!" I make no false assumptions about the value of his character and watch in grim satisfaction as the gun is lifted up and carried away while my clothes whip around my body, stinging my skin. The most horrible fucking screech comes to us on the gale, the death throw of a small car as its open door comes off with a frightening ease. It doesn't have long to mourn its lost limb because up it goes next, spinning away like a toy.

We are so done for.

I crouch down over Turner who can't get up, who can't run and reach for the handle of the door to the venue. It's locked. Locked. Fucking *locked.*

"Go," he growls at me, shoving me back, pushing at me with bloody hands. "Now. Fucking get your ass out of here Naomi. I'd rather have a tree shoved up my ass than see you hurt." I think I'm crying, but who knows

because the tears get ripped away in the wind. Eric continues to lord over us.

"Come with me," he says and in his voice, I hear the magic of a boy who once watched the stars with me. I don't know if it's in his genetics or what, but he's changed. He transformed from that hopeful boy to a disturbed young man. He can't be redeemed for what he's done. There is no *I'm sorry* for Katie. I hope the tornado kills him. "I'll keep you safe, Naomi. That's all I ever wanted was to keep you safe. I helped you clean up the crime scene, didn't I?" I ignore him. He's inconsequential now. We have seconds, if that. "I don't know what Hayden or Katie told you, but I can promise it's a bunch of bullshit. They've been playing me almost badly as Turner's been playing you. He knows everything, Naomi. He's a part of it."

I grab Turner's face between my hands, and I look him in his beautiful, beautiful eyes. If I'm going to die here, I'm going to do it right.

"I fucking love you," I tell him, and he stops fighting me. The gray sky drops a torrent of violent rain on our heads, plastering my hair to my face, drowning me. I slap it away and press my face close to his. "I haven't completely forgiven you for the things you've done, but I love you just the same. I love you. I love you." And then I kiss him, taste his tongue ring, run my fingers

down his face.

And then I'm shoving him onto his back, covering my body with his, waiting to die.

CHAPTER 33

& TURNER CAMPBELL &

I can't describe my next few moments because the English fucking language does not have words for them. All I can tell you is that I've traveled to hell and back, and it isn't pretty. It's ugly as *shit*.

"Naomi!" I scream after the wave rushes us, rides us, fucks us and then simply … stops. The building is missing its roof, the buses are not where they were when we left them and there are bodies everywhere. Some are covered with debris, others are lying bare on the suddenly sunny pavement like they're just out for a tan. I *must've* passed out because I don't remember anything beyond that kiss, that one fucking, single sharing of breath that will define who I am for the rest of my miserable life.

"Naomi!" I push myself up with my elbows and grit my teeth against the pain in my thigh. It's inconsequential right now. I don't care. I don't care about anything but my one woman. My only woman. "Naomi?" My shout becomes a question as I roll her over. She moves limply, pulled only by my arms on her shoulders. I don't see her chest moving. I don't see it. I don't fucking see it.

She's dead.

She's fucking dead.

"Naomi?" That's it, there it is, a sob. A wail. "NAOMI! FUCK!"

I grab her face, lift her head up, tap her cheek. Blood dribbles down the side of her face and turns her blonde hair pink, taints her lips. I pull her body up to mine and listen. *No, no, no, no.* But then, there it is, a faint pulse, a light whisper. She sucks in a breath and groans.

I cry like a little bitch.

I won't lie. I bawl like a baby and go back for more, squeezing her against me, cursing her name under my breath.

"Would you stop shouting," she whispers. "I mean, just shut the fuck up. My head hurts. I can't think straight."

"You stupid, fucking bitch, what the hell were you thinking?"

"I was shielding you, you asshole." Naomi tries to sit

up and whimpers, dropping her body back against mine. I hold her tight and wrap my arms around her as I survey the damage. It's like a fucking apocalypse out here. In the distance, I hear sirens, ambulances probably. The tornado warning has stopped, but I doubt out of choice. I bet that fucker got ripped up and torn up, spit out and eaten alive. Whoever it is that's coming, I hope they get here soon because I don't think either of us is able to move. I press a kiss to Naomi's hair. "You're alive," she says.

"You sound almost disappointed," I whisper, trying to keep the fuck all, screw it rhetoric. I don't want to know how many of those bodies are never going to get up again. Naomi doesn't respond and we wait while leaves skitter around us. Groans are coming from various places across the lot and voices from beyond the chain-link fence. I don't turn and look at them. I can barely fucking move.

And then I remember. Shit.

Dax.

I twist around and try to look, trying not to let Naomi figure out what I'm doing. I spot his emo ass right away, lying motionless where I last saw him standing. God-fucking-damn it. I turn back around and squeeze Naomi's head against my chest. She doesn't need this right now. I just keep my attention on moving my hand through her

hair, nice and gentle and slow.

I notice Eric's blonde head sticking out from under a cluster of cardboard boxes, buried there like a bum in an alleyway. He, unfortunately, isn't as motionless as Dax. I can see his fingers twitching as he groans and crawls forward, straining himself up on his elbows. Behind me, shouts ring out and boots pound the pavement. My neck is fucking killing me, but I stay in that position and watch as some of the police officers and roadies check the bodies.

Naomi starts to fall asleep, but I give her a gentle shake and press another kiss to her head. I think she has a concussion. Ain't no way I'm letting her out of this now. Not after that confession. It was as epic as the fucking storm and ten times as unexpected.

"I love you, too, Naomi Knox," I tell her. "And it'll be alright. It'll be o-fucking-kay." I glance back. Hayden is leaning over Dax with tears on her skinny, gaunt face. She checks his pulse and I wait with bated breath. *One, two, three.* She rubs at her nose and sits down, pulling his head into her lap. It only takes a moment for some of her bandmates to catch up to her. From their reactions, I can tell that Dax is alright. They're worried but not devastated. Good sign. I breathe out a sigh of relief. He might be a fucking rival, but I don't want him dead. I don't want anything around that could hurt Naomi.

"He's okay?" she asks, and I pause.

"Yeah," I say, as I look back and lift my hand to grab Ronnie's attention. He starts towards us in a jog. "Dax is alright." I smile. "Sneaky bitch. I was tying to protect you from that shit." Naomi's orange-brown eyes flicker open and she focuses her watery gaze on the crawling form of her foster brother.

"Turner, don't ever try to protect me from feeling something real. Don't try to protect me at all." She pauses and a tiny smile tweaks her bloody lip. "Unless it's as stupid and egotistical as thinking you can take out a man with a gun without being shot. Kind of like that."

I smile and then pause. My lips turn into a frown.

"The fuck?" Naomi twists just enough to see, wincing as she spots her foster sister, Katie, standing with her dirty dress and plastic purse. She's at the edge of the parking lot, next to a toppled bus. She doesn't look bothered by the devastation. She doesn't even *see* it. Her purse falls to the ground with a crash that sounds too loud for plastic on cement, like something else is falling, too, like her sanity is smashing down right along with it. And then she starts to run, bare feet whispering across the lot as she skitters, moving in a way I've never seen another human move – with grace and fucking violence intertwined around the bareness of her soul.

"Katie?" Naomi asks, but her sister doesn't look at us.

She has black angel wings on her back, guiding her forward, bringing tiny tears from the sky in the form of rain. It splats on our cheeks as we watch. She skids to a stop next to Eric and bends down to pick up a wooden board from his back. At first, I think she's fucking helping the asshole, that this whole plot is even more sick and twisted than it was before, that she has hardcore Stockholm syndrome.

Eric doesn't see her, doesn't even look up.

Katie whispers something that nobody else can hear, that's meant solely for the ears of God. Or the Devil. Yeah, probably for him.

And then she drops the board.

Naomi and I cringe as it hits Eric in the head and drops his chest back to the pavement. He whimpers and tries to stand, but she isn't finished. She hits him again. He collapses a second time with a strangled cry. There's so much going on that nobody but us sees at first. And Katie keeps going. She has a purpose in mind and *nobody* is going to take her from it. The board comes down. Eric grunts. Again. The crack of skull.

"You! What the fuck are you doing?" The gruff voice from behind us doesn't stop Katie. She starts to slam that board down with a renewed vigor, splattering her face with blood, soaking her dress with the spray. "Drop your fucking weapon and put your hands in the air!" Katie

swings again and a warning shot is fired into the gray stillness above our heads. She drops the wood by her side and looks down at the bloody pothole of Eric's skull. When she raises her hands above her head and drops to her knees, tears of joy are rolling down her face.

I hold Naomi close to me and try not to think the one thought that we're both feeling. *There goes the problem. That solves it. This is it, right? The rest of the little details, the unanswered questions, can be worked out later. The threat is over, erased with violence and tiny, porcelain hands so used to abuse they can stand innocent no longer.*

The cops cuff Katie Rhineback and keep guns trained on her tiny form. A man in an *Ice and Glass* shirt checks his pulse. He shakes his head and purses his lips.

In the midst of the chaos and destruction, somebody spins America's silver wedding band around their finger.

Dear Reader,

Thanks for staying on this crazy journey with me. I know it might be tough sometimes, but it'll all be worth it in the end. Look at Naomi and Turner. Match made in Heaven. Or maybe Hell. But it's beautiful either way. But we're not done with Amatory Riot and Indecency yet. There's more to come and you never know who's turn it'll be to tell the story next.

The plot thickens.

And this series will have a definite ending at some point, all questions will be answered, and happily-ever-sometimes will be passed out. Stay with me and we'll get there. Book three coming soon.

Kisses.
C.M.

About the Author

C.M. Stunich was raised under a cover of fog in the area known simply as Eureka, CA. A mysterious place, this strange, arboreal land nursed Caitlin's (yes, that's her name!) desire to write strange fiction novels about wicked monsters, magical trains, and Nemean Lions (Google it!). She currently enjoys drag queens, having too many cats, and tribal bellydance.

She can be reached at author@cmstunich.com, and loves to hear from her readers. Ms. Stunich also wrote this biography and has no idea why she decided to refer to herself in the third person.

Happy reading and carpe diem!

www.cmstunich.com

Made in the USA
San Bernardino, CA
07 September 2013